Her Captain Enchanter

The Worthington Legacy
Book Five

Marie Higgins

ARE YOU SIGNED UP FOR DRAGONBLADE'S BLOG?

You'll get the latest news and information on exclusive giveaways, exclusive excerpts, coming releases, sales, free books, cover reveals and more.

Check out our complete list of authors, too!

No spam, no junk. That's a promise!

Sign Up Here

www.dragonbladepublishing.com

Dearest Reader;

Thank you for your support of a small press. At Dragonblade Publishing, we strive to bring you the highest quality Historical Romance from some of the best authors in the business. Without your support, there is no 'us', so we sincerely hope you adore these stories and find some new favorite authors along the way.

Happy Reading!

CEO, Dragonblade Publishing

**Additional Dragonblade books by
Author Marie Higgins**

The Worthington Legacy
Her Perfect Scoundrel (Book 1)
Her Dreamy Deceiver (Book 2)
Her Adorable Cad (Book 3)
Her Irresistible Charmer (Book 4)
Her Captain Enchanter (Book 5)

Love's Addiction Series
A Wallflower to Love (Book 1)
A Governess to Protect (Book 2)
A Maiden to Remember (Book 3)

Mobs are threatening Lady Sarah Emiline Langston's family because of her corrupt uncle. She must go into hiding, so her father sends her far away to his friend's country estate. In order to keep her identity a secret, she switches roles with her servant and calls herself a lady's companion. Complications arise when Emiline meets the very handsome man, and she suddenly wants him to look at her as a real woman, not a servant.

Captain Hawk's ship is almost captured, and this time it was too close. As a pirate, Broderick Worthington lives a double life, and now he and his crew need to stay low for a few months to keep the men looking for them away. During his stay at his aunt and uncle's estate, he meets the enemy's niece. Because she doesn't know who Broderick is, he will become close to her to see if she knows any more of her uncle's secrets. But the beauty of her companion, Miss Emmie, captures his attention, and her quirky personality keeps him wanting more.

How can he protect them both and play the part of a gentleman when an unknown spy is always one step ahead... and wants Broderick dead?

Chapter One

SOMETHING WAS NOT right.

Unrest flittered in Emiline Langston's stomach, pricking the hairs on the back of her neck as her carriage rocked to a halt outside the family's two-story townhouse. Servants scampered from the house, carrying trunks as they loaded them on a coach.

Curiosity and determination to discover what was going on enveloped her as panic settled in her chest. She gave her hand to the footman as he helped her down from her carriage, and then headed toward the front door. Several soldiers stood guard near the white wraparound porch as if they expected trouble at any moment. They eyed her warily until she walked closer, and then their postures relaxed a bit. She was used to being watched closely, since her uncle was lord chancellor, but today's display of guards greatly unnerved her.

After striding into the house, she tugged on the ties of her bonnet to loosen them. "Can someone explain to me why there are so many soldiers outside?" she asked as two of the servants rushed by.

"My Lady Sarah." The housekeeper scampered toward Emiline from the parlor. "Thank the Lord you are back, but you must make haste. There is no time to lose."

Inwardly, Emiline cringed. Lately, she had been so sick of people using her first name instead of her middle name,

Emiline—the very name her mother used to call her. But then again, since dreaming of her mother last night and how Emmie missed her, how could she not become nostalgic?

"I don't understand why—" Her words were interrupted when the housekeeper hooked an arm around her elbow, whisking Emmie up the stairs toward her bedroom. As they passed by the first two guest rooms, the servants rushed around inside, shoving clothes into trunks.

Emmie glanced at Hester, still pulling her along. Lines of worry etched the older woman's round face at the corners of her eyes and mouth. A sheen of moisture touched the servant's forehead.

"Hester, I beg you, please tell me what is amiss." Emmie glanced into another room and saw the same chaos. "Why is everyone so panicked?"

As they reached Emmie's room, Hester stepped inside first, heading directly to the armoire. Already three trunks sat open on the bed. Emmie couldn't understand why they needed to leave. She and her father had only arrived from Paris five days earlier to stay for the summer.

"My lady, your family is in great danger. A threat has been made against your uncle and his family. Your father fears for your life."

Emmie slowly removed her bonnet as she tried to absorb the housekeeper's words. She didn't approve of what her uncle had been doing all of these years. In her opinion, he should stop trying to control people's lives. But would those people really harm his entire family?

Hester fanned her red face. "Mobs are forming as we speak. They want to punish all of the lord chancellor's relatives."

Terror climbed through Emmie's body, clutching her heart. "Are Father and I returning to Paris, then?"

"No, unfortunately. Because your father has duties here in North Devon, he will stay and protect the family's estates, but he is sending you to Greenwich."

"*What?*" Emmie shrieked. "Why there? That is at least a half-day's journey."

Hester took a gown from the armoire, carefully folded it, and laid it in the trunk with trembling hands. "Some of your father's friends live there—Mr. and Mrs. Crampton."

Recollections of her father telling her about the Cramptons flitted through her mind. Her father probably hadn't seen them since her mother died fifteen years ago. "Do they know I'm coming?"

"Yes, my lady. Just this morning, your father sent a messenger to send them a telegram."

Footsteps pounded on the floor down the hallway. Emmie swung toward the door just as her lady's maid ran into the room. Strands of her dark brown hair had escaped her mop cap and clung to her pale cheeks.

She did a quick curtsy. "Lady Sarah, your father instructed me just now that we are to have you packed and on your way within the hour."

Impossible! There was no way they would have her packed that quickly. "Then there is no time to stand around and converse." Emmie marched to another armoire, swung open the doors, and started yanking out gowns. "I shall help pack." Glancing over her shoulder, she peered at her maid. "Anna, I suggest you start on those drawers in the corner."

"Yes, my lady."

To some servants, seeing Emmie packing her own trunks might seem out of character for the daughter—an only child—of an earl. Still, Lady Sarah Emiline Langston had always been different. As a child, they could only afford a few servants, so she learned to do things herself. Two years after her mother died and her father had been given the title, Emmie had more servants than she needed. Having a father with a new title changed everything, it seemed. She missed doing things with him, just the two of them.

With a wistful sigh, she recalled when they used to go sailing.

He had taught her everything about commanding a boat. How she had loved sailing, only because it made her feel so powerful—so in control of her own life. Her father had even taught her how to ride a horse. She had entered many horse races as a child and won ribbons. As she grew to be a young lady, it was unheard of for a mature girl to compete in horse races, which saddened her greatly. At that point in her life, her father had become more political and couldn't find time for his daughter.

Heavier footsteps thudded up the hallway and stopped at the door. She knew who it was before looking his way. Her father's presence commanded attention, no matter where he traveled or whom he encountered.

Emmie glanced over her shoulder and met her father's stare. "I'm almost packed."

He glanced at the housekeeper. "Will you give me a private moment with my daughter?"

"Yes, my lord." Hester curtsied and hurried out.

Anna turned to follow the other servant, but Emmie's father touched her arm. "I would like for you to stay."

"As you wish." Anna curtsied, too.

After he closed the door, he strode closer, his arms folded over his massive chest. He was a large man and not one to be trifled with. Worry lines creased his forehead and around his mouth. It seemed he had aged several years since Emmie had visited with him this morning. Definitely, the strain from the recent upset had taken its toll.

"Father, what is amiss?"

For a few long and awkward moments, he stood in silence. Finally, he cleared his throat. "I have a wild idea, and I need both of you to do something for me."

Emmie exchanged glances with Anna before she returned her focus to her father. "What is it?"

"Where I'm sending you, there are many people who loathe your uncle. They would rather cause mayhem and make others miserable than try to find peace."

Emmie frowned. "Do you blame them, Father? Uncle Edward isn't very wise—"

"Please," he interrupted, holding up a hand. "Let me finish."

Nodding, she kept her mouth closed—and her opinions to herself.

"Because it's hard to decipher who exactly is sending this threat against our family, I cannot trust those I don't know. It is for that reason I'm sending you to my friends, Henry and Martha Crampton. But because I don't trust their neighbors, I cannot have my daughter in danger with me so far away." He took a deep breath. "Because of that, I have formulated a plan that only we three will know about." He looked at Anna. "Before you reach Greenwich, you both will switch roles. Anna, you will become Lady Sarah"—he met Emmie's wide eyes—"and you, my darling daughter, will be Lady Sarah's maid."

Slowly, Emmie shook her head, not quite comprehending the idea. "You want us to switch places?"

"Yes. Just while you are staying with Mr. and Mrs. Crampton."

"But will they not realize we are fooling them?"

"No." He stepped closer and stroked her cheek lovingly. "Mr. and Mrs. Crampton have never met you. If you and Anna play your parts precisely, my friends will never know of the deception." He motioned his head toward Anna. "You and your maid are only a few months apart in age. You both have brown hair and blue eyes. During your carriage ride, you can instruct Anna on how she needs to act."

"Oh, my lord," Anna said quickly, her voice raised in excitement. "Lady Sarah doesn't need to instruct me. I have been her maid for several years. I know how the daughter of an earl is required to act."

He smiled wide. "Splendid. Then I shall need you to instruct my daughter how to act like a servant." He glanced back at Emmie and winked. "I fear my daughter has been pampered these past several years."

Inwardly, Emmie growled. She was quite certain she would *not* need lessons. "Father, forgive me for voicing my opinions, but I cannot act as a maid. It's just not done. I would be expected to know how to do things. I will certainly mess up and then cause suspicion."

"Hmm…" He nodded and rubbed his chin. "I do see your point. All right, then, instead of Lady Sarah's maid, you shall be her companion. I'm quite certain Mr. and Mrs. Crampton will have a maid to tend to Lady Sarah while you are there."

Without being able to stop herself, Emmie snorted a laugh. "A lady's companion? Truly, Father, I'm not old enough to play that role."

"On the contrary, my dear. Not all lady's companions are old. We will tell Mr. and Mrs. Crampton that you are Lady Sarah's poor relative, and you have been her companion for three years now. You will not be required to do all the duties of a maid, and you shall have more freedom to do other things when you are not with Lady Sarah."

Emmie kept quiet as she considered her father's idea. The more she thought, the more she realized this just might work. "All right. I believe I can handle being a lady's companion."

"Splendid." He kissed his daughter's forehead. "Now that is all settled, I will have only a few soldiers following you during your journey. They will follow until you are close to my friend's estate."

Her heart sank. "But… would the soldiers not draw attention to us if they are following?"

He shook his head. "I shall instruct them not to follow too closely." He took his daughter's hands and squeezed. "I believe your journey will go smoothly. When you reach Greenwich, I want you to enjoy yourself. Think of this as a holiday, if you will. Try not to worry about your papa or your uncle."

Emmie's heart clenched, and she frowned. "That is asking a lot of me. I cannot help but worry about you." Her uncle, however, she would love to forget completely.

Her father pushed his fingers through his graying black hair. "My dear little Emmie, you worry entirely too much about me."

"Father, it's hard not to." Tears pricked her eyes. "I don't want to lose you like we lost Mother."

"Nonsense. Your mother was killed by a pirate ship."

"Exactly. What if they are part of the same group who despise Uncle Edward?"

Chuckling, he patted her cheek. "My dear, you are too intelligent, and you know too much about politics. Rest assured, all will be well."

She released a pent-up breath. "Promise me you will not do anything rash and get involved where you shouldn't."

He offered a sympathetic half-smile. "Not to worry, my dear little Emmie. The Lord will watch over both of us."

Her father turned and opened the bedroom door before leading them down the grand stairs to the front door. Servants loaded trunks onto the coach as Anna climbed into the vehicle. Emmie hugged her father before getting in herself. Once she sat, he reached in and grasped her clutched hands.

"Godspeed, my dear."

"I shall see you soon." She smiled, although she didn't put much effort into the emotion due to her jittery feelings.

As the coach jerked into action, her heartbeat slowed considerably. The next little while was definitely *not* a holiday, no matter what her father tried to tell her. And she had promised to be a lady's companion the whole time.

Good grief, what had she been thinking to agree to her father's plan?

CAPTAIN BRODERICK WORTHINGTON gnashed his teeth as he gripped the ship's railing with one hand and balanced the spyglass with the other, watching the enemy ship coming toward them.

All the crew on the *Avenger* scrambled into action as Broderick shouted orders over his shoulder. His ship was fast, so it was perfect for his needs to find disloyal men and bring them to justice.

One of Broderick's great-uncles, Captain Hawk—also known as Marcus Thorne—had once commanded the *Avenger*. Now the ship was Broderick's, as long as he could get away from the French vessel heading right for them. For a few years, the *Avenger* had taken command of some of Napoleon's ships. Was it any wonder the emperor's armies wanted revenge?

"Captain, we are picking up speed."

Broderick lowered his spyglass and settled his attention on his first mate, Phillip Daughtery. The wind whipped the man's long auburn hair around his face in disarray. Under the sun, the strawberry tint was more prominent. Needless to say, Phillip always stood out in a crowd.

"That we are, Daughtery." Broderick glanced at his crew. "It appears Lieutenant Mercer doesn't know when to give up."

Phillip took a step closer and squinted in the direction of their attacker. "Is that who is after us?"

"It is." Broderick gritted his teeth.

"If I might say, captain, that man will stop at nothing to get his prize. He has a reputation that precedes him. Good men quake in their boots when he is near."

Broderick looked through his spyglass again. "The man has the most wicked eyes I have ever seen, not to mention his ungodly orange hair."

"I must agree with you. Mercer is the spawn of Satan himself."

Broderick blew out an irritated breath. "I feel the wind is on our side today. Let us pray it continues."

He had to trust all would go well. He turned back to the ocean and lifted his spyglass again. "However, I would truly like to know how Lieutenant Mercer knows we were here in the first place. The *Avenger* has been out of commission for a few months.

How would they know where we were headed this time?"

"Do you think there is a spy among us?" Phillip asked in a lower voice.

Broderick swung around and faced his friend. Phillip's panicked expression mirrored the way Broderick felt. "I pray there isn't, but I know not how to explain today's mishap." Sighing, he raked his fingers through his hair. "Today's near capture was too close. I don't want it happening again." He glanced over his shoulder at the vessel that was slowly getting smaller. "If the wind changes, we may not make our escape after all."

From the other ship, a booming noise shook the air around them. The cannonball landed in the water, splashing water on Broderick and Phillip. Broderick strolled to the railing of the quarterdeck and shouted more commands at his crew to pick up speed.

His friend jumped back, his face hard with anger. "What in the blazes do they think they are doing?" Phillip snapped. "Why did they waste a cannonball when they knew it would not get to us?"

"Lieutenant Mercer is arrogant. I believe he truly thought he could hit our ship. Or frighten us into surrendering."

"They are all bloody imbeciles—every last one."

"Indeed." Broderick scrubbed his hand over his unshaven jaw. "Unfortunately, they did get close enough to see us through their spyglasses just as I watched them." He sighed and frowned. "Once we are able to hide the ship and go on land, I think they will be looking for us." His gaze shifted to Phillip's thick patch of auburn hair. "And unfortunately, we are both easy men to spot because of our hair color."

"What do you suggest we do, captain?"

Another cannon boomed through the air, but the projectile fell short of hitting its mark. Thankfully, it wasn't as close as the first one. The *Avenger* was definitely gaining speed. Broderick was confident the crew would reach their destination without getting caught, but they would all have to go into hiding for a while.

"Once we reach Brighton's port," Broderick answered his friend, "I will instruct everyone to go into hiding. I think we all need to stay someplace we haven't been. That's the only way. We also may need to alter our appearance."

"How do you suggest we do that?"

Broderick shrugged. "By any means we can obtain. In fact, I know of a woman—"

"Of course you do," Phillip interrupted with a snicker. "And a lot of women *know* you very well too, captain."

Broderick rolled his eyes and tried not to grin. True, he had become a ladies' man in the past few years, but that was neither here nor there. "As I was saying," he continued, "I know an *older* woman who can dye hair. Perhaps I shall visit her and see what she can do with mine." He scrubbed his raven hair as he peered at Phillip's head. "And I suggest you follow my example."

"I shall, captain."

With a nod, Broderick ended their conversation and strolled back toward the end of the ship so he could finish watching the French vessel that was almost out of sight now. Over the past ten or so years, there had been many times the enemy had nearly captured him. Thankfully, good fortune was on his side.

Doubt snuck inside his mind. Could there be a spy amongst them, as Phillip had suggested? Most of these men he knew from when he was the first mate to Captain Hawk not more than sixteen months ago. Back then, there were many spies, some they didn't know about until Broderick and Marcus almost lost their lives. So why not now?

Growling, Broderick tightened his fingers around the railing. He needed to weed them out, yet how could he accomplish such a feat while he was in hiding? Regardless, he must find a way. His crew depended upon him. He could not... *would not* let them down!

Chapter Two

*C*AN THIS DAY *possibly get any worse?*

Emmie's legs wobbled as she rose out of the mud pit she and her maid were tossed into when the vehicle had thrown them. Her heart still hammered out of control, and the spinning in her head hadn't subsided. She glanced up the small slope to where the vehicle had rolled before stopping in the muck.

One minute they were riding along just fine, and the next minute, the coach jerked fitfully and flipped over. Within seconds, the door had broken open, throwing both Emmie and Anna out.

Anna groaned and rose to her feet but slipped and fell on her backside once again.

"Here, let me help," Emmie offered, holding out a shaky hand.

Once Anna was standing, she tried to swipe the mud off her dress, but it mostly stuck to her fingers. "What happened?" Her voice shook.

Emmie examined the scene closer—an overturned coach with a broken door, but the four wheels were still held together and connected to the vehicle. Where the horses had run off to, she didn't know. "I wish I knew what happened. Perhaps the vehicle hit a large rock and overturned."

"Lady Sarah? I can't see the driver."

Panic raced through her blood. "Neither can I." Emmie lifted her soaked skirt and walked to the knoll not far from them. "He isn't down in the ravine… although our trunks are." She searched again, this time calling, "Sir? Driver? Where are you?" She turned toward Anna and shrugged.

"Heavens, Lady Sarah. Your face has smudges of mud all over it."

Emmie swiped the muck off her face, knowing she'd probably made it worse.

"Oh, Lady Sarah, this has been the worst day of my life, and yours as well. I blame your uncle and his selfishness for putting us in this predicament." Anna pouted and slipped again, but Emmie caught her maid's elbow, steadying her.

Sighing heavily, Emmie nodded. "I agree. Today has been simply horrid. But we must not blame my uncle. Not fully, anyway. This senseless world in which we live has many emotions running high. People don't always make the best decisions when they are angry." She glanced up and down the empty road, searching for their driver. "Sad to think we have only been in Greenwich for a few hours, and already we have had a very trying day."

"And your father's soldiers have already left us." Anna choked on a sob.

"That only means we are near the Cramptons' estate."

"I want to return home." Anna sniffed. "Oh, Lady Sarah, look at your dress." She brushed her hands over Emmie's traveling dress but only managed to smear the caked-on dirt instead of removing it.

"Not to worry, Anna. Since this was something we could not avoid, we should not fret. However, I wonder what happened to our driver." She scanned the area once more. "Without him, how shall we get to our destination?"

"Oh dear. Do you suppose he is terribly hurt from being thrown?"

Silently, Emmie grumbled. If only the soldiers had stayed

with them the whole journey, perhaps she and her maid wouldn't be in this predicament. Then again, in order for Emmie to begin her charade, she'd needed the others to turn back. "I cannot see any trace of him. Unless…" She sucked in a breath and trudged through the mire toward the overturned coach. "I pray he's not trapped underneath."

"Oh no!" Anna moved around the other side of the vehicle. "He isn't here, either."

Worry seized Emmie's throat, and she walked slowly around the vehicle, hoping she didn't see any feet sticking out… or, heaven forbid, a head. "I cannot see him underneath." She prayed he wasn't completely crushed and sucked into the wet ground. But she felt he wasn't. Something else had happened to him.

"I want to go home," Anna whined again.

Emmie nodded, but at the same time, she wished her maid would stop complaining. "Unfortunately, we cannot. Not until my father lets us know it's safe."

"I know, but being in an unfamiliar place is just as frightening."

"Very true."

Anna released another cry and pointed to the bottom of the hill. "How will we retrieve our trunks?"

Heaving a sigh, Emmie rubbed her forehead. The painful tic throbbing behind her eyes threatened to expand into a huge pounding before too long. If only she could go back to this morning and start all over from when she crawled out of bed, maybe things would have worked out better. Or if she could go back to eight weeks ago, she would still be in Paris. Then again, this part of the country was where her mother had been born and raised. Part of her heart wanted to search for relatives she had never met, but she didn't dare.

Emmie adjusted her crooked bonnet and tightened the bows under her chin—now dripping with filth. At least she could act dignified, even though she appeared far from it at the moment.

The rumble of another coach from up the road pulled her

from her thoughts. She held her breath, hoping good fortune had decided to smile upon them after all. Anna scooted closer to her side and clutched Emmie's arm.

The vehicle slowed as it neared, the driver's gaze roaming over both Emmie and her maid. The coach appeared to be one of someone with wealth. The gold crest of eagle wings on the door hinted that the vehicle's owner could be a noble.

Once the horses stopped, the driver shifted on his seat, leaning toward them. "What has happened here?"

Emmie took a step closer. "We are stranded, sir. Our coach overturned, and we cannot find the driver."

The door to the vehicle opened, and a head poked out mere seconds before the man's frame followed. Emmie's mouth hung open as she stared at the man emerging. He was very tall and muscular, and she couldn't believe someone so robust could be so incredibly handsome as well. His light brown hair was pulled back from his face and secured with a leather tie. Dark brown eyes widened as he gazed over both Emmie and Anna. Never in her life had she felt so unclean before, but concern registered on the man's face even though she and Anna looked a fright.

"What happened?" The handsome man glanced at the wrecked vehicle.

"I wish I knew," Emmie answered. "We were riding along smoothly, then the wheel must have hit something, and we were thrown into the mud." She pointed to the sloping hill just off the road. "Our trunks ended down at the bottom, but I can't seem to locate the driver."

He blew a heavy sigh between his teeth, and it whistled. "I'm relieved to know you are unharmed. Where are you heading, may I ask?"

"Mr. and Mrs. Crampton's estate—"

"Henry and Martha Crampton?" His gaze slid over both women once again before his eyes widened. "Are you perhaps their guests from Manchester?"

Emmie hitched a breath in surprise. "Indeed, we are."

He studied them again, slower this time, until he rested his gaze on Anna. He smiled. "Then you must be Lady Sarah Langston."

Emmie held her breath, praying Anna would remember what they had discussed during their journey. *The charade.* But what if Anna forgot… or, heaven help her, what if the maid was too frightened?

Quickly, before Anna could respond, Emmie squeezed her hand and met the man's stare. "Indeed, this is Lady Sarah Langston. I'm her companion."

Anna's wide-eyed expression clashed with Emmie's, but she gave her maid a small, reassuring smile and nodded to follow along.

The handsome man tilted his head toward Emmie. "And does Lady Sarah's companion have a name as well?"

Emmie swallowed hard. "Indeed she does. You may call me Miss Emmie."

He bowed. "It's a pleasure to meet both of you." When he straightened, he turned to his driver and motioned. "Come help me assist these two lovely ladies." He shrugged out of his waistcoat and laid it across the lip of the coach. The driver jumped down. The younger man pointed toward the vehicle. "Let's see if we can turn this aright."

"Splendid idea," Emmie cheered. "I shall help as well." She glanced at Anna, who still looked at a loss for words. "Lady Sarah, please stand over there, so you don't hurt yourself."

"Uh, I—I think I should help, too. More hands are better."

The handsome man held up his hand. "Please, my lady. I fear you may strain yourself if you try to help." He paused and looked at Emmie. "I think you should stand aside with your lady. My driver and I can see to the matter ourselves."

"Nonsense. I'm very adept. I think you should allow me to assist." Emmie lifted her chin, challenging the man.

Shrugging, he walked to the coach. "Suit yourself. My uncle taught me never to argue with a woman."

"Wise man." She chuckled.

Emmie hurried to the handsome stranger, admiring the way he looked in the beige shirt and cravat once he had removed his coat. His wide shoulders captured her attention first, and as her gaze slowly slid down his lean waist and muscular legs, her throat turned dry. Although it was most improper to admire the way he looked so masculine in his clothes, it was hard to stop.

She wanted to wave her hand in front of her face to cool herself from such wicked thoughts, but then he looked over his shoulder at her and smiled, which nearly melted her legs right from underneath her.

"If this is too much for you, Miss Emmie, please don't push yourself. I would hate for you to get injured."

She wanted to chuckle at his remark. Not many people knew that she did things an earl's daughter should not do—and her father had scolded her several times in the past year because of her stubbornness. She rather liked being her own woman. "I assure you, I know my limits."

He nodded, turned, and grabbed a section of the vehicle. Together the three of them lifted, pushed, and set the coach aright. Immediately, Emmie studied the space where the overturned vehicle had lain. Thankfully, her driver had not been trapped underneath. Yet the thought remained… where had he gone?

The nice man placed his hands on each wheel, pulling to ensure they still were in working order. His driver had found where the horses had wandered off, brought them back, and hitched them up. Then the two men lugged the trunks up the hill and lashed them back to the vehicle.

"It appears everything is in working condition, except for the broken door."

"We shall drive without a door, then." Emmie smiled.

The handsome stranger stepped to Anna and offered his hand. "My lady, let me help you back into your coach. I shall have my driver take you to Mr. and Mrs. Crampton's estate."

"What about you?" Emmie asked. After all, he was a gentleman of means, she was certain, so didn't *he* need a driver?

He glanced her way for a second before leading Anna to the coach. "I shall have no problems driving my vehicle, thank you."

"Oh, sir… What about our driver?" Emmie shook her head. "I didn't see him anywhere. He couldn't possibly have been thrown so far from the coach, could he?"

He glanced at her over his shoulder. "If you wait here, I shall go up the road a bit and try to locate him."

"Would you like me to help?" Emmie offered.

The man shook his head. "I fear if he's lying broken or bleeding, that is not the sight a young lady needs to see. Wait right here."

As the man hustled up the road, Anna clutched Emmie's hands. Both of them had been through so much within the past little while, and Emmie prayed the good Samaritan would find their driver. During their wait, the man's driver tried to fix the broken door to their carriage, but there wasn't much he could do without tools. Nevertheless, they could travel without a door, just as long as they didn't have much farther to go.

Soon the helpful stranger returned. A frown marred his handsome face, and he shook his head. "I couldn't see him. When I return to town, I shall summon the authorities and have this investigated posthaste."

Sighing, Emmie nodded. "You are extremely kind, sir. I thank you for taking the time to look anyway."

He helped Anna inside the coach, and she offered a shy smile to the man. "I thank you, sir."

Emmie bit her lip to keep from grinning. Her maid was certainly acting out of character. Usually, her servant flirted outrageously with handsome men. Perhaps Anna was thinking about her new role and remembering an earl's daughter wouldn't be so bold, even though sometimes Emmie was.

Emmie walked to the door, waiting for him to step aside so she could climb in. "Pardon me, but what is your name? How do you know Mr. and Mrs. Crampton?"

"Most everyone around these parts knows of Mr. and Mrs. Crampton. They own a large piece of land and live in a beautiful estate."

"You did not tell me your name."

"I'm Broderick Worthington."

She smiled. "Thank you for your kindness, Mr. Worthington. We certainly appreciate your assistance."

He took her hand and helped her inside. After Mr. Worthington walked back to his vehicle, Emmie looked at her maid and sighed with relief. So far, their disguises had worked.

Anna shook her head. "Lady Sarah, I really don't know what your father was thinking to have us switch roles." She spoke low. "I feel as if I have to think about every word before I say it."

Emmie arched an eyebrow. "But Anna, you told my father you could play this role without any instruction."

A blush stole across the maid's cheeks. "Well, perhaps I didn't know what I was saying. Thinking and *doing* are two entirely different things."

Emmie chuckled. "Indeed they are. But you are doing fine." She nudged her maid's arm. "Besides, you look more like an earl's daughter than I ever did."

"No, I don't." Anna shook her head. "I bet you are glad you made me wear this fancy traveling dress. Otherwise, Mr. Worthington may have been suspicious."

"Indeed, I'm very grateful. I knew we would reach Mr. and Mrs. Crampton's house today, and now we won't have to worry about first appearances." Emmie patted Anna's clasped hands. "No need to fret. Nobody will know the difference."

The clip-clop from the horses' hooves and the swaying of the vehicle lulled Emmie, causing her eyes to droop. Yet her mind wouldn't sleep. Many ideas swam in her head, and excitement danced in her body, keeping her awake.

Originally, she had abhorred her father's plan. But now...

She wanted to accomplish so much without the restrictions of being an earl's daughter hanging over her. She would finally get to ride through the countryside without one of her father's servants escorting her. She could talk the way she wanted, pretty much *do* whatever she wanted, without seeing her father's scowl or hearing his raised voice when he scolded her for being hardheaded and having her own mind.

How would it be if a man could look at her as a woman and not as a wealthy lady? Plenty of men had vowed their loyalty and love to her, but none she believed. How could she when she knew it was her dowry they were after?

Closing her eyes, she leaned back on the seat. A man's face appeared in her mind, and she smiled. *Mr. Worthington.* Would she ever meet him again? Although he rode in the coach of someone who had money, he certainly didn't act like he was used to being waited on. When he'd volunteered to help turn over their vehicle, and then said he would drive the coach himself, Emmie was certain he didn't hold a title.

When the coach slowed, and surprised voices rang out, Emmie snapped her eyes open and peeked out of the broken door. The old trees lining the drive appeared as if they had been tended with care throughout the years, as had the acreage of manicured lawns rolling out as far as she could see. She gasped in awe of its beauty. When a manor came into view, she gazed upon the two-story building that looked like a cross between Gothic and Tudor styles. This, she had been informed, was where the Crampton family liked to spend their off-season.

As the vehicle came to a stop, the front door to the house opened, and an older gentleman, tall, stocky, with thinning brown hair, hustled out. Not far behind him came a woman about the same age, tall and thin, wearing a lovely blue gown. She adjusted her bonnet as she aimed her gaze at the coach.

Emmie smiled. These must be her father's friends, Mr. and Mrs. Crampton.

Anna stirred on the seat. "Have we arrived?"

"Indeed we have, Lady Sarah."

Anna blinked as she looked at Emmie. "Do you know how hard it is going to be for me to answer to that name?"

"You shall do fine. Just remember to call me Miss Emmie."

As the driver hopped down, Emmie prepared herself for a new adventure. Freedom from Society's rules was in her grasp, at least for a little while, and she planned on taking advantage of a perfect opportunity.

Chapter Three

BRODERICK SUBMERGED HIS body fully into the pond. Holding his breath, he hoped the water would not take away his new hair color. The old widow, Mrs. Baker, had changed his hair color to brown and even given him a cut. Gratefully, he had walked out of her house looking like a new man. Now, if he could just keep away from large crowds, all would be well in his world. At least for a few months. He prayed things would get back to normal soon after that.

During his much-needed break, he didn't want to think about the problems in his life. He didn't want to have to constantly look over his shoulder and wonder who was a spy—and especially who might know his true identity. Unfortunately, he couldn't relax now. Not since he knew the niece of the wretched lord chancellor was visiting the Cramptons.

Before the air in his lungs ran out, he rose out of the water and breathed deeply. He swiped his fingers through his hair, pushing the strands back on his head and out of his eyes. Wiping the excess water from his face, he blinked and focused on his surroundings. His uncle's country estate was the perfect place for his sanctuary, and during the next few weeks, he would take advantage of what the property had to offer, which at the moment was peace and solitude.

Sometime while he was here, he would also get to know

Lady Sarah a little better as well. He couldn't really blame her for what her foolish uncle had done, but he would definitely become close to her to see if she knew about the man's plans, because Broderick would surely put a stop to them. The man needed his title removed, and soon.

Taking the brick of soap, he scrubbed it over his face. Within seconds, his eyes began to sting. He cursed, tossed the soap on the grass, and then splashed water on his face, but his eyes still stung and blurred.

The rustle of bushes and snaps of twigs pulled his thoughts away, and he swung around to face the intruder. Ready to give them a sound thrashing, he scowled when his vision didn't quite cooperate. Through his impaired vision, it looked like someone was peeking through the bushes.

The burning sensation in his eyes only intensified. "Please, I need your help. If you will, I need you to bring me that towel over there."

When the person didn't move and continued to stare, irritation flowed through him. "Are you going to stand and ogle my body, or can you hand me that towel?" He pointed to the rock where he had left the towel.

Finally, the person moved out from the bushes, heading for the rock. Broderick splashed his eyes with water again and rubbed them harder.

"Actually," the stranger said, "I thought ogling your body would help pass the time on this dreary day."

Stunned, Broderick exhaled sharply. Words vanished from his mind, and he blinked, trying to focus. The blur finally formed into a person... a woman with her hair wound tight on the top of her head and who appeared to be wearing a baggy dress.

Embarrassment washed over him quicker than the cool water had a few moments ago. What was a woman doing peeking at him while he bathed? Unless... He had known the younger widow from his uncle's neighboring property, and she was always a little forward. Perhaps it was Mrs. Fisher. Inwardly, he groaned.

Now was *not* the time to try to fight off her advances.

"Thank you for your assistance," he said, "but if you were planning on joining me, let me assure you, I'm nearly finished, so your trip here was wasted."

A gasp came from the woman, and her mouth hung open. She lifted the towel from off the rock and stepped closer.

"First off, let me say I'm appalled by your rude behavior from a man who—not more than two seconds ago—asked for my help. Lastly, I don't know who you think I am, but I had no plans on joining your bath."

The voice was definitely not Mrs. Fisher's. Mortification expanded inside him. For the first time in his life, he was rendered speechless.

Quickly, he splashed his eyes with water one last time and rubbed them before focusing on his intruder once again. This time he could see the woman as clear as day. And sure enough, this was definitely not Mrs. Fisher, but a much younger woman. He didn't know who she was, but she was in dire need of a more experienced seamstress. She wore men's trousers and shirt but had on women's boots. And her hair flowed gently over her shoulders and down her back.

He studied her face as she stepped closer to the edge of the pond holding the towel. Now he could see the gentle curves of her cheeks and lips. Long eyelashes framed her eyes. Although her face was pretty, her hair and dress did not fit her loveliness.

Broderick shook his head. "Forgive me for not noticing you at first. I had soap in my eyes and couldn't see clearly. And I apologize for thinking you were someone else."

"Oh. Well then, since you thought I was someone else, you are forgiven for being so rude."

She was forgiving him? When she was the one spying on his bath? Obviously, she wasn't as innocent as she appeared. "Who are you, and where are you from? Did you know you are trespassing on another man's land?"

Instead of the panic he figured to see on her expression, she arched one of her eyebrows. "I have been invited here, but you, sir, have not. I have met everyone who lives and works on this estate, and you are not one of them. Perhaps you are trespassing."

Confusion filled his head. Was she one of his uncle's servants? But she didn't look like any servant he had met before. And why was the woman dressed in men's clothes?

"No, I'm not trespassing." Still in the water, Broderick walked toward her. Just before reaching the point where the water lowered on his body, he stopped. Why did she continue to stare? She didn't have that *experienced* expression on her face. Indeed, this woman was innocent, so then why was she still watching him? "Are you going to turn and hide your eyes, or are you used to seeing a man's nakedness?"

Her cheeks flared a bright red mere seconds before she spun around. "Forgive me. I hadn't realized... I mean, I had forgotten..."

Chuckling, he walked out of the water and stood behind her, taking the towel from her hand. "Nonetheless, I thank you for retrieving the towel for me," he whispered in her ear.

A shiver shook her body, but she stayed rigid and faced the other way. "Sir, you still haven't told me who you are."

He wrapped the towel around his waist and tucked it in the edges. "And you, my little confused woman, haven't introduced yourself either, so I assume we are at a standstill."

"Confused?" she shrieked.

Huffing, she spun around and faced him. Fire nearly shot out from her heated gaze as she lifted her eyes and met his. Being a head and a half taller, he hadn't realized until now how tiny she was. Another thing he hadn't noticed until now was her astonishingly lovely blue eyes—a much darker shade than he had ever seen before.

A small gasp came from her as her eyes widened. "Actually, I believe we have met after all. You are Mr. Worthington, the man who rescued Lady Sarah and myself from the overturned coach."

It was Broderick's turn to inhale a surprised breath. This was

Lady Sarah's companion? *Good heavens!* "Forgive me for not recognizing you, then. You looked different without all that mud covering you—and without a dress."

She shrugged. "It's surprising what a little bath will do." She motioned toward the pond. "As I'm sure you have already guessed."

He chuckled. "Indeed, I have. But now I'm curious to know why you are still standing here talking to a mostly naked man. Most women I know would have run like the devil was on their heels from seeing a man take a bath. Yet here you are, still in front of me."

Although her cheeks continued to glow with embarrassment, she squared her shoulders and lifted her chin as if to challenge him.

"I hate to disillusion you, Mr. Worthington, but I'm not like most women."

"Do lady's companions usually act this way in Manchester?"

"Not many." She shook her head. "But Lady Sarah understands me well and allows it."

He nodded. "Then forgive me for scolding you. It was not my place."

"So, Mr. Worthington, you still haven't told me why you are here on Mr. and Mrs. Crampton's property."

He couldn't believe how surprised he was at this whole situation—almost speechless, which wasn't like him. Strange to think he was still mostly naked, and yet the young lady continued to make polite conversation as if they were at a dinner social.

Shaking his head, he tried not to laugh at her. "I'm visiting my uncle for a spell. Henry Crampton is my mother's brother."

She smiled. "How nice, Mr. Worthington." She scrunched her forehead. "By chance, do I need to address you differently? Are you a lord?"

Not unless his noble relatives had all died... Broderick laughed. "Miss Emmie, you can call me Broderick or Mr. Worthington, either one."

She smiled. "It is very nice to see you again, Mr. Worthington."

He grinned at her stubbornness, and a thought struck him. "Pray, what is a lady's companion doing traipsing throughout the countryside dressed like a man, and by herself, instead of tending to the earl's daughter?"

Smugly, she arched an eyebrow again. "As I mentioned previously, Lady Sarah understands me and treats me differently than most servants. When I'm not tending to Lady Sarah's needs, I am free to dress this way and ride my horse or walk around the grounds. Besides that, a lady's companion doesn't need a chaperone constantly, especially when she is with your aunt and uncle right now."

"You are correct, of course."

An uncomfortable silence hung between them, and she shifted her feet as her gaze moved around the secluded area. He found it strange that he didn't want to talk. Looking at her was fulfilling enough. He enjoyed the way the men's clothes nearly clung to her woman's curves. She was anything but plain. She was quite lovely, in fact.

"Oh, Mr. Worthington, I must ask… Did you discover what happened to my—er, Lady Sarah's driver?"

He shook his head. "Unfortunately, I haven't heard. I summoned the authorities, as promised, but I haven't heard what happened. I told them Lady Sarah was staying with my aunt and uncle, so I suspect if the authorities find anything out about your driver, they will let Lady Sarah know."

"Well, I thank you again for your help in the matter." She offered a smile that didn't quite reach her eyes. "As much as I would like to stay and chat, my time is about up. I should return to the house. Lady Sarah might need me soon."

"As you wish. I trust we shall see each other later."

She nodded. "I'm certain you will."

"Good day, Miss Emmie."

"And good day to you, Mr. Worthington."

As she walked away, he grinned. Although he hated to admit it, he quite enjoyed their little interlude, even if he was half-naked. Now he wondered if she'd even realized it at all. Yet her blush from time to time proved that she did indeed know but had tried to be proper about it.

Broderick retrieved his clothes and chuckled. Miss Emmie was certainly different, and he looked forward to visiting with her again.

What was he thinking? It should be Lady Sarah he needed to get to know—not her companion. Then again, *this* particular lady's companion showed promise of fun-filled days ahead.

EMMIE STOOD BEHIND Anna, helping her prepare for the Cramptons' ball that evening. Although a maid should be fixing Anna's hair, Emmie didn't mind the task, only because she wanted Anna to look her part.

Anna wrung her hands against her middle, and in the reflection in the mirror, Emmie noticed the lines of worry etched on her face. "Mr. and Mrs. Crampton are going to introduce me to their family and friends. Are you certain your father doesn't know anybody besides the Cramptons?"

Emmie weaved a pink ribbon through Anna's dark hair and artfully pulled back the sides with pearl-studded combs to complete the ensemble. "I wish I could tell you, Anna. My father doesn't speak of everyone he knows. He met my mother on a visit to York, and I think her death hurt him so much he doesn't want to talk about that time in his life."

"Oh, forgive me, Lady Sarah. I didn't even think of that."

"Shh... I'm Emmie now, remember that," she reminded Anna.

"My apologies, Lady—eh, I mean Emmie." Anna sighed heavily. "What am I going to do if someone realizes I don't look like your father?"

Emmie snorted a laugh as she met her friend's gaze in the mirror. Sometimes the maid could be so obtuse. "Anna, I don't even resemble my father. I take more after my mother, but you look enough like me that you fit the part."

Anna relaxed. "Forgive me for being so jumpy. I suppose I'm a little nervous about tonight. I don't want to muck things up."

Emmie added the finishing touches to Anna's hair by pulling the ringlets down evenly. "You will do fine. You have given a splendid performance thus far. Mr. and Mrs. Crampton don't suspect a thing, and Mr. Crampton was very close to my father."

Anna nodded. "You're right as always, my lady."

"Anna!" Emmie said in a whisper. "You must not call me that. No one must know of our charade. I don't even want the servants to overhear. Do you understand?"

"Yes," Anna answered softly.

After finishing Anna's hair, Emmie helped her friend brush the gown to free it from the few wrinkles it had gathered. This pink ball dress of Emmie's had always been one of her favorites. The silk sensation had a deep v-cut in the bodice, which she thought made her chest look fuller. Of course, the slim waist and the billowy sleeves of white lace had always made her look elegant. But now, as a different woman was wearing it, it disappointed Emmie a little, because the dress actually looked better on her friend.

She tried not to think about all the parties and functions Anna had been invited to while they were visiting. Emmie would have to stand back and watch her friend be swept away by men on the dance floor. Then again, this could be a good thing. Emmie wouldn't have to hear their lies when they promised her the moon and stars on a silver platter. She wouldn't have people bowing and curtsying every time she walked by, and they wouldn't treat her as if she was precious glass just because her father was the earl. She reminded herself again that the disguise as a lady's companion couldn't be more perfect.

Anna picked out one of the fancier dresses for Emiline to wear tonight. The shimmering gray material was pretty, but just like the dress she had worn earlier, this one practically hung on her. The modest high-neck collar with white lace and long sleeves didn't enhance any part of her body. The color even made her face pale, and her eyes bug out. Then again, the way she wound her hair so tight, that could be the reason her eyes looked funny.

Emmie and Anna left the bedroom together. When they reached the ballroom, Emmie stopped and tapped Anna on the arm. "You shall do fine. Just remember... you are me," she whispered.

Holding her head high, Anna entered the ballroom as Emmie followed. She tried her best not to let anyone really look at her, and thankfully, their eyes were on Anna—who soaked up the attention well. Many people filled the ballroom and greeted Lady Sarah with bows and curtsies. Emmie smiled, knowing Anna had turned out a great performance.

This time...

Chapter Four

IT HAD BEEN quite a long time since Emmie attended a party, and being at this one brought back nostalgic memories. She remembered in her younger years that she loved dressing up in fancy ball gowns. She had danced with the boys, even though most of them stepped on her toes. As she watched Anna dance with Mr. Crampton, Emmie was grateful she had decided to teach her maid how to dance when they were younger.

A few couples strolled past her, not even giving her a dismissive glance. Strange how people treated her like she was a ghost. Once in a while, Emmie received judgmental glares and upturned noses, especially from the ladies, but it didn't happen until after they had looked at her gown. Inwardly, she groaned. Maybe she should spend some of her father's money to purchase newer gowns. After all, Anna only had gowns for servants, not for Emmie's new role.

Subtly, she glided over to a potted plant near the corner of the room and pretended to pick out the dead leaves. When two ladies passed by and eyed Emmie closely, she decided not to act like she was picking apart the plant any longer and slowly wandered toward another wall. Immediately, her attention was pulled to the door of the ballroom. A handsome man strolled inside, his powerful presence demanding attention, which he definitely received.

Emmie grinned. Mr. Worthington looked just as good clothed as he did when he was bathing in the pond. The memory of that most embarrassing moment caused heat to climb up her neck and rest on her cheeks. She'd been so uncomfortable conversing with a half-naked man, yet she had been mesmerized by his charm and good looks, and she couldn't force herself to leave, even though her mind argued how wrong it was to be with a man who had just finished bathing.

Never had she seen a man's bare chest and bare legs. Mr. Worthington was magnificent, and it had been all she could do to keep from touching his muscles to see if they were as hard as they appeared.

She tore her mind from that very heated memory and watched him move from guest to guest. He mingled easily. His smile had her enthralled, and his laugh caused flutters in her belly. The handsome creature then walked to his uncle. The two men talked for a few minutes before Mr. Crampton turned and called out to Anna.

Mr. Worthington's eyes widened when he first looked at the pretend daughter of the earl, and jealousy jabbed at Emmie's chest. Mr. Worthington took Anna's hand in formal greeting, his face brightening by the second.

The next dance was claimed by Mr. Worthington as he took Anna out on the dance floor. Emmie didn't want to admit it, but her maid actually looked good beside him. Anna's eyes gleamed like stars while she danced. How could they not? He just happened to be the most dominant man in this room, and Emmie wasn't the only woman who noticed. Many pairs of eyes followed the handsome man with the muscular body around the room.

Emmie almost wished she could take back her identity, only so she could be the woman dancing in his arms. It was too late for that now. Both she and Anna would be laughingstocks if people were to find out about their charade. In addition, Emmie couldn't do that to Mr. and Mrs. Crampton. And she especially couldn't go against her father's wishes.

After Anna and Mr. Worthington's dance was over, he bowed to his partner and brushed his lips across the back of her hand. Pleasure spread over the maid's expression, which, in turn, made Emmie more upset over the switch of identities. That could have been *her* out there on the dance floor. He could be kissing *her* hand, instead.

Broderick left Anna's side to wander around the room. He took a glass of champagne from the butler and then leaned back against the wall.

Anna made a sharp turn and headed Emmie's way. "I was so nervous during that dance."

"You are doing splendidly tonight," Emmie replied.

"Thank you. I stepped on his toes a few times, though."

"Nobody could tell." Emmie grinned.

Anna whispered her gratitude and returned to the Cramptons' small group.

As Emmie started to head back toward the wall she had been keeping company with the last little while, her attention immediately stopped on Broderick, who stood where she had seen him last. His gaze rested intently on her, causing her feet to stop before reaching their destination. She wrung her hands, hoping he wouldn't say anything about their last meeting at the pond. That was all she needed, for people to judge her for being improper.

Was he the kind of man to mention the time at the pond? She prayed he wasn't.

Broderick Worthington boldly scanned Emmie's attire, from her tight bun down to her gray dress. When his eyes met hers again, his lips turned up into a smile. With a small bow, he let her know he recognized her.

Her heart pounded an uneven rhythm as she returned the smile and curtsied. Following his lead, she looked over his attire—a deep blue waistcoat stretched across his wide chest, a black coat that fit his broad shoulders, and black breeches that snugged against his muscular legs perfectly. His shirt and cravat were pristine white, bringing out the skin tones of his face. She nodded her approval. He chuckled and held up his drink as if in a salute.

Sighing, she stared at his astounding smile. Shame on her, but as hard as she tried, she couldn't get the image of him bathing out of her mind. Never had she witnessed such an indecent sight, even though all she had seen was his bare chest and arms. Now, as she stared dreamily at him, it was as if they were the only two people in the room.

Although she wanted to talk to him, she knew it wasn't her place. Besides, she felt tongue-tied around him, which didn't happen often. Not only that, but she was a *lady's companion*, and she shouldn't be conversing with the male guests, no matter how incredibly handsome they were.

Humor twinkled in his eyes, and she desperately wanted to know what thoughts swam through his head.

When he finally turned away to chat with a group of beautiful young women who flocked to him, disappointment washed over Emmie. Slowly, she went back to her corner of the room to keep the wall company once again.

For the rest of the evening, her form of entertainment was to witness the way her maid interacted with Broderick. Soon, Anna broke away from him and walked toward Emmie. Her heart quickened. She wondered what was going on now.

"Emmie," Anna said when she reached her. "Mr. Worthington has asked me to take a walk with him outside. What should I do?"

Emmie fisted her hands by her sides, wishing once again that *she* was the woman he'd asked to walk with him. "It's polite to accept."

"Then will you fetch my shawl for me? I mean… um, your shawl?" she ended in a whisper.

"Yes, *my lady*. I shall be more than happy to fetch the shawl." Grudgingly, Emmie hurried out of the ballroom and up the stairs to get the shawl. On the way back down, she grumbled under her breath. As she placed the shawl around Anna's shoulders, she whispered in her friend's ear, "Remember who you are and that Lady Sarah doesn't allow men to seduce her."

When Anna met Emmie's glare, the maid's forehead creased. Before Anna had a chance to say anything, Broderick claimed her for their walk. The only acknowledgment he gave Emmie before he escorted Anna out on his arm was a nod.

Emmie rolled her eyes. Why was she feeling this way? She didn't have any claim on Broderick. Come to think of it, he had been quite snobbish to her when they spoke earlier at the pond.

But even though her mind was trying to create bad thoughts about him, she was still curious to find out what the two of them were doing on their walk right now.

She glanced around the hall, hoping nobody would care if she disappeared outside. But since everyone treated her as a ghost, she was certain to not have anyone stop her.

She grinned. Her entertainment was just beginning.

Emmie crept out the side door and onto the terrace. Casually, so as not to draw attention, she walked to the edge of the lawn and scanned the large expanse of grass and trees, hoping to spot Anna. Within moments, she noticed her friend and the very handsome man beside her. Broderick led the love-struck Anna away from the house toward the shadows near the trees. Growling under her breath, Emmie feared the worst. Knowing her maid like she did, she knew exactly what Anna wanted.

Emmie quickly searched for a place to hide and watch them better. Across the way stood a large marble statue, and behind it, some bushes. Since Broderick and Anna headed in that direction at a leisurely pace, Emmie decided she would have time to get to the statue and hide there before they arrived… as long as she ran.

She lifted her skirts to her ankles and sprinted across the yard toward the statue. Broderick and Anna seemed to have eyes only for each other, so Emmie arrived at her hiding spot before the other two did.

Hopefully, her maid wasn't up to her usual tricks and disregarding the rules of propriety. If so, Anna would be in Broderick's arms this very night. Emmie didn't think she'd be able to hide her jealous anger and keep herself concealed if that happened.

She gulped. If Anna didn't take care, Emmie's reputation could be ruined.

BRODERICK SMILED POLITELY at the lovely woman beside him. The longer he was in her presence, the more confused he became. Her charm was evident, yet her shyness was a contradiction. She really didn't talk much, and he couldn't believe he'd actually met a woman who didn't chatter endlessly. Now he'd found one he wished would talk a little more.

So far, he had told her about himself—at least what he wanted her to know—and now he wanted to hear about her. If she would tell him, that was. Every time he asked her about herself, she changed the subject, bringing the topic back to him.

They stopped by the marble statue of a woman with a water pitcher in her hands. Still close enough to the house for propriety's sake, and so as not to anger her lady's companion, Miss Emmie… yet far enough away that they wouldn't be bothered or overheard.

He glanced up at the moon and the few clouds littering the darkened sky. Most of the light shone from the house. Although they were not in total darkness, many shadows crept around them, especially in the bushes not more than five feet away. Prickles of awareness danced over his skin, hinting there was another presence nearby. Over the last ten years, he'd learned to trust his feelings and instincts. Spies were all around, and he must be cautious. Until he could figure out who was watching them, he would be careful.

"Please tell me about yourself, Lady Sarah. I'm certain you grow weary of hearing about my dreary life."

She smiled. "Oh, no. I could never get bored hearing about you." She paused to look at her clasped hands. "Besides, there really is not much to tell you about my life."

"You must be mistaken. After all, you are an earl's daughter. What could be more exciting than that? I'm quite certain you have many stories to tell."

"I assure you, I don't lead the adventurous life you do. My life is quite boring. My father keeps me sheltered. I'm surprised he allowed me to visit Mr. and Mrs. Crampton without his bringing me himself."

"I wonder why he is so overprotective. I assume your father has been in Greenwich before, though?"

"Indeed. He met my mother in Berkshire on one of his visits."

Her tale grew more interesting by the second. At least he wasn't completely bored. "Why did your mother not come with you this time?"

"She died fifteen years ago."

Sorrow filled him, and he frowned. He understood the ache of losing a parent because he had lost both of his. "Forgive me. I didn't know."

"There is nothing to forgive. How could you know when you do not know my family?"

"No truer words were spoken." Broderick offered a slight smile as his gaze traveled over her black hair, wound artfully in a bun, then to her pretty, round face. Big brown eyes stared back at him, long, thick lashes surrounding them. Her nose was small and somewhat pudgy, but not overly so. Her lips appeared thin, and it surprised him that he wasn't tempted to kiss them.

Another face came to mind. Miss Emmie—the one with the smoldering, big brown eyes. Right away, he questioned his train of thought. Why would he think of the lady's companion at a time like this? Quickly, he shook her out of his mind.

"Well, Lady Sarah, I appreciate your kindness in telling me about your family. I do feel as if I'm getting to know you better."

"As do I."

From the corner of his eye, the shadow in the bushes moved. Once again, awareness pricked his skin. They were definitely being watched. Without studying the shadow and drawing attention to himself, he tried to sneak peeks that way while conversing with the earl's daughter.

"Lady Sarah, now that you have been here a few days, what do you think of Greenwich?"

"It's certainly a lovely area, and the scenery is so much greener."

Silence lagged between them, which gave Broderick a moment to take a peek at the bushes again. Slowly, the clouds moved away from the moon long enough for him to see the figure of a woman. Unless his vision was playing tricks on him, the figure resembled Miss Emmie quite a bit. Without studying the shadows any deeper, he knew it was the lady's companion. Although he didn't know much about her, what he did know led him to believe she would do something this daring. He held back a grin.

He debated whether to say something and bring her out of hiding. Then again, he couldn't embarrass her. Instead, he would take advantage of the situation and play it up, just to see how Emmie would react.

Broderick stepped closer to Lady Sarah and took her hands. "My lady?" he asked softly. "Is there a man back home to whom you are promised?"

She looked up at him with wide eyes, then dropped her gaze. "No."

Strange, but he thought she would be betrothed by now. "I cannot believe such a lovely woman doesn't have a beau."

She giggled. "There are men who try to court me, but none have impressed me or my father." She lifted her attention back at him. "My father promised I could choose my own husband. So far, I have found none I could fall in love with."

He caressed her cheek. "I'm certain you will find him soon enough."

She nodded.

He moved closer and swept his fingers along her chin. "Do you think your father brought you here to find the right man?"

Her gaze softened, and he tried not to grin. He should be ashamed for leading the poor girl on, but it had been a while since he flirted this way. Thankfully, he still had that certain touch that made a woman's knees weak.

"I don't know," she replied. "Perhaps."

He scanned her face again and rested his attention on her lips, which were now parted. Although she was lovely, he didn't feel any attraction to her whatsoever. Besides, he only acted this way to make Miss Emmie upset.

"Lady Sarah, I cannot believe how lovely you are." He came closer until her dress rubbed against his trousers and overcoat. "Will you consider letting me kiss you?"

Her throat jumped in what must have been a hard swallow. He waited for a reaction from the hidden, peeping companion. From the bushes, heavy breathing overrode Lady Sarah's ragged breaths. Keeping a solemn expression, Broderick tried not to laugh.

She cleared her throat. "Mr. Worthington, I think it's improper to kiss you at this time. We have only just met." Her voice squeaked.

Broderick hovered his lips above hers, hesitating, making the moment linger. The scent of wine was on her warm breath as it blew against his face. She licked her lips. Staring deeply into her eyes, he watched the fear laced with eagerness on her expression. Her breathing quickened, and he knew he'd better stop this before she passed out.

Slowly, he pulled away. He admired her courage, but more so that of Miss Emmie. So far, the little minx hadn't blown her cover.

"Very well, Lady Sarah. I shall have to bide my time until the moment is right and you approve. Please forgive me for my forwardness."

She shied away again. "There is no need for apologies."

"Come." He held out his elbow. "Allow me to take you back to the party." As he turned, he took a quick peek at the woman still hiding in the bushes. He grinned, continuing on his way. Miss Emmie surprised him at every turn. Remarkably, he wondered what she would do next—and realized he couldn't wait to find out.

Chapter Five

ONCE BRODERICK AND Anna had walked away, Emmie released the breath she was holding in a gust. Thankfully, neither of them had seen her. She was relieved to know that Anna had not let Broderick kiss her. Her maid played a role, and the real Lady Sarah would have not allowed a man to take liberties in stealing a kiss, no matter how handsome he was.

Then again, Emmie had really never known any man as handsome as Broderick. And blast it all, it didn't help that her mind kept picturing him in the water. Perhaps if *she* had been in Broderick's arms, she would have been sorely tempted to let him place his lips on hers.

Breathing slower, she relaxed against a tree. Finally, her heart beat a normal rhythm. She had experienced Anna's thrill of excitement, making her want that very thing herself.

Groaning, she rubbed at the throb starting in her forehead. She wished she knew why she felt this way. It was so unlike her. Had living as a lady's companion become so boring that she suddenly dreamed of improper things? What happened to the freedom she thought she would have in pretending to be a companion? For some reason, it wasn't all she had wanted it to be.

She pulled away from the tree and took slow steps away from her hiding area, taking great care to see if anyone was watching her. Once again, she was grateful that nobody had cared about the lady's companion. She hurried back into the house.

Just as she entered, the announcement came of the last dance for the evening. Disappointed, she watched as Broderick danced with Anna. His joyous smile while he stared into the maid's eyes nearly broke Emmie's heart.

After the dance ended, Anna left Broderick's side and made her excuses to Mr. and Mrs. Crampton. Emmie followed Anna up the stairs toward their rooms. She really didn't want to talk to her friend, since jealousy continued to eat at her gut.

"Oh, Emmie." Anna sighed dreamily. "Can you believe there is a handsome man who wants to be with me? Although I tried my best to act shy, he still continued his pursuit."

Emmie tried to be gentle as she helped Anna remove the gown to ready her for bed, but ended up yanking the material over her friend's head instead, pulling her hair in the process.

Irritably, Emmie rolled her eyes. "Of course he flirted with you. He is an untitled man, and you are supposed to be the earl's daughter. Why wouldn't he vie for your attention? Believe me, I see men like Mr. Worthington all the time, which is why I'm not married."

She refused to believe he was enamored with Anna because she was pretty. Men only wanted to court Lady Sarah because of who her father was, so it had to be the same with Anna. It just *had* to be.

"Oh." Anna sobered drastically.

Inwardly, Emmie cringed. Obviously, she had wounded her friend's pride. But something needed to be said to deflate Anna's enthusiasm.

"After I get you ready for bed," Emmie said, "I'm going outside to take a walk, all right?"

Anna shrugged. "Why are you asking me? *You* are the earl's daughter, after all."

Emmie sighed. "I was just letting you know my plans for the evening."

"Fine," Anna snapped as she sat on the chair in front of the vanity and pulled out the pins in her hair. "I don't care if you go for a walk in the dark this late at night without a proper chaperone."

"You forget," Emmie countered, picking up a brush, "everyone thinks I'm a lady's companion. They are not going to wonder why I'm by myself."

As she finished brushing Anna's hair, silence grew in the room and became insufferable. Emmie realized she shouldn't be so upset, but it was hard not to feel like this. Though she didn't want her maid to think it was her fault she was angry.

Taking a deep breath, she forced herself to smile. "Anna, I forgot to tell you that I think my father would have complimented you on your performance tonight." She chuckled. "You look more like my family than you think."

Suddenly, Anna's eyes widened. "Oh, I just remembered something I overheard tonight." She grasped Emmie's hands. "I heard rumors that Mr. Crampton is related to Captain Hawk."

Confusion filled Emmie's head, and she couldn't quite wrap her mind around what Anna was saying. "Captain Hawk?"

"Yes, the captain of the *Avenger*—the pirate ship that attacked the very ship your mother was killed on."

The shock of the news gusted out of Emmie's lips as she lost her breath. The brush fell from her hand, thudding to the floor as an icy chill ran through her blood. "That cannot be right," she whispered in disbelief. "Mr. Crampton is friends with my father. Would my father not know this?"

"I'm thinking he does not, Emmie."

"But why… why would Mr. Crampton agree to have me stay here knowing it was his relative who killed his best friend's wife?"

"I don't know—unless Mr. Crampton isn't on speaking terms with his relative now, and he must have thought you would not ever know."

Emmie's heartbeat gradually returned to normal as she tossed the idea back and forth in her mind. "What you said makes sense,

Anna. After all, I have a corrupt relative, and I'm ashamed to be known as his niece."

"Exactly."

Emmie sighed and nodded. "That must be why Mr. Crampton hasn't said anything. I shall not blame him."

"You have a forgiving heart."

After Anna climbed into bed for the night, Emmie quickly left the room and made her way down the stairs. Her maid had said she had a forgiving heart, but Emmie didn't feel like she did at that moment. She wanted to know the truth. Who was this so-called relative of Mr. Crampton's? And why was her mother killed so violently? The mystery of her death was never fully explained.

Outside, the cool air stroked Emmie's face, relaxing her slightly. Breathing in deeply, she hoped it would cool her temper as well. This whole night had been an emotional ride for her. First watching Mr. Worthington woo Anna, and now hearing the news about the relative.

If they had only stayed at home instead of coming here, none of this would have happened. Her father wouldn't have had the insane notion of Emmie playing the role of lady's companion, and she wouldn't have had to discover Anna's talent for acting. Moreover, they wouldn't have met the very handsome Mr. Worthington, and she wouldn't be having these strange feelings of jealousy. Emmie always envied her friend for being pretty but had never let it get this far out of control.

In her wandering, she found herself on the back terrace. Most of the guests from the party had left, and only a few servants milled about cleaning up. Luckily, a few lamps were lit on the lawn, giving her the lighting she needed for her walk. Pausing, she leaned against the railing and looked up at the moon. It appeared so big tonight, much larger than she had ever seen, and that was something she'd peered at quite a bit in her lonely life.

"Now, why am I not surprised to find you out here this late after dark, and all alone?"

The man's deep voice from behind made her jump. She

whirled around to face the intruder. When Broderick walked closer, her heart pounded faster. Automatically, her hand flew to her bosom as if to stop the wild beating beneath her chest. Being alone with him out here was certainly not proper. Yet leaving was not an option.

"Mr. Worthington, you frightened the wits out of me."

He chuckled. "Forgive me, but I thought you would have heard me coming. I made enough noise to wake the neighbors."

She grinned. "I suppose I was lost in thought and didn't hear."

He moved closer until he stood next to her, leaning his hip against the railing. "What, may I ask, were you thinking? It must have been enthralling to keep you from hearing my loud entrance."

"No. It was not that intriguing. I was just thinking of home."

"Are you homesick?"

She nodded. "I have never been this far away."

"I'm sorry. Is there anything I can do to help you keep your mind occupied?"

A teasing glimmer sparkled in his eyes, letting her know he wasn't serious in trying to give comfort. This look was definitely different from the way he'd looked at Anna tonight. "I thank you for your thoughtfulness, but there is nothing you can do."

He grinned then glanced over her attire. She shifted, uncomfortable under his close scrutiny, yet a heated shiver ran over her, warming her considerably.

"I have to admit," he said, "you do look different somehow."

She arched her eyebrows in question. "Is that good or bad?"

He laughed deeply. "If you don't mind my candidness, I think your dress looks slightly outdated, and it's a little large on your petite frame. This particular style of dress doesn't match your bold personality. Your outfit at the pond definitely fits you much better."

She couldn't hold back from laughing. Wouldn't he love to know why? "Well, I'm sorry you don't approve. Maybe Lady Sarah and I can travel into town tomorrow to find a dressmaker.

Would that make you happy?"

He shrugged. "I would have to see what style of dress she picks for you first."

She shook her head. There was no point trying to convince him what kind of dress she would look better in. It would just waste her time. She ran her gaze over his attire, noticing he had discarded his coat, making her realize just how broad his shoulders really were. Very masculine, indeed.

She grinned. "I hope you don't think I'm forward in saying that you look just as superb in fancy clothes as you do when donned in a towel."

His eyes widened mere seconds before he tilted back his head and howled with laughter. "Oh, you are a humorous one, Miss Emmie. And although it was rather forward of you to say, I appreciate your boldness. It's not very often I find a woman who is so openly honest."

One side of her mouth lifted in half of a grin. "Now, is *that* good or bad?"

"That is good."

She smiled fully. "I thank you, then."

He continued to boldly scan her with his enticing gaze, wearing his all-too-cocky grin. "You probably noticed I spent a lot of time with Lady Sarah tonight."

Emmie lost her smile. "Indeed, I did."

He turned, leaning his back on the railing as he looked up into the night sky. "Lady Sarah is a very beautiful woman, but you have probably heard men say that about her before."

"I have," she mumbled.

"She doesn't talk much, though."

"She is a little demure."

He looked down at her. "She really didn't tell me that much about herself, and so I cannot understand why she is like that." He paused briefly then continued. "You must know why she is so shy. Couldn't you give me a little information about her?"

Emmie pulled herself away from the railing and slowly

walked to the side of the terrace, sliding her fingers along the wooden gate as she went. "Forgive me, Mr. Worthington, but I cannot help you. Lady Sarah is always reserved around people she doesn't know."

"Why?"

She shrugged without looking his way. "That is just the way she is." Emmie didn't want to tell him it was because she couldn't trust men. Usually when they proclaimed their love, it was only to be the earl's son-in-law and receive her dowry.

"How long have you been a lady's companion?"

She stopped at the end of the railing where a rosebush was in full bloom, and gently ran the tip of her finger around one of the yellow petals. "I don't know if she told you this, but we are distant relatives. I became a lady's companion a few years ago when I needed to find employment to help provide an income for my poor family. Her father was very generous to allow me this position in his household." She looked at him over her shoulder. "Why do you ask?"

"I just wondered why some of your personality didn't rub off on her, since the two of you have been together for a while."

She shrugged, turning her attention back to the rose. "We have only been together a few short years, as I mentioned. She grew up with privileges, and I did not. Whether or not that gave me a bolder personality, I couldn't tell you."

"Do I hear resentment in your voice?"

"I don't know. Do you?" She peeked over her shoulder.

"You almost sound like you don't like that you grew up differently."

She forced a laugh. "That's preposterous."

He moved away from the railing and came to stand by her once again. "Tell me honestly, Miss Emmie. Do you ever wish you could trade places with somebody else?"

She snapped her head around so fast that she was surprised it didn't bounce off her neck. As she stared deeply into his eyes, she wondered why he'd asked her that. *Oh goodness.* He couldn't possibly know the truth.

"Do you ever wish people would treat you differently?" he continued. "That you could perhaps be in someone else's place for a while? Sometimes I wonder if people would treat me differently if I were… Well, say I was a wealthy man with nice lands and a large estate. Would people treat me the same as they do now?"

She couldn't believe he was saying this. Could he read her mind? "No. You would not be treated the same. People would treat you differently because you have money." His enchanting chocolate-brown eyes met hers, and she continued. "Take, for instance, Lady Sarah. All available men are after her hand in marriage, even some of the married men." Lord Richard came to mind. The arrogant fool had married her cousin two years ago, yet continued to act as if he wanted Emmie as his wife. "It would not matter to them if Lady Sarah was pretty or ugly. They would try everything to get her attention and conquer her heart."

He nodded. "I do know how it is. That is why I sometimes wish I were a wealthy man, and even though women may think I'm attractive, I will never be anything more to them than just amusement. Women don't want to marry me."

She studied him closely. From his words and tone of voice, he felt the same way she did about marriage, which made her feel closer to him. "Is that why you are after Lady Sarah?"

Confusion clouded his face. "Pardon me?"

"Are you trying to get Lady Sarah to fall in love with you because you are an ordinary man without a title?"

His blank expression finally turned into a grin. "Is that what you think I'm trying to do?"

She shrugged. "I have seen it before. A charmingly handsome man tries to sweep the earl's daughter off her feet when he knows he has no liberty to do so."

He chuckled. "Is that why you followed us out to the statue tonight?"

Emmie gasped, her heart hammering as heat shot up her face,

nearly scalding her cheeks. How did he know? Could she lie herself out of this?

He arched an eyebrow. "Were you trying to keep Lady Sarah from falling in love with an untitled man?"

Words seemed to disappear from her mind, which rarely happened. How did he know she had spied on them? Apparently, she hadn't hidden herself as well as she'd thought.

Stepping closer to her, he gently grasped her shoulders, bringing her body against his. "Or did you want to watch me kiss another woman and envision yourself in my arms instead?"

Shock waves crashed over her and her mouth hung open. His words were so appalling, even though they were close to the truth. "How dare you insinuate—"

"Miss Emmie? Do you want me to hold and kiss you, instead of Lady Sarah?"

Her breathing grew faster, and although she should slap his face, this was exactly how she felt. Excitement and anticipation shot through her. Against her will, she was being lured into his charm.

He bent his head, brushing his lips softly against her mouth. "Tell me. Do you want me to kiss you? Is that the reason your gaze followed me around all evening?"

Their closeness made her head swim and her body weaken. At the same time, his actions and truthful accusations disturbed her.

She pressed her hands against his chest and shook her head. "Mr. Worthington, you have gone too far."

He grinned. "No, I haven't, but I will now."

Pulling on her shoulders to bring her closer, he lowered his head. When she fell against him, he placed his mouth over hers. His warm lips moved sensuously back and forth across her stiff ones. She should struggle and break his hold, but his determined kiss convinced her to yield. His mouth remained soft as he pecked at her lips, urging her to open for him. Once her lips parted, his tongue slipped inside. Fireworks exploded in her mind as dizziness assailed her.

One at a time, his hands moved from her shoulders as they slipped around her back, pressing her more intimately against him. Fire consumed her the longer they kissed. Helplessness washed over her, and she hated feeling that she had no control. Her body wouldn't listen to her mind, which screamed at her to stop and push away. The strength in her hands slowly disappeared, and her lips softened and relaxed to his passionate kiss. She had never been kissed like this before, and strangely enough, she didn't mind feeling so vulnerable… if even for a few seconds.

At her surrender, he growled and turned the kiss wild. She sighed and gripped his shirt, fitting herself closer to him. But as soon as the thrill began to build, he broke the kiss and stepped back.

Her strength returned just in time. Before she melted to the ground, she steadied her legs. As the shock of the situation finally hit, disgust ran rapid inside her, more so over her weakness than his actions. Anger streaked through her, and she slapped his face.

"Indeed, you have gone too far," she said, her voice deep, still laced with passion.

His blank expression didn't change as he stared at her. She didn't know if he was angry or hurt, and she wished he would say something to let her know. His chest heaved with quick breaths, the same way hers was doing.

Finally, he nodded. "I beg your forgiveness."

He continued to stare at her for several long, agonizing minutes while she tried to get her breathing regulated. Her body shook, and she cursed herself for feeling this way around him.

Emmie gained control of her senses. She lifted her skirt to her ankles and ran into the house, all the way back to her room, where she knew she would feel safe.

Her heart beat erratically. She could not stop thinking about Mr. Worthington and that earth-shattering kiss.

Chapter Six

BRODERICK STOOD STUNNED. Not because he had kissed Emmie, but because he enjoyed it so much.

Usually, he preferred more experienced women, and those who dressed better. Certainly, she wasn't the kind of woman he would usually seduce. Yet he had been thinking about doing that very thing since noticing her hiding behind the statue.

He shook his head and turned back toward the house. His uncle and aunt were saying their goodbyes to the last of the guests who just wouldn't leave, and Broderick really didn't want to be included in that, but he had to go inside nonetheless. As he opened the door and stepped inside, he noticed a friend from earlier who was speaking to Uncle Henry. Broderick hadn't wanted to say anything to his friend before, since there were too many gossipmongers about, but now would be a good time.

Just as Broderick reached them, his uncle walked away. Broderick stood in front of the other man, eyeing him warily. He tried not to grin, but his lips pulled upward. "I'm hesitant to ask if this is a coincidental meeting... Mr. Daughtery." He chuckled softly. "I honestly didn't expect to see you here."

Phillip grinned and folded his arms. "Ah, my good friend, Mr. Worthington. I almost didn't recognize you." His gaze lifted to Broderick's hair. "You actually look better with brown hair, I must say."

Broderick laughed. "But I think you used too much black when you changed your hair color."

Phillip ran his fingers through his crop of hair. "Yes, the person who helped me was not as talented as the one who assisted you."

"Obviously."

"Tell me, Worthington, why are you here?"

"Mr. and Mrs. Crampton are my uncle and aunt." Broderick took a quick glance around the empty room. "Who are you here with?"

"My cousins, if you must know. I had nowhere else to hide out but with them."

Broderick nodded. "I understand, my friend." He clapped his hand on Phillip's shoulder.

His first mate took a step closer. "I'm sure you were surprised to learn the lord chancellor's niece was staying with your aunt and uncle," he said, lowering his voice.

"Very much so." Broderick dropped his tone as well. "Apparently her father is acquainted with my uncle. However, my uncle doesn't want others to know who her uncle is. While she is here, she is just the earl's daughter."

"How very interesting." Phillip arched an eyebrow. "This is something we could use to our advantage."

"Believe me, I have already thought of that. I'm not going to let this matter rest. I plan on finding what the woman knows about her uncle's plans."

"Is that why you took her outside earlier?" Phillip scratched his chin. "Or was it the normal reasons you take a woman out under the moonlit sky?"

Broderick rolled his eyes. "Trust me, I do *not* have plans to seduce Lady Sarah."

Phillip chuckled. "If you say so."

"I do," Broderick snapped, not appreciating that his friend jumped to conclusions.

"Very well, I shall leave you to Lady Sarah. I had thought to woo her tonight, yet she was always dancing with other men. I ended up dancing with your cousin, Miss Rebecca, and getting to know her."

"I'm sure she loved your attention as well as your company."

"As did I. I found her delightful."

Holding back a laugh, Broderick bit his lip. Was his friend addled? Rebecca was exactly opposite of that. "I suspect she was putting on a grand performance if you found her delightful. Most of the time she is more like…" He scratched his chin. "A shrew."

"Oh, come now, Worthington. Your cousin was very pleasant."

"I'm glad you think so." Broderick folded his arms and glanced around the room again. "So tell me, did the rest of the crew go into hiding as I instructed?"

"Indeed they did. They were all looking forward to the much-needed rest."

Broderick felt more at ease. "I wish I knew how long we need, but for now, at least two months."

"Aye, captain."

Broderick glared at Phillip. "Keep your voice down, man. We do not need others hearing."

"What others?" Phillip snickered.

"Servants have ears, too," Broderick clipped out. Taking a deep breath, he stepped away from his first mate and, in a louder voice, said, "It was good to see you, Mr. Daughtery. I hope we can meet up again soon."

"As do I."

"In case I need to contact you, where are you staying?"

"Joseph and Mildred Caldwells'. They live just down the lane from the mill."

Broderick nodded. "I'm sure my uncle will be able to direct me in their path if I cannot locate them."

"I'm sure he can."

After the men shook hands, Phillip quit the ballroom and the house. Broderick scrubbed his hands over his face. Exhaustion set in, and he couldn't wait to rest. Making his way to his room, he realized he might not sleep tonight anyway. Not with his mind occupied with the passionate kiss he had shared with Emmie.

BRODERICK ROSE EARLY in the morning and quickly dressed in his riding clothes, preparing to spend a leisurely afternoon doing nothing but enjoying his solitude in the countryside. It had been two weeks since he came to stay with his uncle, and boredom had begun to consume Broderick's mind. He had led a busy life of spying these past few years, and time for leisure was rarely heard of.

After flying down the stairs, he hurried across the wooden floor and made his way to the front door. When he neared his uncle's study, Broderick slowed and trod softly, hoping Henry wouldn't see him. This was one time he did *not* want to be bothered. Unfortunately, as Broderick passed the room, his uncle looked up from behind his desk and motioned with his hand.

"Broderick? I would like a word, please."

Broderick sighed in defeat, walked into Henry's study, and closed the door. "Yes, Uncle?"

"We need to have a serious discussion," Henry began.

Broderick sat in the wooden chair near his uncle's desk. He breathed in the pipe scent that drifted through the air—the same brand his father used to smoke. It brought back a pang of homesickness and sadness, but he quickly dismissed it as he met his uncle's gaze.

Henry held up a piece of paper. "I received this missive earlier from your father's half-cousin, and I fear you won't like the news." He paused, staring into Broderick's eyes as his frown deepened. "You have grown up carefree and not expected to become a responsible adult. Yet whether you know this or not, you have inherited your father's brother's title—Marquess of

Wilshire."

Confusion filled Broderick, and he leaned forward, grasping his knees. "My father rarely spoke of his older brother who lived in London. From the stories I heard, Father was disowned by his father years ago, before he married my mother."

"That he was. Unfortunately, circumstances change throughout the years. Your grandfather is dead, as well as his son and your uncle's son."

"Why was the missive sent to you and not to me?"

"Apparently, your family's solicitor didn't know your whereabouts, so he sent it to me hoping I would." Henry sat up straighter in his chair. "You, my nephew, are now the only living male heir. The title is yours."

Not really knowing how he should act, Broderick went with his first instinct and laughed. Actually, a snort was what came out of his mouth and nose. His reaction made his uncle jump back, and his eyes widened.

"Uncle Henry, forgive me, but—" Broderick laughed harder as he stood, now towering over his uncle. "Moving to London and becoming a marquess is just not what I want to do with my life."

Within seconds, a deep scowl appeared on Henry's face, emphasizing his many wrinkles. "But you must."

A sharp pounding started in Broderick's forehead, and he rubbed the irritation. "Is there not a distant cousin that the title can go to? I mean, I have several cousins throughout England."

"But this one belongs to you and none other. Why do you want to give it to a cousin who is already titled? Your father would want you to have it."

Broderick didn't want to explain the reasons why he didn't want to live his life as a marquess. "Uncle Henry, I really need to think this over before making a decision."

His uncle gasped. "What is there to think over, boy? The title comes with a large estate and lands. Many men dream of having such a thing handed to them. You are very fortunate."

Broderick shook his head and walked to the window. He peered out into the yard and gazed upon the predawn sky scattered with billowy clouds. "I'm aware of that, but I have made my own life, and I don't want to change it yet." He heaved a sigh. "Will you give me time to think this over?"

"Yes, but don't take too long."

"But Uncle, I cannot make a rash decision." He looked back at the older man. "This is my future. If I step into a nobleman's life, I would surely be expected to take a wife and have heirs."

Henry nodded. "Just as it's supposed to be."

"But I'm not ready for such a responsibility."

Henry slapped his hands on the desk and stood. His brow creased with irritation. "Then it's time you took on that challenge. You are not a lad living the carefree life any longer. You need to bring respect back to your father's name, and this is the only way you can accomplish such a feat."

"But I want a normal life."

The corner of Henry's mouth lifted in a smirk. "Broderick, I believe you have never had a normal life, especially now."

Curiosity got the best of Broderick, and he wondered exactly what his uncle knew. But he couldn't ask. He didn't want to admit his secret life as Captain Hawk.

"Please, give me time to think about this important decision, Uncle."

"I will."

Broderick left the room in a hurry, wanting to ride, but now he would be in a grouchy mood. Did his uncle know about his secret life? He certainly couldn't tell him he'd changed his hair color to hide from the enemy.

His long strides carried him to the stables, and within moments, he was atop one of his uncle's stallions and riding away from the estate. It irritated him to think his uncle would reprimand him, yet he could see how much Henry worried about his welfare. As his uncle pointed out, it wasn't every day a title was handed over to a commoner.

He growled in frustration and pushed the horse faster. Ideas of what he could do with a title such as this floated through his mind, but he didn't want to be in London, so close to those soldiers who might arrest him for piracy.

Broderick slowed his horse to a trot as he wandered aimlessly along the path ahead, canopied by the trees. A gentle breeze caressed his face, bringing with it the heady scent of wildflowers nearby.

He stopped the horse on the top of a knoll and looked out over the countryside, breathing the fresh air. He relaxed slightly. Soon he would have to make a final decision about his future, but right now, this break refreshed him.

Out of nowhere, something Miss Emmie had said to him came to mind, making him chuckle. She'd accused him of trying to make Lady Sarah fall in love with him because he was a penniless man. The lady's companion would probably faint dead away if she knew exactly how much money he had in his coffers—and that he was just given a title. But to her, he was a normal man.

He grinned wider. At least he knew he was playing his part well.

Miss Emmie was a strange little woman. Over the past two days, he had taken Lady Sarah on a few carriage rides, and even on picnics. Emmie had made it obvious through her glares that she didn't approve. Sometimes he wondered if he courted the earl's daughter just to get a reaction from her companion.

It was rather funny, now that he thought about it, because Emmie hadn't met his gaze since their kiss. However, she still watched Lady Sarah closely and had an even closer eye on him.

He had also made it a pastime of late to watch the lady's companion. He couldn't understand why he thought Lady Sarah looked out of place, and especially why she didn't act as bold as her companion. Yet bold as Miss Emmie was, she still displayed a face of innocence. Her crimson blushes gave it away.

Swiping his hand across his moist brow, he kicked the horse

into a gallop and rode in a different direction. Since the weather was warmer than it had been in a few days, he decided to take another swim in his uncle's pond. Just thinking about the cool water cascading down his heated body made him urge the animal faster.

He neared the secluded spot and stopped the horse. As he tied the reins to a tree branch, the sound of splashing permeated the air. Tall trees surrounded the pond, so he couldn't exactly see who had invaded his bathing place. He hurried toward the water, and the first thing he saw was an ugly gray dress lying on a rock.

Broderick shook his head and held in a chuckle. *Miss Emmie.* He really should leave so that she could have some privacy. He was, after all, a gentleman—when he wanted to be, anyway—but currently, he was in the mood to tease a little. Actually, this time he would tease a lot. How could he not, since it had been his first instinct since meeting her?

He waited until she emerged before doing or saying anything. The water slapped against her shoulders and around her creamy breasts. Unfortunately, he couldn't see much, since the water covered her. Stringy, wet brown hair fell around her face and down her back, making her look more like a woman… and that much more alluring. Something must have gotten in her eye, because she vigorously rubbed that spot with dainty fingers. After a minute, she swiped the hair out of her face, shaking her head in the process.

This was absolutely the most enticing thing he'd ever witnessed, and what made it more appealing was that she didn't know she had an audience. The woman was naturally sensual, and this knowledge brought a tightening to his chest as his heart hammered out an uneven rhythm.

Once she opened her eyes and saw him, she gasped. Her arms crossed over her chest to hide what he really couldn't see anyway, and she squatted in the water until the liquid bobbed up around her chin.

"Mr. Worthington?" Her voice squeaked high in panic.

"What are you doing here?"

Her gaze combed slowly over him. Desire flowed through him from her adorable expression. May the devil take him, but he liked seeing her all flustered. Her red cheeks made her brown eyes darker.

Wetting his dry lips, he exhaled through his nose, trying to remove the indescribable feelings pumping through his blood. What was wrong with him?

He tried shaking himself out of the trance she'd put him under. "Good day, Miss Emmie. I was just passing by when I heard someone in the pond. I took it upon myself as the nephew of this estate to see if there was perhaps an intruder on my uncle's lands."

"Well, now that you see I'm not an intruder, will you be so kind as to leave me to my privacy? It is *not* proper for you to be watching me bathe."

"And when you watched me bathe the other day, was that any different?" He shook his head. "I think not, my sweet."

"That is neither here nor there." Her cheeks reddened even more, if that were possible. "Please, Mr. Worthington, leave me alone."

He grinned, deciding this was the perfect moment to start teasing. "Actually," he began as he started releasing the buttons of his waistcoat, "I thought I might join you. The weather has been warm today, and I was in the mood for a swim." He stepped toward the water.

"No!" She moved back farther. "Please, Mr. Worthington, don't come any closer."

He removed his waistcoat and cravat quickly, leaving his neck and upper chest open for her view. Stepping to the edge of the pond, he grinned. As much as the idea of sharing the water with her sounded most entertaining right now, he was only teasing.

Now if his heart would quit hammering from the pleasure flowing through him from just watching her, he'd be able to think rationally.

"Are you certain you would not enjoy some company?" he asked.

She shook her head, and once again, her gaze moved over his chest, resting momentarily on his exposed throat. "Yes, I'm most certain."

He sighed heavily and shrugged. It pleased him to see that her innocent gaze couldn't stay off his body.

"Can I help you out?" He looked around the area where her clothes were located. "I think you will need a towel, but I don't see one."

"I-I-I will be fine, Mr. Worthington. I assure you."

He looked back at her and grinned. "I gather you have never shared a bath with a man."

A deeper blush filled her face, verifying his curiosity. Her reaction was everything he thought it would be, and he wouldn't have traded it for all the money in the world—or his new bloody title. The look on her face was priceless. He loved the fact that he could make her respond in such a way.

"Mr. Worthington, I don't believe it's any of your business, but no, I have *never* shared a bath with a man."

"I don't suppose you would want to start your first experience now?"

"I would not," she said pertly.

"Is there any way I can convince you otherwise? I assure you, I will show you a most enjoyable time."

"My answer is still no."

"Then alas, my work here is of no avail. I suppose I shall have to leave. Have a pleasant bath, Miss Emmie." He gave her a wink before turning and leaving the woods.

Slowly he made his way to his horse, thinking the whole time that maybe he should go back and spy on her. No, that wasn't like him. When a woman said no, he accepted that as the final answer. However, he quite enjoyed riling her.

He wished he knew why she brought out his wild, rebellious side.

As he mounted his horse and rode off for the house, he realized that today's run-in with Miss Emmie, brief as it was, had certainly brightened his day.

Chapter Seven

"BRODERICK? WOULD YOU come here for a moment?" Henry called as Broderick stepped outside through the side doors, preparing to head toward the stables.

He swore under his breath. *Not again!* It had been a few days since he had talked to his uncle in the study. Broderick didn't want to have to rehash the same words.

Hesitantly, he turned away from the stables and made his way to the green patch of lawn where his aunt, uncle, and cousin stood with Lady Sarah playing trundling hoop and roll. Henry looked dashing in his tan coat covering a white shirt and matching tan breeches. Indeed, he looked as if he was headed to a political meeting instead of playing outdoor games with his family.

Aunt Martha always dressed properly in her silver and white day dress with white neck lace kerchief covering her neck and shoulders, and a bonnet sitting on her head. Rebecca wore something similar to her mother, just without the kerchief, and her sleeves were not as long. In fact, the bodice of her gown was lower cut, as well. Ringlets circled his cousin's head underneath her bonnet. To be sure, Rebecca appeared most wanton in her attire, and Broderick pitied the man who wound up married to his cousin.

By far, Lady Sarah's gown was of a more expensive cut, and

almost fit her too tight. She wore the neck lace kerchief, yet he could tell it didn't do her justice because it didn't hide how her bosom almost spilled over the top of her bodice.

He walked toward Henry, who came his way. "What can I do for you, Uncle?"

"I thought you would like to play a game with us. Lady Sarah mentioned she had learned a new game that expands on trundling hoop and roll, but she doesn't quite remember how to play." Henry ran his fingers through his salt-and-pepper hair and gave Broderick a crooked smile. "With your traveling abroad so much, I was hoping you had learned this game as well."

Broderick moved beside his uncle toward the little group and stopped beside the earl's daughter. "Good day, Lady Sarah," he greeted her with a smile and a bow.

"And a good day to you, Mr. Worthington." She curtsied.

"My uncle tells me you are having a problem remembering the game."

She laughed lightly. "I must admit, I cannot recall exactly how to play, but it was very enjoyable."

"Do you remember who played this game with you?"

She nodded. "I was with Emiline... er, I mean Miss Emmie, and she taught me... um..."

She stopped abruptly as if she had said something wrong. Broderick was happy to learn the companion's full name—although Emmie suited her much better for some reason.

All eyes turned toward Lady Sarah as they waited for her to finish her story.

Broderick's cousin, Rebecca, snorted a rude laugh. "Your companion taught you how to play? Are you saying this game is a *servants'* game?"

"Uh, well... yes, she taught me—however, I don't think it's a servants' game. I haven't played in a couple of years, but I remember it was so much fun." Lady Sarah frowned. "It is most unfortunate she isn't here right now. Perhaps she would do a better job of teaching it to us."

Broderick slapped his hands together and laughed. "I think that's a splendid idea." Everyone swung their head toward him, and their eyes widened. "Lady Sarah? Where is Miss Emmie? I shall fetch her at once and bring her into the game." Suddenly, the idea of having to play this insipid game didn't seem as boring.

Henry held up his hand. "Oh, but Broderick, I don't think—"

"But Uncle, it's a perfect suggestion. As it stands right now, I'm the odd man. If we bring Lady Sarah's companion into the game, it will make our game even with players."

As he stepped away to search for Emiline, his cousin huffed. "Father, I don't think this game needs teams."

Henry grumbled irritably, "It doesn't."

Broderick chuckled but hurried away before someone tried to stop him. He only had to ask two of his uncle's servants before finding Miss Emmie's whereabouts. It surprised him to think she was spending time in the library. But then, he was certain that most lady's companions were bored easily.

When he stepped into the library, he spotted her immediately. Today she wore an ugly brown dress—so very drab, and it didn't suit her at all. And, as before, it practically hung on her petite frame. Apparently, she hadn't made it into town to visit a dressmaker.

She sat curled on the couch with her legs tucked underneath her, shoes gone from her feet and lying haphazardly on the floor. Miss Emmie looked deeply engrossed in a book, and guilt overrode his emotions. He couldn't believe he was going to interrupt her private time just so *his* day could be more enjoyable. She made such a lovely picture all cozy on the couch, wearing a serious, but pleasant expression. He liked the soft color in her eyes, and the way her lips parted slightly.

He stepped closer and cleared his throat. "Good day, Miss Emmie."

Her head snapped up and she rested the book against her bosom. He was suddenly jealous of the object so close to her heart.

"Good day, Mr. Worthington." She scrambled to her feet, the book now resting where her bottom had been only moments before. "Forgive me for reading, but I was caught up with my duties, and I... um, well, I—"

"Miss Emmie," he interrupted her. "No need to fret."

"Is there something Lady Sarah needs?"

"I'm not sure about Lady Sarah, but I need you." Had his voice really deepened just now? Heavens, why had he said it *that* way? Her cheeks reddened and her eyes widened. Although he loved teasing her, he decided he'd better tell her why he'd sought her out. "My family requests the pleasure of your company in a game they are playing out on the back lawn."

She blinked slowly. "They do? Why?"

"Lady Sarah inadvertently let it slip that you taught her how to play a more entertaining game of trundling hoop and roll. Can this be true?"

Emmie stared at him for the longest time, her chest rising and falling at a fast clip. "It is true."

"Then you know the game well?"

"Yes."

"So, you wouldn't mind playing with me... um, I mean, us?"

"Are you certain your family requested my presence?"

"They will be delighted to have your company."

Taking a deep breath, she nodded and slipped on her shoes. Broderick remained standing where he was until she finished, and then he held out his elbow for her to take. "May I escort you outside, then?"

She looked him directly in the eyes before her gaze slipped to his mouth. A blush stole across her and she quickly looked away. "Mr. Worthington, you needn't escort me as if I were a lady of nobility. In case you have forgotten, I'm her companion—just one of Lady Sarah's poor relatives who needed employment."

Actually, he had forgotten, although right now, he didn't know why. Nonetheless, he wanted her touch on his arm. He wanted her so close he could inhale her sweet fragrance of roses—the same fragrance he had smelled that night they kissed.

"Fine, you don't have to hold on to my arm, but will you walk beside me?"

Slowly, she nodded. "I can do that."

He smiled. "I would like that very much, Emiline."

She stumbled and bumped against him and then quickly righted herself. The color in her cheeks had left, and her eyes now were laced with panic. "Who told you my name was Emiline?"

"Lady Sarah let it slip. Is there a reason you don't want me to use that name?"

"Uh, no, that's fine. Just make certain you refer to me as Miss Emmie in front of your family."

"I can do that. I think your name is lovely, and if you ask me, it suits you better."

Side by side, they walked outside to the lawn where Lady Sarah waited with his family. Broderick noticed how uncomfortable Emiline seemed when all eyes were upon her, and he thought it was probably the first time his uncle, aunt, and cousin had really gotten a good look at the woman. She tugged at the waist of her dress then smoothed her hands down the material.

Broderick decided to break the silence. "Now that we are all here, let us allow Miss Emmie to teach us how to play."

He glanced at his uncle and aunt, who stared blankly at Emiline as if the girl had two heads. Irritation ran through Broderick. Were his relatives appalled to actually be playing games with a lady's companion? He would talk to them alone about their behavior and give them a piece of his mind. After all, Emiline was a guest here, just as Lady Sarah was.

Henry cleared his throat and nodded. "Broderick is right. We shall let Miss Emmie teach us this new game." He smiled wide at his wife. "I, for one, am quite bored of trundling hoop and roll, after playing it for so many years."

"Uh…" Martha's gaze switched between Emiline and Henry a few times before she shrugged. "I think that is a splendid idea, Mr. Crampton."

Relief washed over Broderick at the knowledge that his uncle and aunt were not going to cause a scene—although Rebecca just might. Broderick handed a stick and hoop to Emiline and gave her an encouraging nod.

A shaky smile appeared on her lovely face as she took the items. "Actually, the way I have changed this game is that we will need a wooden ball as well. If you do not have one, I'm certain my ball of yarn will work."

Rebecca snickered and smartly folded her arms across her chest. "A wooden ball? Pray tell, is this a *child's* game?"

"Actually no, Miss Crampton," Emiline replied quickly. "Although I'm quite certain children could play without difficulty." Her grin widened, and she suddenly didn't appear as shaky as before. "So, I'm very certain *you* will have no problem catching on to the game—as well as everyone else, of course."

Rebecca gasped, her mouth agape. Broderick slapped a hand to his mouth to keep himself from laughing and covered his quick movement with a cough. Remarkably, his aunt and uncle didn't comment.

"Uh, I do believe we have a small wooden ball," his aunt finally said, and turned to a nearby servant. "Linus, do you know to which ball I'm referring?"

"Yes. I will fetch it right away."

During the few minutes the servant was gone, Henry and Martha directed a few questions to Emiline, inquiring about her stay here in Greenwich. The companion's tone of voice was quite different than when she had first spoken to Rebecca. Rather than showing her as the bold woman Broderick knew Emiline to be, her answers were soft, and she rarely met his aunt and uncle's gaze.

The more he studied the lady's companion, the more he wondered why she acted so differently. In front of him—and even Rebecca—she was as brash as any woman he'd ever met. Yet in front of Henry and Martha, she acted extremely shy.

When the servant brought back the small wooden ball,

Emiline changed into a different person again. Confident and self-assured, she explained the new game and even demonstrated how to smack the sticks against the ball, making it roll from one end of the lawn to the other until reaching its destination inside the hoop. Indeed, Emiline was brilliant. This game would be much more enjoyable.

Soon the game began. And even though it wasn't prearranged, the group did eventually divide into partners. Broderick willingly partnered with Emiline, Rebecca with Lady Sarah, and his aunt and uncle were together.

Rebecca stamped her foot and scowled as she faced the ball. Slowly, she turned her back to the group, but it was obvious she kicked the ball instead of hitting it with the stick. When the ball didn't reach its mark, she grumbled, "This is a very senseless game, and in my opinion, the rules were not thought up correctly."

"Now, Rebecca," Henry warned. "The rest of us are enjoying it. I suggest you relax and enjoy it as well."

She huffed and planted her hands on her hips. "I don't know why we have to play this. And really, why did we pair off?" She pointed at Broderick. "He is stronger than any of us, so naturally *he* is going to win. It's not fair." She glared at Emiline. "And *she* is cheating. I just know it!"

Emiline stood beside him, hitched a breath, and squared her shoulders. "Forgive me, Miss Crampton, but I assure you I'm not the one who is cheating. I don't have to kick the ball in order to make it move."

"Augh!" Rebecca aimed her fiery blue eyes at the lady's companion. "How dare you accuse me of kicking the ball?"

"Rebecca, dear." Martha moved to her daughter and grasped her arm. "Please, just calm yourself and play the game right."

Rebecca flapped her hands in the air. "What are you saying? Do you think I'm cheating too?"

"I believe it's my turn," Henry said quickly, and moved into place.

Broderick didn't think he had ever seen his cousin so out of sorts, but he loved how Emiline could irritate the redheaded woman. When she turned her attention back to him, he winked at her, silently letting her know he approved.

"Your rules are impossible to follow," Rebecca snapped as she swiped a reddish curl off her forehead. "I cannot seem to hit the ball. It's too difficult."

"May I show you another way?" Emiline asked calmly.

Rebecca shrugged one shoulder and rolled her eyes.

"If you will," Emiline began, "imagine the ball as a head." When Rebecca gasped, the lady's companion held up her hand and continued. "Think of the head as someone you loathe and would love to take out your frustrations on." She adjusted her stance with her stick close to the ball. "For instance… if someone has been belittling me on a daily basis, and I want to take my frustrations out on that person but know I can't"—she arched an accusing eyebrow toward Rebecca—"instead, I just swat this stick against the ball as hard as I can to relieve my anger."

Focusing on the ball, Emiline nibbled her lower lip as she aimed and swung. *Whack!* The ball sailed across the lawn perfectly. She stepped back and pointed toward the ball. "Ahh, I feel so much better now." She grinned haughtily. "See, Miss Crampton? It works perfectly."

Rebecca grumbled and stormed toward her parents. "Did you see that?" she whined. "She was thinking of me, I just know it!"

When Broderick's cousin reached his aunt and uncle, their whispers couldn't be heard. He grinned at Emiline as she made her way back to him. Chuckling, he shook his head. "I don't know what you are trying to prove with my cousin, my dear Miss Emmie, but I'm having the most enjoyable afternoon watching you."

One side of her mouth lifted more than the other. "Prove? Pray tell, what would a mere *lady's companion* want to prove with your cousin?"

"Oh, I don't know, unless it's showing you are not afraid of her."

"I don't fear many people, Mr. Worthington, and most assuredly not your arrogant cousin."

The game continued, and to Broderick's greatest delight, the winner was Emiline. He held himself back from taking her in his arms to give her a congratulatory hug, only because he worried that once she was in his arms, he'd want to do more than just hug her.

He quickly shook the thought from his head. What was wrong with him lately? Why couldn't he stop thinking about the charming woman? Had he basked in their kiss that much?

He grinned. Apparently so.

"That was a splendid game," Henry cheered. "What shall we do next?"

"As much as I hate to leave this cheerful group," Broderick answered, "I have other duties that need to be dealt with at this time, so I shall wish all of you a good day and see you at evening meal." He bowed slightly and turned to leave.

"I, too, have things to do in order to get Lady Sarah's dress ready for this evening's social," Emiline added quickly. "Thank you, Mr. Crampton, for including me in this game. I really do appreciate your kindness, but I need to get back to my duties." She bowed and turned toward the house, passing Broderick on her way.

"Emiline, hold up there," he called.

She glanced at him over her shoulder. "Mr. Worthington, I really need to go—"

"Emiline, I just wanted to tell you what a good game you played, and I wanted to thank you for teaching my cousin a lesson."

She stopped and faced him. "I taught your cousin a lesson? When did I do that?"

"Dear Becky couldn't stand the fact that you won the game." He laughed. "I thought it was the best medicine she had ever tasted."

A small smile tugged on the corners of Emiline's tempting mouth. "If you think that is a good thing, then I'm certainly glad I was able to help."

"My cousin needs to be brought down a notch or two in her life, and I was happy to see it happen." He stroked her cheek with his knuckles. "Especially from you."

Her gaze dropped to his mouth, and once again, she blushed profusely.

"I thank you, Mr. Worthington," she said, stepping away from him as she reached to open the side door. "I really must be getting back. I promised Nancy I would help her get Lady Sarah's dress ready, and give her some tips on how to style her hair correctly."

The statement struck him as funny. Miss Emiline knew how to style hair correctly, when hers was always pulled back so tight her eyes nearly popped out?

Shaking away the confusing thought, he stepped past her and took hold of the door. His hand brushed against hers, and she quickly withdrew. Her eyes sparkled as she looked into his eyes. There was a certain glow about her, and it wasn't due to the sun shining on her face. Curses, she was pretty!

"I thank you, again," she whispered.

"Yes, well, I'm sorry for keeping you. Have a good afternoon, and I shall see you later."

Her smile widened as she curtsied and then quickly walked into the house. Although she was a mere companion—a poor relative, as she kept reminding him—he felt like a grand gentleman while holding the door for her. He looked forward to doing things for her just to see her radiant smile. And her eyes…

He took a deep, cleansing breath. Those mesmerizing eyes could make a man weak in the worst way.

Chapter Eight

WITH A SIGH of apathy, Emmie closed the book she'd finished reading and rested it on her lap. It had been three weeks now since arriving in Greenwich, and as the days lagged on, she realized just how dull the life of a lady's companion was.

She attended *Lady Sarah* like a dutiful companion—well, at least as well as she could. She helped Anna dress every morning, since the Cramptons' maid was busy with Miss Rebecca. Emmie accompanied Anna downstairs for breakfast, but usually, they were the only ones in the room eating, since Mr. and Mrs. Crampton had already partaken of the meal, and Rebecca was still dressing. After breakfast, Emmie and Anna took a stroll through Mrs. Crampton's flower garden, but after that, Rebecca controlled Anna's time pretty much the rest of the day.

Slouching on the sofa, Emmie parted her legs in an unladylike manner underneath the overly large dress as she slid her stockinged feet on the polished wooden floor, thinking about what to do next. Did her boredom stem back to her masquerading, or did the useless feeling come from watching Broderick court Anna? Lately, she'd been thinking about asking him about Mr. Crampton's relative—Captain Hawk. But would Broderick be so open with her about the notorious pirate?

For some reason, Mr. Crampton had given Emmie permission to ride his horses any time she wished. It seemed odd that he would say that, but she wasn't about to argue. She loved riding, even if it was sidesaddle—although she did prefer astride—but after weeks of riding, even that became boring.

During these times, she thought of her father. She prayed he fared well in this time of turmoil, but in the back of her mind, she wished it would all come to an end. She worried that someone would know she was the lord chancellor's niece, and they would blame her for the double role she played.

She noticed that Broderick also played double roles. Although he acted interested in Anna, he also tried to keep Emmie entertained. Because she had to accompany *Lady Sarah* whenever Broderick took her on a ride or a walk, sometimes it seemed he talked more to Emmie than Anna. During these times, her heart softened, and she became weak in the knees. The steamy kiss they had shared not too long ago was permanently in her mind, and it wasn't healthy to daydream so often.

And the pond...

Sighing, she slipped farther down into the cushions of the couch, lifting the book to cover the cheeks she knew were flaming from the memory. She didn't know how much of her body he had seen, but it was so very improper. Yet why did she receive flutters in her stomach every time she thought about how he'd wanted to take a bath with her?

Loud footsteps echoed in the corridor outside the library, and she straightened to see who was coming to invade her private time. When Rebecca and Anna walked inside, Emmie sat up straight and slipped back into her role.

Anna's brown eyes jumped with excitement, but before she could say anything, Rebecca smiled haughtily.

"Miss Emmie? Might I have a word?"

"Certainly, Miss Rebecca."

"My father and mother are taking Lady Sarah and myself to London tomorrow to do some shopping, and then to see an opera afterward. We will be gone for two, perhaps three days. I need you to get trunks packed for the journey."

Emmie's heart picked up rhythm. London for the opera? How thrilling. She tried not to express her joy but kept a pleasant smile when she nodded. "Lady Sarah and I will be ready, I assure you."

Anna stepped to her and clasped her hands. "Oh, Emmie, this will be so fun. I can hardly wait. We will have the grandest time—"

"We?" Rebecca cut in.

Anna glanced at the other woman. "Yes. My companion and I—"

"Heavens no, my lady. Miss Emmie will remain here."

Emmie's heart dropped to her stomach, and although she wanted to ask why Rebecca didn't want her to go, Emmie already knew. That woman was so mean and selfish, Emmie would probably spend most of the trip teaching her manners, she was sure. She glanced at Anna and frowned.

Anna shook her head. "Miss Crampton, Emmie *has* to come."

Rebecca's false smile pricked Emmie's temper, making her want to physically lash out at the obtuse woman.

"Miss Emmie won't be needed, since you will be with me and my parents." Rebecca threw a glare toward Emmie then quickly diverted her attention back to Anna. "Our maid Nancy will be traveling with us, and she'll help you however you need. Besides, Nancy is used to hard labor and will do an exceptional job."

Anna's happy expression disappeared when a frown claimed her face. Emmie pursed her lips tight. Apparently, Miss Crampton didn't think Emmie worked very hard.

She nodded to Rebecca then looked at Anna. "I will have your things ready, Lady Sarah." Then, before she was tempted to put Rebecca in her place, she quickly spun around and left the room.

Storming into Anna's room, Emmie yanked open the closet doors and pulled out the trunks. "I'm not used to hard labor?" she mumbled to herself as she stuffed a dress into the trunk. "Who does Miss Crampton think she is to judge me so harshly?"

The bedroom door opened, and Anna flew in. She ran to Emmie and grabbed her hands. "I'm so sorry. I didn't know—"

"Anna," Emmie interrupted. "I realize what Miss Crampton thinks of me. Most of the Cramptons' servants think I am slothful, too, so it's only natural for Miss Crampton to think her maid can do more."

"But what should I say to change her mind?"

Emmie shook her head. "There's nothing you can say. Leave it alone. I will be fine right here at the estate. You go and have fun for the both of us."

"But it's not right."

"I know that, but we must let the matter rest. There is nothing either of us can do or say, since we are both guests here."

Frowning, Anna nodded as she moved to one of the armories and pulled out a gown. Emmie didn't stop her, only because she lacked the strength to say anything as discouragement sat heavily on her heart. They both packed the trunk in silence. Once in a while, Emmie glanced at Anna, but when she noticed her friend's watery eyes, she quickly looked away before she started crying, too.

Soon, the swishing of petticoats against the skirt of a dress was heard in the hall. Seconds later, Rebecca stood in the doorway holding two teacups. Her expression wavered between happiness and irritation. Emmie wished she knew she could read the other woman better.

"There has been a change of plans," she said. "Apparently, my father thought it best that we invite Miss Emmie to go with us."

Emmie's heart lifted. What a wonderful man! If he were standing here right now, she'd probably hug him.

"How exciting!" Anna cheered as the tears disappeared from her eyes. "Now we must get *your* trunk packed."

"Yes, um… that's what I thought too," Rebecca said in a rush. "So I brought up some tea for both of you." She handed Emmie a cup first, then Anna.

Emmie eyed the other woman carefully. Rebecca was certainly acting out of character—being nice, that was.

"Thank you, Miss Crampton." She took the teacup from her.

Anna took hers and sipped. As Emmie drank her tea, she watched Rebecca over the rim of the cup. Something was definitely not right. From the way the other woman's sinister eyes watched Emmie, the hairs on the back of her neck stood. Did she *want* to travel to London with such a calculating woman?

Sighing heavily, Rebecca offered a faux smile, turned, and hurried out of the room. Emmie was even leerier of the woman's actions now.

Once they were finished packing, Anna returned downstairs, but Emmie wasn't feeling well. By the time dinner was served, her stomach was roiling, and she stayed upstairs in her bedroom. The tang of the tea still lingered in her mouth and tasted very different from what she'd drunk before. For some reason, her stomach didn't like whatever it was Rebecca had given her. Yet Anna seemed just fine.

The night passed too slowly. Emmie couldn't sleep because she was running to the chamber pot too often, upheaving whatever it was that irritated her stomach. By the next morning, she was too tired and weak to even get out of bed. When Anna and Rebecca came to Emmie's room, she didn't have the strength to even smile.

"Oh, dear." Anna touched her hand to Emmie's cold face. "Miss Crampton, I don't think we should go to London with Emmie this sick."

"How sad," Rebecca said with entirely too much bounce in her voice. "Well, everything is already in place for us to travel." She pouted, although Emmie knew it was all for show.

"Go on without me," Emmie whispered brokenly.

Rebecca tapped Anna's arm. "I'll let our servants know to take special care of Miss Emmie while we are gone."

Confusion caused Anna's eyes to narrow as her forehead creased. "I don't know. Maybe I should stay—"

"Absolutely not," Rebecca said quickly. "Miss Emmie will be

just fine." She glared at Emmie. "Won't you?"

If this were any other day, Emmie would have loved to argue with her. But she just didn't have it in her now. "Yes, I shall be just fine. I'm actually feeling slightly better than I did last night," she lied.

Frowning, Anna folded her arms. "Well, all right, if you insist."

"I do," Emmie whispered.

When the two women left, Emmie groaned and turned in her bed, pulling the blanket up higher. She needed rest badly.

By midafternoon, she was back to feeling normal. It was strange that the stomach ailment would affect her in such a way. Her mind was working better as well, and she *knew* Rebecca had put something in her tea to make her so sick. That was the reason the insufferable woman had acted the way she had.

On the second day, Emmie decided she wasn't going to sit around and be bored, and would do something instead. She changed into her riding habit—not Anna's, but *hers*—and left the house. This particular riding habit wasn't as new as her others, but because it had been her favorite for over a year, it was well worn, so she didn't think any of the Cramptons' servants would question why she was wearing one of Lady Sarah's outfits.

Emmie ran right to the stables. As she entered, the stable boy stood talking to another person. She couldn't see who it was until she moved closer and noticed Broderick. His gaze met hers, holding her prisoner. It was too late to leave now.

Staring at him nearly caused her to have heart palpitations. Every time she'd seen him before, he was dressed in fancier clothes. Now he looked more like a farmer, but he was absolutely breathtaking in his fawn-colored shirt, brown breeches, and black knee-high riding boots.

He stopped the conversation with the stable boy, who then turned to fetch a horse. Broderick smiled at her, so she returned the gesture. She still felt uncomfortable under his close scrutiny but tried to be polite, nonetheless.

"Good day, Miss Emmie. What are you doing here?" he asked.

"I have come to ride one of Mr. Crampton's horses."

He lifted an eyebrow in disbelief. "Indeed? Have you done this before?"

"Yes. Mr. Crampton gave me permission not long after Lady Sarah and I arrived."

Slowly his smile widened. "Splendid. Now we can ride together."

Her heart pounded with uncertainty, yet the idea did sound exciting. It was either that or be very bored. "Why didn't you travel to London with your aunt and uncle yesterday?"

Tapping the whip against his thigh in a steady rhythm, he moved closer. "I can do without big cities, and most especially the people there. They are just a bunch of gossipmongers, if you ask me." He paused, tilting his head as he studied her. "Why didn't you go? I heard my aunt and uncle were taking Lady Sarah to the opera. Won't you need to assist her?"

She shrugged. "According to your cousin, her maid will suffice just nicely for both of them. Miss Rebecca was determined that I shouldn't go with Lady Sarah."

He stood beside her now. His gaze roamed slowly over her face, making butterflies dance in her stomach. Taking a deep breath of courage, she inhaled his intoxicating scent of leather and spice.

"I must apologize for my cousin. She can be very manipulative sometimes."

She arched an eyebrow. "Sometimes?"

He chuckled. "You are correct. She is manipulative *all* the time."

"Indeed."

"You look disappointed that you were not able to go," he said.

She nodded. "I, too, would have liked to see an opera in London. It would have been nice to partake of the scenery and pleasures."

"Maybe someday you will."

She shrugged. "Perhaps."

There was silence between them for the next few moments. Broderick glanced at her a few times but mostly watched inside the stable. When his attention wandered her way, a different expression touched his face. It was as if a light flickered to life in his head. His eyes widened as he turned them to her.

"I have a message for Lady Sarah. I received this yesterday, but she was out. Do you mind if I tell you instead and you can relay it to her?"

"Of course," she replied.

"Remember your carriage accident on your way to my uncle's estate?"

"How could I forget?"

"Well, apparently the authorities found your driver."

She gasped and stepped closer. "They did? Was he terribly hurt?"

"Just the opposite, in fact." Broderick shook his head. "He was drunk and spouting the truth. Apparently, he knew Lady Sarah's uncle was lord chancellor, and the driver wanted to harm her as a way to get back at her uncle."

Emmie slapped a hand over her mouth. Indeed, her father had been correct to assume his daughter might be in trouble. Breathing slower, she lowered her hand. "But we switched carriages before we even set foot in Greenwich. How did the driver know?"

"I'm assuming the first driver you had told him."

"That could have happened."

"Apparently, the second driver released the horses before jumping off the vehicle just as it traveled down the slope. That's why the coach turned over the way it did."

She nodded, blinking back tears. Was her family safe anywhere? Still, if these citizens knew that she really did side with them and not her uncle, perhaps they would not want to harm her. "I thank you for letting me know. I shall inform Lady Sarah as soon as she returns."

"Yes. She would definitely like to know."

Panic welled in her chest, and she grasped Broderick's arm. "Mr. Worthington, could I ask you a favor?"

"Anything," he said in a soft voice.

"Please don't say anything about the lord chancellor being related to Lady Sarah. That is why we are here. The earl wanted to protect his daughter."

"I understand. I only hope the driver and the authorities haven't gossiped about it."

"I hope not, too, or Lady Sarah's father will be sending us somewhere else."

"No." Broderick slid his palm against hers. "I will protect you. Both of you."

At that moment, the stable boy brought around an amazing black stallion, temporarily taking her mind off her troubles. Emmie knew a purebred when she saw one, and this horse was top of the line. Her father owned several, which she rode back home.

Broderick looked at her again with a gleam in his eyes. "Emiline, would you like to join me for a friendly and relaxing jaunt around the countryside?"

She still didn't know if she dared be alone with him. Her body had betrayed her before, not only with the kiss but when she was in the pond. Good thing he couldn't read her mind at that time, since it was full of improper thoughts.

But now… She wanted to be with someone. Anyone. Loneliness didn't make a good companion. If they became better friends and he started to trust her, then she might ask him about his relative, Captain Hawk.

"All over the countryside?" she asked. "Not just inside the estate, but outside of it, also?"

His smile was full now, showing off his straight, pearly white teeth. "You have seen enough of the estate, so why not see more of England's beautiful country?"

Returning a smile, she quickly made her decision. "I would love to join you, Mr. Worthington."

"Splendid." He turned to the stable boy. "Put a sidesaddle on Princess so that Miss Emmie can ride her."

"Actually," she quickly cut in, "I prefer a regular saddle."

Broderick glanced over her riding habit. "Are you certain?"

"Yes. I'll be able to ride just fine in this." She picked at her skirt.

Not much time later, the stable boy brought out a white thoroughbred mare, the most amazing horse she had ever seen. "Oh my," she gasped, and walked to the horse, patting its nose. "You are going to let me ride her?"

The young lad looked at Broderick, who gave him a small nod, then back to her. "Yes, miss. You can ride Princess."

The boy moved to give Emmie assistance, but she flipped her hand to move him away. "Thank you, but I can mount by myself."

The stable boy shrugged and turned to help Broderick, but he mounted without any assistance. The boy threw up his hands and walked away.

Without thinking, Emmie pulled her skirt up almost to her knees, helping her to mount better. Once she was sitting astride and had her garment in place, she glanced at Broderick. His eyes were wide and still directed at her legs. Inwardly, she groaned. If her father knew she'd just given a man a glimpse of her stockinged legs, her hide would be raw by nightfall.

After clearing his throat, Broderick switched his focus to look straight ahead as he pulled the reins and turned his horse. Emmie followed him until they trotted side by side. He rode with ease and skill. So refined. So much like a nobleman. She was certain he would have made a fine man of peerage. It was too bad his circumstances had left him untitled.

After a few awkward minutes, she finally breathed a sigh of relief that Broderick hadn't commented on her improper display not too long ago, and she finally let the excitement of their ride consume her. Although being alone with Broderick made her nervous, she couldn't stop giddiness from filling her as he began his tour of the countryside. Not only was her heart beating witlessly, her mind jumped everywhere at once.

"You know," she began, speaking her thoughts as they came, "I used to ride a horse just like yours back home when—" She quickly stopped then mentally scolded herself. She shouldn't have told him that. After all, she had told him a story of how she was a poor relation, and people like that didn't own thoroughbreds.

Broderick raised his eyebrows in question. "You rode a stallion? Just like this one?" he repeated. "Was it your horse or Lady Sarah's?"

"It was… Actually, it was her father's horse, but Lady Sarah allowed me to ride it, and she rode the mare." His gaze narrowed on her. She quickly thought of something to add. "Because of my upbringing, she knew I could handle the stallion better." Once again, she silently chided herself for saying whatever was in her mind. After all, how was a poor relative going to handle a thoroughbred better than a mare?

"Pray tell, Miss Emmie, why don't you tell me about your most curious upbringing?"

Think, Emmie! "Perhaps I will when the time is right." She lifted her chin and pushed her horse a little faster. He kept her pace with his animal.

"How good are you at riding?" he asked with a twinkle in his eyes.

Her heartbeat picked up rhythm. "I'm actually not as good at riding as I am at… racing." She dug her brown calf-high boots into the sides of the mare, taking off ahead of him, laughing over her shoulder as she passed.

He shouted with laughter before the thunder of the horse's hooves caught up to her. Knowing him, he would try his hardest to show her that a woman didn't know the first thing about racing. After a few moments of him still being the one in the rear, she hoped he would change his attitude about her.

She glanced behind her. His hard expression let her know he was serious in his pursuit as he leaned forward in his saddle, pushing the animal faster. When she finally allowed him to catch up, his expression changed. Now he looked hurt, yet surprised.

She stopped her horse, and he did the same. "I apologize, Mr. Worthington. Please forgive me for laughing, but if you could see the look on your face right now…" She couldn't hold it back any longer and laughed harder.

He growled, and his brown eyes darkened. Fear grasped her as her blood turned cold. Upsetting him was the last thing she wanted to do, especially now that they were becoming friends. She needed to think of something to change his attitude quickly— or at least make him smile.

Chapter Nine

IRRITATION ROILED IN Broderick's stomach. He hated to be bested. He especially didn't enjoy being outdone by this slip of a woman. Determination settled in his bones. There was no way he was going to lose a horse race to a woman. Even in her outdated riding habit—that actually fit her better than the other dresses had—she was all woman, soft and desirable. Excitement flushed her face, causing her eyes to gleam. Lips, soft and red, turned up in a smile.

When she laughed, her whole face lit up with enthusiasm. Of course, now she wore a panicked expression. Probably because she sensed his frustration.

It took him a few moments, but he finally gained control over his emotions. He sighed deeply and smiled, which made her pretty face light up again.

"Emiline? Would you please call me Broderick?"

The laughter disappeared quickly from her face as she lost her smile. Her forehead creased. "Why?"

He shrugged. "Because all of my friends call me by that name."

"And you consider me amongst your friends?"

His grin widened. "Yes. Don't you?"

The corners of her mouth lifted as if she fought showing him any reaction. "Well, I… Um, all right, Broderick," she ended, giving him her full smile once more.

"Much better, thank you. And now, since we are friends, it's only decent of you to let me have another chance at winning. So, if you will play honestly during our next race, I would like to prove to you that I'm as admirable as you are."

"When was I not playing honestly? I will have you know I am quite ethical when sporting."

"But you got a head start."

When she laughed, her eyes danced with merriment. "No. I think you held yourself back because I'm a woman."

"And what if I did?"

"I don't want you to hold back this time. I want you to push yourself to the limit."

Suddenly, an idea took root, and he held back the mischievous spark of energy within. "Would you care to make a wager on our little race, then?"

One of her perfectly shaped eyebrows rose. "What did you have in mind?"

He couldn't believe what he had in mind, but he would definitely not tell her about his improper thoughts. "If I win, I will require you to dress like a genteel woman for an entire week."

She gasped. "Are you jesting?"

"No. I'm quite earnest."

"You don't think I dress like a woman now?"

"Well, let me rephrase that. I want you to dress a little more... what's the word... *appealing.*"

She released an unladylike snort. "Appealing? My gowns aren't appealing?"

"Let me clarify a little better. I want you to wear gowns that fit you, and I want to see your hair styled like a young woman your age. I don't want you to dress like an old woman."

"All right, I understand now. So, what if I win? Are you going to wear a bath towel all week for me?"

He howled with laughter. This tiny woman certainly knew how to keep him on his toes. She had a quick wit, and he adored it. "Is that what you want to see me in?"

"No. I was just making a comparison."

"All right, I will do anything *but* wear a bath towel."

Leaning forward on her horse, she studied him in quiet deliberation. What wild wager would she require? Would he play along? She was sure he would, especially if he won. Seeing her wearing lovely dresses would give her more of a mature appearance—more alluring. Most of the time she looked out of place anyway.

Finally, she smiled wide. "If I win, for an entire week you have to treat me as if I'm a princess."

He chuckled. "How can I treat any woman like a princess if she is wearing baggy and plain dresses with her hair wound so tight?"

"I suppose you will just have to try."

He remained silent for a second, staring at her stubborn—yet pretty—face. He didn't plan on losing, so he would agree. "I will take your challenge. If you win, I will treat you like a princess, but if I win, you will have to wear enticing women's dresses for an entire week." He reached out his hand to seal the bargain. "Shall we close the arrangement with a handshake?"

She smiled, slipping her small hand into his and giving it one good squeeze. "Yes, we have an accord."

Lining their horses up, they prepared for the race.

"On your mark… get set…" he started.

"Go," she yelled, and took off. Broderick was prepared for her trickery and wasn't far behind. He laughed. She really wasn't being dishonest, just sneaky.

The thoroughbreds ran neck to neck along the countryside. At times, Broderick was ahead, but then, discouragingly, Emiline always seemed to catch up. At one point she broke ahead of him, but soon enough he caught up. Obviously, she was determined to win, but so was he.

One mile away at the stream was their ending point, and both reached the bank at the same time. By the time he pulled his horse to a stop, he laughed merrily, and she joined in.

Broderick dismounted first and moved to help her down. "You surprise me, Emiline. I have never known a woman who could maneuver a horse as well as you." He took her small waist and lifted her down from the horse slowly.

"Thank you, sir. That is quite a compliment coming from you."

Still holding her by the waist, he stared down into her huge eyes. Excitement shot through him. He became breathless standing so close. The yearning to kiss her again spread through him like wildfire. The sudden spark of heat confused him, so he released her and stepped back.

Taking a deep breath, he tried to calm himself from the brief contact. "Now what do we do in this situation?"

Her eyes widened. "What situation?"

"The race. We tied."

She blew out a gust of air and smiled. "Yes, the tie. I don't know what to do in this situation, because I'm usually the person who wins."

"You are very good—for a woman." Amazed, he shook his head. "But what I think is done in situations like this is that we both have to pay the consequences."

"What? You still expect me to dress myself as an *enticing* woman?"

He nodded. "Yes, just as I will treat you like a princess for a whole week."

Emiline bit her bottom lip as silence stretched between them for a few seconds. "I think you are getting the better end of our wager."

He chuckled. "No. I think you are. Can you imagine what my relatives will think when they see me treating you as if you are royalty?" He laughed harder. "Just think about what Lady Sarah will do."

A grimace quickly touched her mouth. "I will explain things to her, so she understands."

He turned and walked to the water. "Is it really difficult for you to dress that way?" He bent and plucked a long weed from out of the grass, noticing a bunch of summer snowflake flowers nearby.

"Hard for me?" Her laugh sounded forced. "I will have you know—" She stopped suddenly, biting her lower lip.

He received the impression she had been about to divulge a secret. Now he wanted her to continue. "Go on," he encouraged her.

"Um, I will have you know that… Well, that I do know how to dress that way." She walked to him. "I have been Lady Sarah's companion for a couple of years, and I have watched her closely. I know I could dress as she does, but I have chosen not to. My father was not very strict with me as a child, and he let me traipse around the estate doing things only a boy would do."

Chuckling softly, he shook his head. "And Lady Sarah still wanted you for her lady's companion?"

A flicker of hurt flashed through her eyes and her expression sobered. She lifted her chin stubbornly. "As I told you before, I was a poor relation, and she wanted to help me out by giving me the position as her companion."

He hadn't meant to hurt her—he thought he was stating the obvious. He reached down and plucked the white snowflake flower and then touched it to the end of her cute little nose. "You must have done fabulously, because look at Lady Sarah now."

She took the flower from him and smelled it as she walked past him toward the stream. "I thank you—I think."

He chuckled. "Yes, that was a compliment."

She knelt by the stream and ran her fingers through the water. Leaning against the tree near her, Broderick studied her, wondering why she had suddenly become quiet. The gentle breeze lifted the wavy strands of her hair that had miraculously escaped her tight bun. His gaze traveled further to her ears and neck, which was actually beginning to tempt him to lean down and kiss her skin. Strange how hard it was to hold back from doing so.

As he studied her, he realized she would be the hit of London if she were a real lady. If she arranged her hair the right way and wore elegant dresses that fit, she would indeed make one very beautiful woman. She carried herself as a lady, and talked as one, too, which was quite surprising—but then, he suspected it was because she had been around the earl's daughter for a few years. Strange, but Lady Sarah didn't speak as eloquently as her companion, nor did she carry herself as well. Yet Emiline was the one who was the poor relative. Very confusing.

Her pretty eyes were surrounded by dark, thick lashes, almost like butterfly wings. Soft skin and high cheekbones made her face appear more delicate. Indeed, she was one very handsome woman. Then again, so was Lady Sarah, yet... There was something not quite right, and he couldn't pinpoint the problem.

"Emiline?"

She didn't take her eyes off the water. "Yes?"

"I was just wondering about something."

"What is that?"

Curiosity got the better of him. "Why do you know more and seem more educated than Lady Sarah? You mentioned earlier you rode a stallion, yet once when I was with Lady Sarah, she said she had never been on one before. Can you tell me why this is?"

Her hand froze in the water, and she stiffened.

Now he *knew* she had a secret.

EMMIE CURSED UNDER her breath. Dare she weave more into her web of lies? Or could she trust him with the truth? As much as she *wanted* to trust him, the simple fact was that she didn't know Broderick very well at all. She didn't know the Cramptons, either. Would they frown upon her father's decision to keep his daughter's identity hidden? She doubted they would understand.

She tried to steady her heart as she looked up at him. "I was born to a struggling farmer and his sickly wife. My mother died when I was young, and my father raised me to help him around the farm. He also worked as a horse trainer for the wealthy, and he taught me that trade. When he became ill and couldn't make a living, that is when he sent a letter to his distant cousin—Lady Sarah's father—to ask for help. The earl agreed to have me be his daughter's companion until she married. So, I suppose you can say I received the best of both worlds while growing up."

Broderick's eyebrows rose in curiosity. "That certainly explains why you can ride a horse astride so well."

She nodded. "Exactly."

"But that doesn't explain why Lady Sarah cannot."

"Um… She has terrible allergies around horses."

He knelt beside her, touching another summer snowflake flower to the tip of her nose. "I suppose that is what makes you so special."

"Not being allergic makes me special?"

He chuckled. "No, being raised the way you were."

She gazed back into his eyes, and heaven help her, she couldn't look away. A few minutes ago, his jabbing remarks about Lady Sarah's feelings had really irritated Emmie, and yes, jealousy crept into her mind. Now his kind words were like sweet honey.

She didn't reply to his comment. She couldn't. Trapped in his mesmerizing gaze, she felt her heart hammer faster, shooting vibrations through her insides until they threatened to melt. Something needed to stop, or she would soon find herself swooning in his arms.

He slowly slid the flower petals down the bridge of her nose to drop on her lips, his eyes following the path. Automatically, she parted her lips, and the tip of the flower rested on her lower lip. The urge to kiss him became strong, and she wanted to bring back the heated excitement flowing through her when he had kissed her before.

Her mind argued this wasn't right, but the tingling in her body countered, reminding her how incredible his arms had felt around her.

Unfortunately, she couldn't get involved with a man like him. Her father wouldn't approve.

She forced herself to stand and move away from him as she cleared her throat. "So, is this the only part of the countryside you are going to show me?"

For a minute, she thought he looked disappointed, but instantly the expression was gone. Could he have wanted to kiss her, too? *Probably not.* Those fantasies were only in her mind.

"You want to see more?"

She nodded.

"Come. I will show my lady princess anything her lovely heart desires." He grinned and bowed slightly.

She chuckled as giddiness consumed her once again. "It would be unscrupulous to start our wager now, since I'm not adorned in a fancy dress."

He scratched his head, his gaze roaming over her length. The familiar chills danced over her skin, bringing back her erratic heartbeat. She tried pushing the feelings aside, but the way his mouth lifted in a grin made her heart sing.

"If you wish, we could always go back to the estate and let you change."

"No. Let us just continue on our way. We shall start the wager tomorrow."

"That is a grand idea." He nodded and held out his hand for her to take. "Then let us be on our way."

He helped her to her horse and set her atop the mare, even though she repeatedly told him she didn't need his help. She realized just how much she'd missed being treated like a lady. This time, she made certain she didn't show him so much of her legs when she adjusted on the saddle.

They rode everywhere, or at least it seemed that way. She had never seen so much land without farms or houses occupying the space. Everything was so green. Red, violet, yellow, and pink flowers sprinkled the fields like a rainbow, but her favorite was the summer snowflake, because it would remind her of this wonderful day. She'd adored every second she was out here with Broderick.

Occasionally he stopped, pointed to something, and told her a little history behind the object. It amazed her how educated he was, and it pleased her more than it should.

They came upon acres of wildflowers and stopped to eat. She was grateful the cook had prepared for a big appetite, because there was enough food to fill her belly. After eating, she walked around the field looking at the different types of flowers, some she had never seen before. She thought it rather funny that he knew the names of every flower.

Soon, they rode away from the field and through a few villages. The people waved and greeted them—some even asked if she and Broderick would like to come into their homes for a cup of tea, but he refused for the both of them.

She conversed easily with Broderick, and she liked how being in his presence comforted her. Not once did their topic turn intimate, and she was grateful that her body didn't react with heated tingles anymore.

It wasn't until the sun began to disappear behind the horizon when she realized the lateness of the day. "Oh, goodness." She pulled her horse to a stop. "Do you realize what time it is?"

"Not until now," he replied.

"How far away are we from your uncle's estate?"

Broderick chuckled. "Far enough away for me to know we will not be able to get home before dark."

The mere idea of them alone together in the moonlight made her panic. After all, she was a lady and had been taught the importance of decorum. "Whatever shall we do?"

He remained silent as she surveyed their surroundings. "If I'm not mistaken, I believe there's another village just west of here that will have an inn for us to lodge in."

"And what if you are mistaken?"

He chuckled and met her stare. "Then we will sleep underneath the stars."

Just thinking about being with him alone, out here in their night-filled wonderland, had her smiling. Tilting her head back, she gazed up at the sky to see if that was a possibility, praying that it was. When she didn't see any stars, she frowned. "What stars? All I see are clouds."

He too looked up. "Drat! I didn't think it would rain on us, or I wouldn't have taken us this far away from home." His gaze met hers. "See what being with you does to me? I can't think straight." He laughed.

Her heart flipped, but knowing Broderick, he was probably just being humorous. "Will we be able to make it to the next village before it starts to rain?"

He watched the clouds for a moment. She glanced up at the sky again. Within seconds, the gray clouds thickened and the sky became darker. Even the air cooled quickly.

"I suppose we will, but just barely, and only if we hurry."

"Then let's be off. We have no time to waste." She kicked her heels into the mare and took off in the direction he had pointed to, praying they would not get caught in the storm. What would they do then? She dared not think of how he'd help her to stay warm.

Chapter Ten

EMMIE HUDDLED CLOSER to the horse for warmth as the sheeting rain fell in buckets around her, soaking her clothes. The rain had come earlier than expected, and as she and Broderick searched through the small village for a place to stay, the town seemed too busy closing their shops for the night to help the two weary—and drenched—strangers.

As they passed through the muddy streets, the prospect of finding a place to stay seemed bleak. Desperation fell over Emmie, and she would take anything, even a stable, just to get out of the rain. She glanced at Broderick, and his droopy expression let her know he felt the same hopelessness.

The next man they came across, Broderick urged his horse in the stranger's direction. "Hold up there, if you will." When the man stopped and turned, Broderick stopped the animal. "I'm looking for a place of lodging. Is there one close by?"

The man bundled his coat around his body and shook his head. "No, sir. Our town is too small."

Tears stung Emmie's eyes. She wanted to get out of the cold and find shelter soon, or she would indeed start crying—or freeze to death.

"However," the stranger continued, "an old widow woman just up the lane is very generous and has a large house. I'm certain she will let you stay there for the night."

"I thank you for your assistance," Broderick said before tossing the man a coin.

The man's eyes widened before he smiled up at Broderick. "God bless you."

Hope grew in Emmie's chest as she followed behind Broderick. Just as the man had directed, at the end of the lane, a large house sat up on a hill. She urged her mount faster until both she and Broderick reached the place. A few windows glowed with welcoming light. After Broderick dismounted and helped her down, he quickly put the horses in the barn. He grabbed her hand, and they ran toward the house.

He knocked, and within minutes, a short, heavyset old woman with a white cap covering most of her gray hair answered the door. She held up her lamp to see them better in the dark.

"Please forgive us for bothering you this evening, madame," Broderick began, "but we were just passing through town and were caught in the storm. We were informed you might have an extra room for us to stay the night. I would be willing to pay."

The old woman scanned both Emmie and Broderick before her expression softened and she smiled. "Oh yes, you poor dears. Do come in and warm yourself by the fire." She motioned them toward the fireplace.

Still holding Emmie's hand, he led them inside and to the fireplace. Her body shook as she rubbed her hands together, praying to feel the warmth quickly.

Leaving their side for a moment, the older woman moved to a cupboard and pulled out two woolen blankets. "People around these parts call me Georgia," she said, handing each one a blanket.

"I thank you, Georgia. My name is Broderick Worthington, and this is Emiline."

All Emmie could do was nod at the woman in appreciation as she wrapped the dry blanket around her wet body. Unfortunately, shivers overtook her, making her unable to speak due to her chattering teeth. She couldn't ever remember being this cold in her life.

"It's a pleasure to meet you. What, may I ask, were you two doing out in the rain?"

Broderick chuckled lightly. "We had been out riding and didn't notice the day slipping by. We also didn't realize the rain clouds were moving in."

Georgia shook her head. "You unfortunate souls. Let me leave you two for a moment and prepare a room. You are probably freezing in those wet clothes, and you will need to change before catching your death." She turned and hurried up the stairs.

Emmie moved even closer to the fire, staring down into the orange flames. Gradually, the feeling returned to her limbs, but it wasn't quick enough to suit her. Broderick stepped closer, wrapping his arms around her. She turned to face him as he gathered her against his body, sliding his hands up and down her arms and over her back, trying to get her warm. Although he was wet, too, she had no desire to move away or tell him how improper this was. His body's heat blended into her limbs quickly.

"I apologize for this," he said softly in her ear. "I had not planned on the weather turning bad."

Tilting her head, she looked at him. "I under… stand. You… didn't… know." Her teeth continued to chatter.

"But I still feel guilty, since it was my suggestion to keep riding the countryside."

She managed a small smile. "At least… you got us… out of the… rain."

As his hands continued to move up and down her arms, coziness settled over her, and she wanted to close her eyes and enjoy it.

"It was pure luck that we are here," he said. "I didn't think we would find a place to stay. People usually are not this friendly to strangers."

"It must be… your exceptionally handsome looks… that got

us a… place, then," she teased.

"Or yours," he replied with a wink.

His eyes deepened to the color of hot coffee. The longer she stared, the more she melted. Smiling at him once more, she rested her head against his chest, snuggling closer for more warmth. It wasn't until he moved the bulk of her hair aside to rub her neck that she realized her hair had fallen out of the bun.

"Your hair is down," he whispered. "It's a lovely color."

"The color is called… wet."

He chuckled. "I'm happy to know you still have your sense of humor even while you're chilled to the bone."

"Me too." Standing against him this close to the fire as he continued to stroke heat back into her body was very relaxing. She didn't want to move from her spot against his chest. "Do you think it is raining in London?"

"Possibly. Why?"

"I wondered if the rain would keep your aunt and uncle from their opera."

"I highly doubt that. Uncle Henry is determined, and so it will happen. Besides, he has three females with him, which means they will get their way."

"You know, I didn't tell anyone where I was going today. None of the servants know. Well, besides the stable boy."

He chuckled. "I didn't tell anyone, either."

The swishing of Georgia's skirts announced her presence before she entered the room. "All right, I have your room ready and a roaring fire to warm you two up."

Broderick kept one arm around Emmie as they followed the widow upstairs to the second floor, and the guest room. The heat from the fire touched Emmie's face as she walked inside. She closed her eyes for a brief moment, still enjoying both the warmth and the comfort of being in Broderick's arms.

When she finally surveyed the room, it surprised her to see it was larger than she had expected. Against the far wall was a huge bed with quilts that had been turned down. The floor had a lovely

Oriental carpet lying in the middle. The widow must be wealthier than Emmie first suspected. Even the armoires, drawers, and tables were made of the finest quality.

The cozy room beckoned to Emmie, giving her a confusing sense of being at home in North Devon. Strange she would feel this way, since she hadn't received that feeling at Mr. and Mrs. Crampton's house.

Once her mind cleared, something struck her—jolting her out of Broderick's arms. There was only one bed. Georgia couldn't possibly think they would share a bed, yet what else would the older woman think? She must assume they were married.

Panic consumed Emmie, and she took another step away from Broderick, looking up at him with wide eyes. When she opened her mouth to rectify the most improper situation, Broderick slid his arm around her once more and squeezed so she couldn't move. He shook his head as if warning her not to say anything.

"Take off those wet clothes and leave them outside the door." Georgia didn't notice Emmie's dismay. "I had a few extra changes of clothes that my children left behind, and I laid them on the bed for both of you to wear for the night."

Broderick smiled at the older woman. "Thank you, Georgia. You are an extremely kind woman."

"Let me know if you need anything else." Georgia opened the door to step out, but then stopped and looked back. "Are you two hungry? I could put together a light meal for you, if you would like."

"That would be greatly appreciated," Broderick answered.

"I shall bring the food up when it's ready." She turned and left, closing the door behind her.

Emmie yanked herself away from his side once the door was shut. "Why didn't you tell her?" she asked. "Now she thinks we are married."

Broderick shrugged. "I considered our choices. I could have let her know we are not married, and then she would have wondered why we were alone together all day long without a proper chaperone, and I didn't want her thinking you were anything less than a lady, or she would have turned us out." He dropped the damp blanket to the floor and began removing his shirt. "Or I could have told her nothing, letting her believe we are married, and she wouldn't have known otherwise. Now, which choice would you have me make?"

The second he pulled off his shirt, she suddenly forgot their conversation. Once again, she was able to look upon that wonderfully handsome, masculine chest of his. But she couldn't leisurely ogle as she had done that time by the pond.

"Wh—what are you doing?" she shrieked, while her heart fluttered rapidly.

"I'm taking off my wet clothes and replacing them with the dry ones Georgia set out for me." Pausing, he looked at her standing in the middle of the room, still shivering in her damp blanket. "I suggest you do the same before you become ill with a fever."

He was right, but she didn't think she could undress in front of him. In the back of her mind, she could hear her father's tirades on those times she didn't act like the fitting daughter of an earl. She didn't want him ashamed of her.

Then again, did she really have a choice?

Scanning the room, she looked for any signs of a dressing screen, but there was none. How could she take off her clothes and still be modest about it?

Her gaze moved back to Broderick, and he was wiping his chest dry with one of the many towels Georgia had left for them to use. Maybe Emmie would wait until he was finished and then ask him to leave the room so that she could change.

After drying his hair, Broderick rested the towel over his shoulder and began to undo his breeches. "Unless you want to see the rest of my body, I suggest you turn your head, Emiline."

Gasping, she quickly spun around and faced the fireplace. Heat filled her body, more stifling than the fire, making her face blaze so hot that she feared she wouldn't need a towel to dry off now. Nervously, she threaded her fingers through her hair, finishing removing the pins that were left. She heard when Broderick pulled the wet breeches from his body, and when they flopped to the floor. She waited a few seconds more before she heard the material flap in the air as he put on what Georgia had left for him.

"I'm decent now," he told her.

Slowly, she turned and looked. The long nightshirt he wore looked too small for him. Instead of hitting his calves like nightshirts were supposed to, this one barely covered his knees. He certainly had some muscular legs.

Silently, she grumbled. How dare he make her think of such wicked thoughts? But she had to admit that he was right to make Georgia think they were married. Emmie couldn't have her reputation ruined, especially if the truth that she was the real daughter of the earl ever came out.

Broderick carried his wet clothes to the door and set them outside in the hallway, closing the door after he was done. He turned around and gave her a grin. "Do I need to help you?"

"No."

"Then why have you not started to undress?"

"I'm waiting for you to leave first."

Chuckling, he walked past her and to the bed, where he plopped himself down. He leaned back and folded his arms across the back of his head, stretching his legs out in front of him, sighing heavily. "I think not, my dear *wife*. I'm staying right here." He shrugged. "Besides, how would that look to Georgia if she knew the husband had to wait outside the bedroom while the wife undressed?"

She scowled. "Will you at least have the decency to close your eyes?"

He gave her one of his teasing grins then closed his eyes.

The insufferable man! He could be so impossible sometimes. Between one hand and her chin, she tried to keep the blanket as her shield as her other hand fumbled with her clothes. Needless to say, she failed miserably.

"Would you like some help?" Broderick asked without opening his eyes. "I can hear your grunts of frustration and moans of despair."

She growled, knowing she could not do it without him. "Do you promise to keep your eyes closed?"

The corners of his mouth lifted in a grin. "Yes, but can I look now before I walk to you?"

"Of course."

He moved off the bed, grabbed a few towels, and draped them over his shoulder before coming to stand in front of her. Taking hold of the blanket, he held it together.

"Now close your eyes," she instructed him.

"Why? I will not see you with the blanket around you."

She scowled. "Just do as I say."

Wearing a wide grin, he shrugged and followed instructions. She couldn't stop herself from smiling, grateful he couldn't see. Even with his help, she still struggled, but it was easier than before. She managed to slip off her riding habit, but not her underclothes.

"Keep your eyes closed." She grabbed a towel and tried to dry herself as much as possible while still standing circled by the blanket. Then she removed his hands from the edges of the blanket and hurried to the bed to retrieve the nightgown. After slipping the gown over her head, she quickly pulled off her wet undergarments. Hastily, she patted the towel on her head to soak up any wetness her hair still held. She then picked up all her clothes and dropped them outside the door beside Broderick's. Once this was accomplished, she ran to the bed and hopped in, yanking the blankets up to her chin. "All right, I'm ready."

He opened his eyes and looked at her, then chuckled. "Why are you being so modest? Your wet riding habit showed me more of your womanly curves than that nightgown."

She scowled. He was right. The nightgown billowed over

her, yet she still felt so exposed. "I cannot help how I feel. What we are doing here is wrong, and you well know it."

He laughed again then walked back to the bed, picking up a dry towel on his way. "You know why I'm continuing with this masquerade." Sitting on the bed, he draped the towel over her head and left it there. "Your hair is still wet. If you don't dry it, then your nightgown will get wet, as well as the bedsheets and pillows."

Emmie suspected she looked silly sitting on the bed with a towel over her head while she clutched the blanket with both hands to her chin. She was afraid of letting go of the covers because they might fall away from her.

With one hand she held the blankets, and with the other toweled her hair. When she was done, she threw the towel to the floor and then ran her fingers through her hair, straightening out the tangles, still keeping the blankets from dropping any lower than her chin.

Broderick lay on top of the covers, resting on his side as he watched her. He must think her silly to be so cautious. Although she was supposed to be the earl's poor relation, she still had morals. She wished he would remove that teasing grin from his face.

"What do you want now? Why are you staring at me?" she snapped self-consciously.

"I'm just trying to figure you out."

"Pray tell, what is there to figure out?"

"Your actions. Sometimes I can predict what you're going to do and say next, but other times you take me totally unaware."

"I'm sorry if I confuse you. I didn't plan to befuddle your mind."

He shook his head. "There you go again, talking all educated. Especially for a *poor relation*." Leaning over, he propped himself up on his elbow. "Sometimes I feel that things are uncomplicated between us because of the way we get along so well, almost like one friend to another. Then you turn completely around and start acting like a well-bred woman, which makes me feel differently about you."

He was entirely too close, and feeling his warm breath against her face turned her insides to mush. His eyes were the dark brown she loved gazing into, and at this moment, she never wanted to look away. He appeared so relaxed as he met her stare. His expression was so very tender, and she melted the longer she gazed at him. "How *do* you feel when I'm acting like a well-bred lady?"

A lazy grin touched his mouth. "I feel the same way I did that first night after we met."

Her heart hammered quicker. "That night when… you kissed me?"

His eyes slowly traced her face before coming to rest on her lips. "Yes."

She swallowed hard. "Why would you feel like that about a lady's companion?"

He grinned. "Because sometimes you can be so desirable, and all I want to do is take you in my arms and kiss you."

Tightness consumed her chest, making it hard to breathe, yet her breast rose and fell so quickly, testifying that she was breathing just fine. She didn't know what to say. Maybe she didn't want to say anything.

His attention moved over her face and came to rest on her mouth. Perhaps she should let him kiss her. Yet her mind argued that they were on a bed and the situation was very improper. The longer she studied his lips, so full and inviting, the more she could actually feel herself being lured into temptation, and right now, she almost didn't care if they were in their nightclothes and on a bed.

"You… wouldn't… dare," she whispered, then wondered why she'd said that. Was she trying to goad him into doing it?

Chapter Eleven

B RODERICK'S GRIN WIDENED and his eyes sparkled. "I wouldn't dare?" He moved his head closer to hers as he took a lock of her hair and caressed it. "Are you certain of that?"

Emmie sank into the bed, but his face continued closing in. Did she really want him to kiss her? Heaven help her, yes, she did!

She closed her eyes just as his mouth touched hers. His lips were so soft this time, and she wasn't prepared for the jolt of passion shooting through her. She wasn't going to fight him, especially when he moved his upper body and lay across hers, pinning her down.

He slid his hand around her head and brought her face closer as he continued with the astonishing kiss. Pleasure filled her. She had been kissed a few times by other men, but they had always disgusted her. Not Broderick. He was completely different.

She relaxed and released the blanket she'd been clutching, sliding her hands up his broad shoulders to his neck. She stroked his rippling muscles and marveled again over how well he was put together. He was such a strong man, yet lying on top of her he was very gentle, and she wasn't frightened in the least.

"Oh, Emiline," he mumbled against her lips. "You are so adorable."

She held on to him as she met his urgent kisses, loving the heady sensations building inside her. She loved the way he stroked her neck, moving his fingers to the neckline of her nightshirt as he toyed with the embroidered collar. Heat flowed through her faster, and she yearned for more. This new feeling was so exhilarating, so pleasurable, that she didn't want to stop. Ever.

But she had to. This was improper, and she shouldn't even be with him on the bed. They were wearing their nightclothes, for heaven's sake. Her father would certainly have Broderick's head on a platter for this stunt, and probably hers as well.

Before she could pull away, there was a knock at the door.

"I brought your meal up."

Georgia! How could Emmie have forgotten about her?

She and Broderick pulled away at the same time, staring at each other in silent communication. His hot breath fanned her face, and she knew her heavy breathing matched his perfectly. He gave her a sly smile then quickly moved off her and slid underneath the covers.

"You can come in, Georgia," he called out.

Emmie hoped she didn't look as ravished and confused as she felt. Hopefully, Georgia wouldn't mention it if she did notice.

The older woman brought in a tray of food and took it right over to the bed, setting it down on top of the quilt. It was an assortment of meats and cheeses, and even some fruits and bread.

"This looks wonderful," Broderick said. "God certainly blessed us by leading us to your doorstep."

Georgia's cheeks turned pink. "I'm the one who is blessed. Do you know how long it has been since I have had any real company? My children and their families don't visit me enough, and I rarely get out and visit with my neighbors. My body is just not what it used to be." She patted her hips gently.

"Then we are happy that you are happy," he told her.

Georgia turned her gaze to Emmie in a slow inspection. She prayed the older woman couldn't see the passion still lurking inside her. Slowly, she pulled the blankets up to her neck.

"Where are you two from?" Georgia asked Broderick.

"York," he answered quickly.

Emmie glanced his way, wondering why he'd given her the wrong answer.

Georgia shook her head. "I have never been there. What did you say your last name was? You look very familiar to me."

Broderick stiffened. "Worthington. But I have relatives all over England."

She drew her silvery-brown eyebrows together in confusion. "I fear I have never met any of them." She turned her attention to Emmie. "And what about you, my dear? What was your maiden name?"

Emmie pulled herself up slightly. *Oh, good grief!* Now she had to think of another lie. "Um… Snow." Well, that wasn't exactly a lie, since her mother's maiden name was Snow.

Georgia opened her old brown eyes in surprise. "Snow, you say?" Emmie nodded. "Who are your parents, child?"

Quickly, Emmie thought before answering. She had told Broderick that her father was a farmer and her mother was dead. As long as she stuck with that story, she would be fine. "My mother is dead, but her name was Camilla, and my father's name is Abner." That wasn't altogether a lie either, since that was her father's middle name.

Georgia's face fell. "Oh, I don't know them. It's rather strange, because I have the same last name as you."

Emmie's heart pounded faster as she studied the older woman. Her last name was Snow? She sat up straighter. "Indeed? That is rather strange, is it not?"

"Yes, and what is even stranger is that you resemble my daughter Daphne quite a bit. She, too, has large blue eyes, but her hair was a lighter brown."

Daphne? Emiline caught her breath and held it. This could not be! Her mother's name had been Daphne.

Emmie studied the older woman's face—oval, like her mother's had been, with eyes like her mother's. They even twinkled the same. Could Emmie actually be talking to her maternal grandmother? The older woman did resemble the miniature Emmie had of her own mother.

All of this was too strange for her, and she tried her hardest to keep her eyes from watering with happiness.

Georgia chuckled. "However, now Daphne's hair is almost gray because of her age, but it used to be your color."

Emmie forgot about the blankets she clutched to her chest as numbness spread through her, and the covering slipped to her lap. Her heart stopped. If the Daphne they were discussing was indeed the same lady, that meant...

But no. It couldn't be. Emmie's mother had been dead for fifteen years.

"You know, I believe I have a miniature of her," Georgia continued. "Let me go retrieve it and show you. The resemblance between the two of you is quite remarkable." She turned and hurried out of the room.

Once Georgia had disappeared, Broderick moved the tray of food aside and wrapped his arms around Emmie. "Georgia is a sweet lady, but I wish she would leave so that we could get back to what we were doing before she came."

He kissed Emmie's neck, and she automatically stiffened. He withdrew, his brows pulled together in worry. Cupping her face, he turned it toward his.

"Emiline? What's wrong?"

She couldn't tell him. Not since she had lied to him about her identity all this time. But she had to say *something*. She was almost certain he would understand.

But no, she would keep her little secret.

"I suppose I'm just hungry." She took a piece of cheese off the tray and brought it up to her mouth. She nibbled but didn't taste anything.

"Are you certain that is all? You have lost all the color in your face."

She tried to calm down, inwardly forcing herself to breathe normally, although it wasn't working as well as she hoped.

Turning toward him, she managed a small smile. "Yes. That is all it is. I assure you, I'm fine."

His worried eyes studied her, and she knew he didn't believe her. When his gaze rested on her lips again, his expression softened. He cupped her face, moving his thumb gently across her bottom lip.

"Do you know how much I still want to kiss you?" he whispered huskily.

This wasn't the time. She wanted to be kissed, but she had too much on her mind right now. Her mother may still be alive. If she was, what was her reason for falsifying her death instead of being with her husband and daughter, who had needed her so desperately?

"But Broderick, it's really not proper. We shouldn't even be sitting on the same bed, much less alone together," she answered softly.

He waggled his eyebrows. "But since we're here, we ought to make the best of it."

Georgia chose that moment to come back, so once again, Broderick and Emmie pulled away from each other.

"Here it is." Georgia handed the miniature to Emmie, who took it with a shaky hand.

Glancing down at the picture, she tried to keep herself from crying. The lady she stared at was indeed her mother, except an older version. Her father had kept a picture of her in his bedroom, which helped Emmie to remember. This was the same woman.

She forced herself to breathe normally again. "I—I—would like to meet her one day," she squeaked.

"Yes. I'm sure I could arrange that. Daphne is living near the border of Brighton now. She's the companion to a wealthy widow, Lady Estelle Winterbourne."

Emmie lifted her gaze and met her grandmother's eyes. "Is your daughter not married?"

The old woman's face fell in sadness. "She was married once

with a child, but the ship that carried her husband and daughter was attacked by pirates, killing all on board."

What? Emmie's heart stumbled as her mind came to a screeching halt. This couldn't be right. Georgia had just outlined the same way Emmie was told her mother had died. What was going on?

"I suppose I should let the two of you get some rest," Georgia said, taking back the miniature portrait. "Sleep well, young ones, and I will visit some more with you in the morning." Georgia left the room, shutting the door behind her.

Emmie remained silent as she thought over everything Georgia had told her. This was so much to take in. Her mother was still alive.

SOMETHING WAS DREADFULLY wrong.

Broderick had been studying Emiline since the older woman handed her the picture. Being hungry had nothing to do with what ailed her now. "All right, my darling Emiline. Are you going to tell me what is amiss?"

She turned and met his gaze. "What do you mean?" Her voice shook.

Broderick gave her a sympathetic look, then reached up and wiped her tears falling down her face. "You're crying, love. Tell me what ails you. I'll not relent until you do, and you know how stubborn I can be."

Her mouth cracked a smile, which made him smile. She was so pretty, even crying.

Biting her bottom lip, she looked hesitant to speak, but finally, she took a deep breath. "The picture Georgia just showed us is a picture of my mother."

Confusion filled him. "But I thought you said your mother was dead."

Emiline shrugged. "I don't understand any of this." She sniffed and wiped the tears still streaking down her face. "For fifteen years, I have believed my mother was dead. Yet Daphne is my mother. That miniature is my mother—but older."

He clutched her hands. "Then we must bring Georgia back and have her explain."

Emiline tightened her hands on Broderick's fingers. "Not yet. There is much I need to straighten out in my mind first."

"But Em—"

"Broderick, please. Trust me on this."

Uncomfortable silence stretched between them as Broderick's mind scrambled to sort this story out. Emiline's actions were not making sense. He stroked her knuckles, enjoying the closeness they shared—almost as much as he relished holding and kissing her.

"Emiline, love, are you embarrassed that your mother will disapprove of your station in life?"

One of her perfectly shaped eyebrows lifted. "My *station in life?*"

"Yes. Because you are a lady's companion and your father is poor."

Uncertainty flickered in her brown orbs before she shook her head. "That is not all of it, Broderick. Please do not ask. I'm not ready to tell you."

He leaned against his pillow, folding his arms across his chest. "You will feel better if you talk about it."

"I will." She touched his arm. "Just not right now."

"Oh, my sweet Emiline." He took her in his arms and gently rocked her while caressing her back tenderly. "My heart is breaking because I don't know how to help you." He rubbed his lips across her forehead.

"Holding me is helping."

"Then I shall hold you all night, if that is what you wish."

She wrapped her arms around his waist and buried her face against his chest as sobs racked her small body. Snuggling them down into the bed, he held and comforted her, all the while cursing the uncontrollable urge to become intimate with her. They were definitely closer now than they were before, and he had always been a ladies' man…

He inwardly groaned. Now was certainly not the time to act like a lovesick boy. She needed his comfort right now, no matter how badly he longed to kiss her. Unfortunately, holding her like this would be his downfall.

Indeed, tonight would be torture.

Chapter Twelve

E MMIE PULLED HERSELF from a deep slumber. It took a lot of strength just to peel her eyes open. Exhaustion had taken its toll on her last night, and she felt as if she'd been running for three days straight. Her eyelids were heavy, and her head throbbed, yet at the same time, exhilaration blossomed in her chest. Her mother wasn't dead after all, and the thought of finding her lifted Emmie's spirits. Finally, they could be a family again. Perhaps then her father would cease this inane idea of trying to protect his corrupt brother.

Awareness surrounded her, and she realized she wasn't in the bed she occupied while staying at the Cramptons' house. As her mind started working properly, she recalled being in Broderick's arms and kissing him. He'd held her so tenderly last night, and just the thought made her sigh with happiness.

She turned her head to look at him, but he wasn't on the bed. Propped against a cushioned chair, Broderick slumbered on the floor with a blanket over him near the fireplace. He looked so handsome lying in an awkward position, and her heart melted to think he'd chosen to stay on the floor. Even though he didn't act like it at times, he really was a gentleman. It pleased her to know he wasn't going to take advantage of her situation and try to seduce her.

He'd been so gentle with her last night—so caring. It would

be hard for her not to let her heart get involved. But she must stop this insanity now. Loving this man would come to no good. It didn't matter if kissing him felt so right—loving him would be so wrong.

Quietly, she slipped out of bed and threw on a wrapper Georgia had brought to her last evening. What a dear woman— to be so kind to two strangers. And to think, she was Emmie's grandmother.

Once the garment was around Emmie's waist and tied, she tiptoed to the full-length mirror in the room, fixing her hair so it wasn't so disheveled. For some reason, the weather of late must be helping with its fullness, because she hadn't had such wavy hair before. Acting as a lady's companion, she naturally wanted it pulled tightly back in a bun, but as she stared at her reflection, she realized that she didn't want it that way ever again. She wanted to be the enticing woman Broderick suggested she could be.

"Good morning, my lady."

Broderick's voice startled her. She jumped and turned around. He was still on the floor, stretching his arms over his head. His eyes met hers, and he smiled tenderly. Panic surged through her. Why did he refer to her as *my lady*? He couldn't possibly know her true identity, and she prayed he hadn't gone to talk to Georgia sometime during the night to discover the real story.

"Forgive me. Did I wake you?" she asked.

"Not at all, my lady. I didn't sleep well, so hearing you awaken was quite a relief."

Good grief! He'd called her *my lady* again. Had she talked in her sleep? "Broderick, why are you calling me *my lady*?"

Rubbing his forehead, he closed his eyes. "Oh, blast it. I'm not quite awake, forgive me." He looked at her again. "I should have called you princess, instead."

"But why?"

"Because of our wager. Remember? Today starts the beginning of the week."

She breathed a sigh of relief. "That's right. I had forgotten."

"Well, luckily, I have not." He whipped off the blanket and stood. Thankfully, he was back to wearing his regular clothes.

After another stretch, he ambled over to her and kissed her forehead. "How do you feel this morning, love?"

Her heart fluttered from his endearment. "I have a headache."

"That's to be expected. You received quite a shock last night."

She nodded. "I also did a lot of thinking."

"What about?"

"I want to find my mother."

"Of course you do." He winked.

"Will you help me?"

His expression wavered between panic and confusion as silence hung thick in the air. She waited for him to tell her he couldn't help her, but the longer he stared, the softer his gaze became.

"Yes, of course."

"Even if it means going to Brighton with me? I recall you saying how much you loathe places like that."

He chuckled lightly, sat on the edge of the bed, and took her hands loosely in his. "I cannot believe you remembered that. But yes, I will go with you."

She smiled. "Thank you. You are such an exceptional man. You may not be of noble birth, but your actions show you should be."

Broderick's expression changed slightly. His eyes turned darker—just the way she liked them—as he wrapped his arms around her waist and pulled her closer. His gaze held hers captive even as he lowered his head and placed his lips on hers. The kiss started out soft, but when sparks ignited inside her, she clung to his shoulders and answered his passionate kiss.

This was what she needed. This would help her feel better again. He definitely knew how to kiss a woman to make her swoon, because dizziness was assailing her quickly.

She participated fully in the kiss. With every breath, she seemed to draw closer to his body. She loved sliding her palms over his muscular shoulders and threading her fingers through his thick hair.

Although she took pleasure in kissing him, she knew she shouldn't. Nothing could ever become of her love if she chose to give her heart to him. Her father would definitely not approve of the match.

Emmie slowed the kiss before pulling away and gazing into his eyes. They were so dreamy they made her knees weak. "As much as I would love to stay and continue this, I need to find Georgia."

"What for?" he asked, his voice deeper than she'd ever heard.

Heat bathed her face. "Uh… womanly needs."

Chuckling, he withdrew and stood. "Then, by all means, go find Georgia."

Embarrassment washed over her, yet Broderick didn't seem to mind. As she moved toward the door, he kept his heated stare on her until she walked out of the room.

The house was remarkably quiet as Emmie glided downstairs to the first floor. In the front room, the roaring fire in the hearth warmed the air considerably. Daring to go further into the house, she moved to the next room and walked through the archway. The dining room remained empty, too, but as she turned to leave, a clanking of pots came from the adjoining room.

She opened the door and peeked inside. Georgia stood in front of the stove with a white apron pinned to her bodice. The older woman turned and looked her way.

Automatically, a friendly smile claimed her face. "Good morning, Emiline, dear."

"Good morning, Georgia." Emmie moved into the kitchen more. "Forgive me for disturbing you, but I wonder where you have placed my clothes."

"Amy is just finishing with them. She will bring them to your room when they are ready."

"Amy?"

"She is a lady who helps me out once in a while." Georgia's gaze roamed over Emmie's face and hair, then her smile widened. "Emiline? Would you like to borrow one of my daughter's dresses for today? I'm certain wearing a lovely gown will flatter your slender figure more than the old riding habit you had on last night."

As much as she would like to turn Georgia down, Emmie couldn't because she really wanted to feel like a lady today. Last night and this morning, Broderick had stirred such tender emotions inside her, and she wanted that feeling to continue. She also wanted to impress her grandmother and make her proud of what she'd turned out to be.

Emmie smiled. "As long as it's not an inconvenience."

"Heavens no." Georgia set down the wooden spoon then took the pot off the stove. "Come. Let me show you where my daughter's dresses are." Walking past Emmie, she led her to a room on the second floor.

The room was right next to the one she'd stayed in, except it looked more feminine, decorated in pink and blue flowers. Georgia went straight to the window and pulled open the drapes, letting the sunshine through.

"This room was my youngest daughter's. A few years ago, she married well, and so didn't think she needed any of her clothes." She chuckled. "Her husband buys her anything her heart desires. I worry that he is spoiling her rotten."

She walked to an armoire and opened it to reveal several dresses. "My youngest daughter, Victoria, has the same build as you do—slender. I just thought you might like to wear something that will highlight your lovely face and eyes."

Emmie studied each dress, realizing they were made from the finest silk. Every dress was lovely, but what was more thrilling than the pretty gowns was that these dresses were actually from an aunt she had never known, whom she knew her mother loved dearly.

"Pick anyone you would like. My daughter will not wear these anymore, so you might as well get some use out of them."

"I thank you, Georgia," Emmie told her with a catch in her voice.

Georgia moved toward the door to leave. "There are some undergarments in the drawers by the bed. Just snoop around to see what you need. Let me know if you need any help dressing. I will send Amy up if you do."

"No need. I have been dressing myself for quite a while now."

"All right. I will leave you to get dressed, then. But can I have her come fix your long, lovely hair?"

Broderick's words rang in her ears, reminding her that she hadn't had pretty hair since starting her role as lady's companion. "I would love that."

"Splendid. I'll send her up. Oh, and the chamber pot is behind that screen." Georgia left the room and closed the door behind her.

Emmie eyed each gown carefully. Most of them still looked new, and she could tell the cloth was an expensive cut, as well. Out of all the fine gowns, only one caught her eye. The blue-mint velvet dress had short sleeves and a scooped neckline. Without a second thought, she grabbed it and laid it on the bed. Looking through her Aunt Victoria's drawers, she found other things needed to make her attire complete and then proceeded to change.

After hurrying with her necessities, she stood in front of the full-length mirror fully dressed. An entirely different woman stared at her from the glass. She couldn't believe how pretty this dress made her appear. The color enhanced her face, which made her blue eyes stand out more.

The material hugged her bosom and emphasized womanly curves Emmie never thought she had. All in all, this dress fit her better than any dress she had ever worn. As if it was made for her.

She took pleasure in looking this pretty and wanted to look even lovelier, so she went to Aunt Victoria's vanity table and finished her toiletry by brushing her hair until it shone.

A knock came upon the door, and when she called out to have them enter, a woman—perhaps in her thirties—walked in and introduced herself as Amy. The woman took the brush from Emmie and fashioned her hair so beautifully, it left her in awe.

By adding a little blush to her cheeks and a rose-colored cream to her lips, Emmie tried making her face appear more feminine. She couldn't believe the difference it made. For the first time in her life, she thought she looked beautiful. Not just passively pretty, but exotically lovely. Maybe even more so than Anna. Emmie couldn't wait to show herself to her grandmother and, most importantly, to Broderick.

The more she thought about him, the more her mouth stretched into a grin. She couldn't believe she'd let him kiss her those few times, because certainly the earl's daughter didn't allow men such liberties. But how could she stop him? He was so very passionate and tender, unlike those men who tried to court her and forced their unwanted attention on her.

Amy smiled and gave Emmie an encouraging nod. Nervously, she left the room and made her way back downstairs. Voices rose from the dining room, those of Georgia and Broderick. Pausing before going in, Emmie took a deep breath for courage and tried to keep her heart rate under control. How would he act seeing her this way? She'd find out in a moment.

"AND THIS IS a miniature of my wonderful husband, God rest his soul."

Broderick smiled and sat patiently as Georgia showed him nearly every picture she had in her house. She was such a dear woman, and it was obvious she didn't have many guests stop by. It surprised him that her house was so grand, mainly because Emiline hadn't mentioned having a wealthy family.

"And after the birth of our youngest daughter, Victoria, my wonderful husband had this house built."

Broderick nodded, hoping the older woman hadn't realized he wasn't paying much attention to her storytelling. "And what a fine house it is, Georgia."

She smiled as her cheeks flourished with color—so much like her granddaughter.

There had to be a reason Emiline was fearful of getting to know her grandmother. But more importantly, how could he get the woman he couldn't stop thinking about to trust him—to open up and share her thoughts and dreams with him? To tell him about her life? Deep down inside, he worried that she was holding some deep, dark secret.

Then again, he held a secret from her, so he shouldn't expect something he wasn't ready to give himself.

When he had first come down the stairs and found Georgia, he asked about Emiline's whereabouts. Georgia told him she was upstairs in her daughter's bedroom changing. Now as he sat at the table talking with the older lady, he waited for the woman he wanted to cuddle with, to kiss. To hear the small sighs when he touched her. He didn't know how much time had passed since he'd last laid his lonely eyes on the pretty girl, but it seemed like hours.

This morning had been wonderful, and the kiss endearing. He hadn't wanted it to end, and even now, he wondered when he could kiss her again. Would she allow it? She hadn't seemed repulsed by what they'd shared earlier, so perhaps she was growing to have feelings for him just as he was for her.

When Georgia's chatter suddenly stopped, he snapped out of his thoughts. Her gaze was pinned to something behind him, and her blue eyes widened as a smile graced her face. She nodded as if approving of what she saw.

He turned to see what she was looking at... and almost fell out of his chair. Emiline stood just inside the room, a vision of loveliness swathed in a bluish-green dress. He'd never seen anything so beautiful before. For a moment, he had lost his breath until it all came out in a gust.

Although he'd seen her in dresses before, they had always looked out of place on her. Now he knew why. Emiline didn't belong in plain, ugly dresses. She belonged in a dress made for a princess, which was what she looked like now.

And her hair! Never had he seen it so beautiful—nor had he seen *any* woman's hair done so artfully and perfectly. Instead of being pulled tight in a bun, her hair was in a loose coil on top of her head as thick tendrils graced her ears.

Slowly, he stood, not taking his eyes off her. His mouth dropped open in awe. He took in every detail, from the top of her styled hair to the toes of her dainty slippers, and everything in between. This dress fitted her body perfectly, showing off all of her womanly curves—curves that were usually hidden by her other dresses.

He didn't even realize she had moved until she stood in front of him, peering into his eyes. He had no idea if she spoke, because all he could hear was his heart thumping wildly in his chest.

She smiled, and his heart melted even more. On impulse, he circled her waist, closing the space between them as he pulled her body next to his. He still couldn't think of any words to say because her beauty and grace left him dumbfounded—and really, the only thing he wanted to say was best said with his lips.

He bent his head and pressed his mouth to hers. Thankfully, she responded the way he wanted. Her arms circled his neck, and she kissed him back tenderly, yet passionately. It was really only a few kisses, but there was emotion behind each one that made the moment so special.

When she pulled away, her face flamed red. "Broderick, we mustn't do this in front of Georgia." Her voice squeaked.

He stared mystified at her again but at least managed a smile and a nod.

Beside him, Georgia laughed. "Oh, no, you two go right ahead with what you were doing. I will just go into the kitchen and fix our breakfast." She bustled off.

Although he wanted to pull Emiline back into his arms, he held himself back from doing so. They would only get interrupted when Georgia returned.

Emiline walked past him to the table. Before she sat, he quickly pulled out the chair for her.

Her bright gaze met his, sparkling as she smiled. "I thank you, Broderick."

He really needed to get a hold of this situation. He didn't understand why he was acting so lovestruck. Seeing her dressed like this was quite a shock, but he needed to somehow gain control and get his speech and actions back together the right way.

He sat, still without taking his eyes off her. He couldn't even if he wanted.

"Broderick." She giggled. "Would you stop staring at me like that? It's most embarrassing."

Chuckling lightly, he relaxed in his chair. "Forgive me, Emmie love. You have put me under a spell I have no wish to break. I'm not used to seeing you look so... so..." He partook of her loveliness once more. Slower this time, enjoying everything about her once again.

"Do I at least look like a lady?"

He brought his gaze to her sparkling eyes. "No. You look like a princess."

Her cheeks went red again. "I have never heard more flattering words." She presented him with a soft smile. "With me dressed this way, will that make it easier for you to follow through on our wager?"

He grinned. "Definitely."

Georgia hustled in, carrying a tray with three bowls on it. She set the bowls in front of Broderick and Emiline, then took one for herself.

"I hope oat porridge is all right."

Emiline nodded. "Yes, it is. I have not tasted porridge in such a long time."

She and Broderick were silent as they ate, although Georgia rattled on, trying to keep the conversation flowing. Broderick kept sneaking glances at the adorable woman next to him, and when she peeked back, he grinned even if food was still in his mouth.

He was extremely thankful that they were away from his uncle and aunt's house. With Emiline wearing such enthralling attire, his family would certainly swoon to see his making a total fool out of himself because of this enchantress.

Inwardly, he groaned as dread washed upon him. Reality hit him head-on. They had to return to the estate today. Emiline would change into those ugly, large dresses, and he could never kiss her again.

Chapter Thirteen

A FTER BREAKFAST, EMMIE hurried back to their room to clean up, but when she entered, the bed had been made and the room looked as if she and Broderick had not stayed here at all. The only evidence that she had stayed the night was that her riding habit was folded up neatly on the end of the bed. Broderick couldn't have possibly done this. Perhaps it was Amy.

Emmie picked up her clothes then returned downstairs to thank her grandmother.

As she passed a front window, a movement caught her eye. Broderick stood in front of the stable getting their horses ready. She smiled, loving the way he looked. So handsome and refined. So strong. And the sweetest man she had ever met. If they had been introduced under different circumstances, would she have liked him at all?

Dishes clacked together in the kitchen, pulling her out of such heavenly thoughts. She stepped inside the room to tell her grandmother goodbye. As she suspected, Georgia had packed a lunch for their ride home.

"Georgia?"

Her grandmother turned and smiled brightly. "Are you ready to depart, dear?"

Emmie nodded. "As much as we would love to stay and visit more with you, we both have obligations back home."

Georgia folded a cloth over the picnic basket and handed it to her. "I packed you a light lunch. I hope you don't mind."

Emmie grasped the handle of the basket. "You really should not have done this, Georgia. You have helped us so much already."

"I know, but I would not feel right if I let you two leave for your long trip home without any food." She walked closer and softly touched Emmie's cheek. Tears gathered in her eyes. "Besides, it's the least I can do for my own granddaughter."

A gasp sprang from Emmie's mouth, and her own eyes filled with tears. "How… how did you know?"

"Two reasons, actually. One, because you look too much like my family to not be related, and two, that handsome man of yours let it slip that Lady Sarah and her companion, Emiline, were staying at his uncle's house for a while. Do you not think I would remember my own granddaughter?" She paused for just a second. "From the way I understand it, Broderick thinks Lady Sarah and Emiline are two different people. He doesn't know you are the earl's daughter. Am I correct?"

Emmie grasped her grandmother's hand, panic flowing through her. "No, he doesn't, and I want to keep him from knowing my true identity for now. It's for my own safety. Please say nothing to him."

Georgia tilted her head. "Tell me something, Emiline. Is Broderick your husband?"

Shame swept over Emmie, and she hung her head. "No." Slowly she lifted her eyes and met her grandmother's stare. "But let me assure you that nothing happened between us last night. If I hadn't been in the downpour last night and chilled to the bone, I would have thought things out more clearly and asked for two separate rooms." She sighed heavily. "I allowed Broderick to make the decision for me, which was wrong, I know." She paused, then asked warily, "Do you believe me?"

"I believe you, only because God works in mysterious ways, and He led you to me last night. So who am I to pass judgment?"

"Georgia—"

"My dear child, please call me Grandmama. I would appreciate it very much."

Emmie smiled. "All right, Grandmama. The reason I don't want him knowing about my identity is because Father wanted me to switch roles for my own protection. Although I want to tell Broderick, I just don't dare. Not yet, anyway."

Georgia caressed Emmie's cheek again. "I understand, but really soon Broderick is going to realize you aren't who you have pretended to be." She glanced out the window into the yard. "He has strong feelings for you, I can tell."

Emmie's heart fluttered. "Well, for now, I want him thinking of me as just Lady Sarah's companion."

Georgia nodded. "All right. I shall not say a word."

Emmie threw her arms around her grandmother and gave her a big hug. "Do you know how much I missed having a grandmother when I was growing up?" Her voice broke with emotion as tears fell freely down her face.

Georgia held her tightly. "And I have missed my granddaughter." She pulled away and looked into Emmie's eyes. "Your mother missed you terribly, too. It broke her heart when she thought the two people she loved the most were dead."

A lump formed in Emmie's throat, and all she wanted to do was bawl her eyes out—to cry for not having a mother all of those years. "Grandmama? What happened? Father and I were told *her* ship was the one attacked by pirates."

Sadness crossed Georgia's face. "I wish I knew, dear. Daphne didn't talk much about it. You will have to find out the whole story from her."

"Do you think I should find her?"

"Oh yes, my dear. She will be overjoyed when she sees you. She hasn't been the same since your death—or what she thought was your death." She paused again, but only for a moment. "Does your father still love Daphne?"

"Oh, indeed. I still catch him staring at her picture. If we had known Mother was alive, Father would have moved heaven and earth to find her." Emmie kissed the older woman's cheek and pulled away. "I will find her, and thank you, Grandmama, for everything."

"Good luck with that handsome man of yours."

Emmie smiled. "I will definitely need it."

BRODERICK HOOKED BOTH horses to the buggy he'd purchased from Georgia. At first, she just offered it for his travels today, telling him she never used the vehicle, but he couldn't go without giving her some kind of payment. Finally, he convinced her to take his money.

Emiline walked toward him carrying a basket, and his heart leapt. She now wore a cloak that matched her gown, with a white scarf over her hair, which, thankfully, didn't hide much at all. Curses! How would he be able to handle being so close to her without wanting to take her in his arms and smother her with kisses? Her lips were sweet like honeysuckle, and her skin soft as a rose petal. Strange how in one day she'd turned from being a friend he took pleasure in teasing to a woman he wanted so much to pour his affections on.

She stood next to him, and he smiled. "I bought this buggy from Georgia. I hope you don't mind if we take this instead." He glanced at her gown again. "I thought this method of transportation would be easier because you are dressed as a princess."

Her eyes twinkled. "You are too kind. I would very much enjoy riding in a buggy."

He bowed then offered his hand. She slipped her fingers against his palm, and once again, desire burned inside him. As he helped her into the vehicle, he fought the impulse to pull her against him.

He climbed on the seat, took the reins, and urged the horses into a trot. Immediately, he could tell the journey home would be horrendous. Emiline kept bumping into him, making him more and more aware of her. Not that he wasn't already. How could he forget after what happened last night and this morning?

A few minutes of silence passed very slowly before she turned to him and cleared her throat. "Broderick, I would like to thank you for what you did."

Confusion filled him, and he looked into her innocent, wide eyes. "Which was?"

"You accidentally—on purpose—let it slip about Lady Sarah and her companion visiting the Cramptons. You knew Georgia would figure it out soon enough."

He smiled. "Did Georgia say something to you?"

"She did, and we talked." She softly laid her hand on his arm. "I don't think I could have mentioned it to her, but because of your help, I was able to open up."

He moved his attention back to the road. "I suspected you were scared to say anything, so I thought to help you in some way. I'm relieved you are not upset with me for sticking my nose into your business."

She squeezed his arm. "No, I'm not upset. I'm very grateful for your help. This whole mess has left me so confused that I don't know what I would do without you."

"I cannot fathom how you must feel right now, learning that your mother has been alive all this time." He snuck another glance at her. "How exactly did she die?"

"We were living in France at the time, and she was sailing to England, and her ship was attacked by pirates." She shrugged. "At least, that is the information we received."

Curiosity niggled his mind. "Pirates, you say? And she was on a passenger ship?"

"Yes."

"Most pirates that I have heard about do not attack passenger ships. They are only after treasure of some kind."

"I heard the same thing, but when we received the letter

about my mother's death, it stated her ship was attacked by none other than the fearsome pirate, Captain Hawk."

Broderick swallowed wrong and nearly choked. Yet he didn't want to cause suspicion. "How long ago did this happen?"

"Fifteen years."

Impossible! The title of Captain Hawk was started by his great-uncle, Marcus Thorne, approximately forty-six years ago, and handed down through the family on Broderick's mother's side. He had taken the title not even a year ago.

"Forgive me, love, but it's hard to believe that her ship was attacked by that pirate, since I heard Captain Hawk's only mission is to stop deceitful men in England. However, I do know that his first voyage was across the sea to the Americas."

"Then why would someone tell us it was Captain Hawk if it wasn't?" She rested her palm on his arm. "Broderick, if you know anything else about this pirate, please tell me."

His breath caught in his throat and his blood froze. "You think I should know something?"

"Well, I did hear a rumor, not long after Lady Sarah and I arrived at the estate, that Mr. Crampton was related to Captain Hawk." She licked her lips. "And if he is related, then surely *you* must know him as well."

Broderick didn't know what bothered him more—the rumors that someone knew his true identity or that there might be a spy in the family. Although he didn't want to lie to Emiline, nor could he confess the truth. Not yet. "If I'm related to this pirate, this is the first I have heard about it."

A heavy sigh escaped her, and she brought her hand back to her lap. "Then perhaps the rumor was false."

"Perhaps. You know how rumors can get out of hand. The fact that a pirate attacked a passenger ship tells me this rumor is indeed false, since this particular pirate wasn't known to do such things."

"I'm sure you are correct." She sighed again and smiled at him. "I'm most appreciative of your knowledge."

He winked. "Anytime, princess."

She chuckled and shook her head. Once again, his focus turned to the lovely vision beside him. He skimmed his gaze over her enchanting face, resting it on her tempting mouth. His own mouth watered as he remembered the way her lips had tasted when he kissed her.

Shaking himself out of such wicked thoughts, he quickly diverted his eyes to the road. In order to keep her in a pleasant mood—and her thoughts away from Captain Hawk—Broderick must change their conversation.

"You know, Emiline, I get the impression that you are actually enjoying looking so lovely today. Am I correct?"

She laughed lightly. "What I enjoy is the way you look at me. You look at me as if I were a real princess, and that makes me giddy."

He chuckled. "I suppose it's fun to be treated differently, is it not?"

"Indeed. Would you like me to treat you differently, also?"

"Pray tell, how would you treat me?"

She leaned toward him and touched his arm again. "I would treat you like a king."

"A king?" He laughed. "Not if I'm treating you like a princess. That would mean you would be my daughter." He scrunched his face, making her laugh. "Why not treat me like I'm a... marquess?"

She shrugged. "That will work, I suppose. You are truly a gentleman."

"Such kind words, princess."

"You know, I have changed my mind. You are more like a king, and you can treat me like a queen instead of a princess."

"If I do that, then instead of being a daughter, you would be..." Laughter quickly disappeared when he realized where his thoughts were leading. He swallowed hard and stared deeply into her eyes. "My wife," he ended softly.

She, too, became serious. Her body remained so close to his, and the heat between them grew more powerful by the second. Why did he like the idea of her becoming his wife? Although she was a mere lady's companion, Emiline came from a fine family— apparent by the wonderful and kind grandmother they had met. Besides that, she could pass for a real lady, as she was today.

He continued to stare, not caring that the horses had stopped. He couldn't look away. Her eyes were so illuminated with desire that he was mesmerized. His heart pounded a quick rhythm, and he loved the way happiness flowed through his blood.

He shouldn't have made that bet with her yesterday. If she had remained in those ugly, plain dresses, perhaps he wouldn't feel as dumbfounded right now. Then again, she took his breath away no matter what she wore.

He dropped his gaze to her mouth. She ran her tongue across her sultry, wine-colored lips, and he wanted nothing more than to taste the sweetness he had found this morning.

"Broderick?" she whispered.

"What?"

"We have stopped."

It took all of his effort, but he snapped out of his dreamlike state of confusion. "I suppose we have."

He still didn't move as they stared at each other. Soon, her smile lifted. "We aren't going anywhere yet."

"No, not yet. I must do something first." He cupped her face, pulled her in, and captured her mouth.

A sigh gurgled from deep in her throat as she leaned against him, opening up for his torrid kiss. He moved his hand down her neck to the tie holding her cloak together. In one quick motion, he opened her cloak and moved his hand over her shoulder and lower, brushing the tips of his fingers over the edge of her bodice.

If only they weren't in the buggy…

Catching her breath, she withdrew, folding her arms across her chest. Slowly, she shook her head. "No, Broderick. It's too soon."

He closed his eyes and silently groaned. She was correct. She wasn't that kind of woman, and he didn't want to turn her into that kind, either.

Exhaling deeply, he sat up straighter and looked to the road, flicking the reins to urge the horses to move forward again. Heaviness settled in his chest. He wanted her so much it hurt. Why did his feelings confuse him so?

They didn't talk much more during the ride back, and if they did, nothing personal was brought up. Broderick talked a little about his life, without mentioning his true identity. She talked about growing up without a mother, and with a father who was always too busy with politics to spend much time with his daughter.

They stayed on neutral ground.

Dusk sprinkled across the sky when they arrived at his uncle's house. Instead of taking the buggy around to the stables, as he would have done with the *old* Emiline, he stopped in front of the house. He jumped down first, then turned and helped her out. He wanted to pull her against him, wrap his arms around her, and never let her go. Once she walked in through that doorway, his fantasy would end.

She stepped away and broke the contact. "Broderick, I had a wonderful two days with you. The best two days of my life, in fact. I thank you so much."

He smiled at her angelic face. "I had a splendid time as well. I'm glad you were able to find your grandmother."

"Thanks to you." She touched his hand, and he quickly grasped her fingers. "Will you still help me find my mother?"

"Yes. I told you I would, and I always keep my promises."

"I thank you again." Slowly, she closed the space between them and lifted on the tips of her toes, pressing a kiss on his cheek.

Immediately, Broderick turned his face so her lips would meet with his as he slid his arms around her waist, holding her tight. Heat ignited in his chest, and he didn't want to pull away.

Apparently, she had other thoughts, because she broke the

kiss and stepped out of his embrace. Her face darkened with a deep blush.

"Good night, Broderick."

"Good night, my queen."

She smiled. "You know, I don't expect you to carry out the wager for the whole week. It has been enough that you treated me this special for today. I'm quite certain it was difficult enough for you, and because of that, I won't hold you to our wager."

He caressed her cheek with his knuckles as he gazed into her twinkling eyes. "What if I *want* to continue?"

"Just know you don't have to."

"Are you trying to tell me you do not want to wear pretty dresses any longer?"

"No. I just don't have that many gowns to wear as Lady Sarah's companion. I haven't made it to see a dressmaker yet. But rest assured, it has been rather fun feeling pretty today."

He shook his head. "Emiline, you are not just pretty, you are resplendent. And it wasn't hard for me to treat you as such, especially since you look so very lovely in the gown your grandmother gave you." He raked his gaze over her dress once again, wishing it didn't flatter her womanly figure so. "You were definitely made to wear gowns like this. Not plain dresses only fit for old lady's companions."

The sultry look in her eyes had him spellbound. Her eyes had always made him this way. He liked the way she looked upon him as if he were the most gallant man in the world.

At that moment, the front door swung open, and his uncle and aunt stood on the other side. The passionate mood quickly disappeared.

"You are back," Henry cheered as he stepped outside and gave Emiline a hug. "Oh, child, we thought something horrid had happened to you."

Broderick narrowed his gaze on his uncle. Why was he acting this way toward the companion? From over his uncle's shoulder, Emiline looked at him with confusion in her eyes. Aunt Martha stood behind Henry clasping her hands against her middle, her eyes moist.

Very strange behavior from both of them.

"Uncle? Is something amiss?" Broderick asked.

Henry quickly moved away. "Uh, well… When we returned home earlier, our servants said five men came looking for something we had that they wanted." He shook his head. "It wasn't until Levi heard one of the men say Lady Sarah's name when he realized what they wanted, and when we returned home and saw you were gone…" He paused, looking at Emiline as he laid a hand over his heart. "I thought those men might have taken you."

"Uncle, did the stable boy not tell you she was with me?" Broderick asked. "He was the only one to see us together."

Henry rolled his eyes. "Levi didn't know who was with you, Broderick."

Emiline hung her head, wringing her hands against her middle. "Forgive me, Mr. Crampton. I didn't mean to upset you. We went riding and lost track of time, and—"

"Miss Emmie?" Broderick interrupted her, and she looked up at him. "I shall explain things to my uncle. You hurry upstairs and let Lady Sarah know that you're all right. She is probably worried sick."

Henry nodded. "Oh, yes. She is very distraught."

"Excuse me, then. Good night, gentlemen." She curtsied then entered the house.

Broderick couldn't take his eyes off her as she gracefully floated into the main hall and up the stairs. He took a deep breath, calming himself from the passionate moment they had shared not too long ago. He expected tonight would be miserable until he could see her again. Yet his conscience dictated he couldn't act this way around her. His life was too complicated as it was, and bringing a woman into his world would only bring heartache.

Henry shook his head and chuckled. "The girl certainly looks different wearing that fancy dress. It's almost as if she was supposed to wear that instead of the servant's attire."

Broderick nodded, relieved they shared the same opinion. "I agree, Uncle."

Henry turned to him. "Now, Broderick, would you kindly inform me what is going on? Where were you the past two days, and why did you take that, er… that particular woman with you?"

"Come inside, Uncle. Let us adjourn to your study, where we can discuss this matter in private." Walking into the house, Broderick headed straight to the study, and then to the liquor tray, and poured himself some brandy.

Henry and Martha followed and shut the door behind them. His uncle folded his arms across his chest and glared. "Now will you tell us what's going on between the two of you?"

It was lucky Henry hadn't asked Broderick to explain his feelings for the young woman, because he still had mixed emotions about her. Confusion had been his constant companion for two days, along with pure enjoyment. All he knew was that Emiline entranced him, and the longer they were together, the more his attraction grew.

"Yesterday morning I was about to take a refreshing ride around the countryside when I happened across Miss Emmie doing the same. I suggested we ride together, only because it would keep us both entertained." He paused, sipping his drink. "She had been extremely disappointed because *dear Rebecca* made it clear that she didn't want Miss Emmie traveling to London with Lady Sarah. Seeing how Miss Emmie was a guest at your house just as Lady Sarah, I can imagine her disappointment." He directed that harsh comment to his aunt.

Martha lowered her head and twisted her hands. "But Broderick, I didn't know at first… but when we did, your uncle told Rebecca to invite her. The night before we were to leave, Miss Emmie came down with a stomach ailment, so we left—"

Henry waved his hand through the air as he looked at his wife. "It doesn't matter now." He aimed his focus on Broderick again. "You should not have been alone with her. I'm sure you are aware that you probably ruined her reputation."

The hilarity of the comment made Broderick laugh. "Reputation as what? A lady's companion? A servant of Lady Sarah's?"

Henry scowled. "Well, just see that it doesn't happen again, and for heaven's sake, let us know if you take her away in the future."

Broderick finished his drink and set the glass down on the liquor tray. Why did his uncle suddenly want to step into the role of his guardian? Broderick didn't need to tell Henry everything he had to do, especially with Emiline. "I promise I will inform you when I deem it necessary, Uncle. Rest assured you shall be the first to know." He turned to walk away, but his uncle grabbed his arm and stopped him.

"Broderick? You didn't… um, compromise her, did you?"

Broderick didn't know whether to laugh or get upset. His uncle acted as if Broderick had been with a real lady for two days—and one very magical night. He chose to chuckle instead of being angered. "Are you asking if I seduced her? Did I take her to bed? Ravished her, perhaps?" He laughed harder. "No, Uncle. I was the perfect gentleman." *Well, maybe not completely.*

Henry shifted his feet as his wife blushed. "Fine." He swiped his fingers through his graying hair. "Now that we got that out of the way, we need to find out who those men were that came while we were gone, and why they want Lady Sarah."

Martha moved next to her husband and touched his arm as her eyes locked with Broderick's. "We think they may return, and next time we may not be as fortunate."

Chapter Fourteen

BRODERICK HURRIED TOWARD the stable the next morning, his long legs taking wide strides on his way. Questions swam through his head, and he couldn't focus. It didn't help when all he could think about was his beautiful Emiline.

Quickly, he brought his thoughts to a halt. His Emiline? That was utterly ridiculous. He could not—ever—think of her that way. For now, she was simply a diversion for him while he was in hiding. He really needed to get back to his original plan when he discovered the lord chancellor's niece was here. Spending time with Emiline had been so pleasing, he'd forgotten that he still didn't know very much about what Lady Sarah's uncle was up to.

Inwardly, he cringed. What would his crew think of him now? They would certainly think he was slacking in his duties and that he had a weak mind—neither of which was something Broderick wanted to be known for.

Levi sauntered out of the stable, brushing straw off his trousers. The boy—perhaps not a boy any longer, since a small patch of facial hair grew on his chin—had been working for Uncle Henry for several years. If memory served, Levi's family were also servants here.

"Boy, hold up there," Broderick called out.

Levi scratched his ear. "Yessir?"

"I need to talk to you about those men who came looking for

Lady Sarah yesterday. Do you remember how many were in the group?"

Levi nodded so quickly, his hat nearly slipped off his head. "Five, sir."

"What were they looking for, exactly?"

"Well..." the boy said, tapping his finger on his chin as his attention lifted to the tree above Broderick's head. "When I first saw them, they were still on their horses. They rode to me, instead of going to the house first. The one who seemed to be in charge had evil eyes and hair as orange as the sun."

Unease washed over Broderick. *Evil eyes...* There was one man who fit that description. Lieutenant Mercer—the very man who nearly captured the *Avenger* several weeks ago. Broderick's stomach churned with worry. "What age was this man?"

Levi met his stare. "I suppose he was somewhere around his fortieth year, sir."

Broderick nodded. So far, the description of Lieutenant Mercer fit perfectly. "Continue."

"Well, the man asked the whereabouts of Mr. Crampton. He said my master had something these men needed. I kept telling them that Mr. Crampton wasn't here, but they acted like they weren't listening to me, because they all started talking to each other at once."

"Do you know what they were saying?"

Levi shook his head. "They were arguing about something, but I couldn't tell what it was."

"Then what happened?" Broderick folded his arms.

"I heard one of them say Lady Sarah's name." Levi shrugged. "That was all I heard before the man with the evil eyes looked at me again and asked where Lady Sarah was. I told them she was with Mr. Crampton."

"Was that all, or did they say more?"

"No, that was all they said, and they left upset."

Releasing a pent-up breath, Broderick ran his fingers through his hair. None of this made sense, yet he needed to find out what was going on. More than likely Lady Sarah was in danger. After all, her uncle was a bad man, and their driver knew it and had probably blabbed to his friends, thinking he had killed Lady Sarah and her companion when they traveled here.

The problem was, Broderick didn't know if Lieutenant Mercer was after Lady Sarah—or after Captain Hawk. He didn't know why the lieutenant would want Lady Sarah, unless to kidnap her.

Things were getting more confusing by the second.

"Levi, do you remember when they said they would be back?"

"No, sir. I didn't hear anything of the sort."

"I thank you for your assistance." Broderick swung around and marched back toward the house. He needed to figure out this mystery soon before Lady Sarah was taken, or before Mercer realized the fearsome pirate was staying here as well.

The more and more Broderick thought about staying low, the more he realized that going with Emiline to Brighton looked better and better. His aunt and uncle must not let their servants know of their journey in case Mercer decided to follow. It could be done. Broderick would see to it personally.

This meant he needed to let his uncle know *why* it was so important for Broderick to stay hidden and away from Mercer. But before he did that, he must discover where Uncle Henry's belief really lay… and which side of the ocean he supported in these perilous times.

Quickly, Broderick stopped and turned back toward the stables. Levi was still out, thankfully. "Levi, will you get my uncle's horse ready—and one for me as well? We shall go riding very soon."

"As you wish." Levi rushed into the stables.

Broderick smiled. Levi had always been so obedient. That was a good quality to have in a servant.

He hurried into the house and straight to his uncle's study. The door was cracked open slightly, and his aunt was inside discussing something with his uncle. Broderick really didn't want to disturb them, but his much-needed conversation with his uncle couldn't be put off any longer.

"But what if her father finds out?" Running his fingers through his hair, Henry snapped at his wife. "He will certainly blame me for not putting a stop to it."

"You are overreacting again, Henry," Martha replied. "She is still young and doesn't understand the consequences of her actions. I'm quite certain her father will sympathize."

"Truly, this is utter nonsense. I need to stop this charade—" Henry stopped in mid-sentence and swung his head toward the door.

Embarrassed at being caught eavesdropping, Broderick straightened his shoulders, took a deep breath, and entered. Both his uncle and aunt wore wide-eyed, surprised expressions.

"Forgive me for intruding," Broderick began, "but I needed to speak with you, Uncle."

His aunt grinned and came to him, stopping to pat his cheeks. "You are not intruding, dear. Mr. Crampton and I have finished our conversation anyway." She threw a final glare toward her husband before quitting the room.

Henry stretched his arms above his head and faked a yawn. "What a lovely morning it is."

"Yes, it is, Uncle, which is why I would like you to take a ride around the estate with me."

"Splendid idea, my boy."

After they had retrieved their riding jackets, they met back at the stables. As promised, Levi had both animals ready. Broderick and his uncle mounted then took off.

Collecting his thoughts, Broderick didn't know how to start the conversation. Earnestly, he prayed to say the right words to make his uncle understand.

Henry slowed his horse down to a trot, and Broderick did the same. "I must say, Broderick, you picked a wonderful time to go riding."

A slight breeze flitted through the trees around them, and the sun peeked through the limbs and leaves. "Yes, the weather has agreed with our outing, I believe. I enjoy riding when the land is so peaceful, but then it makes me wish the whole country could be as content."

Henry eyed him warily. "Yes. These are certainly troublesome times."

"Indeed, they are. I have witnessed quite a lot during my travels." Broderick took his attention off his uncle and focused on the trail ahead. "So many people are angry, and… forgive me if I speak out of turn, but I can see why they act out in such a way." He paused. "I'm sure you have heard about the lord chancellor?"

Henry's jaw hardened. "I have."

"Many men want revenge."

"They do." Henry still watched Broderick through hooded eyes.

Broderick sighed. "I can see now why Lady Sarah's father sent her here to hide."

"Indeed, however, I fear she is still in danger."

"I share that same feeling." So far everything was in Broderick's favor. Yet what his uncle had said really didn't tell him what he wanted to know. "Uncle, I heard a rumor not too long ago that has me greatly confused."

"What is it?"

"I heard that you are related to that fearsome pirate, Captain Hawk, who sails the *Avenger*."

"What is this?" Henry's eyes widened. "Out of all the rumors circling about that pirate, I'm surprised my name was mixed up in it."

"I'm assuming the rumor is false, then?"

"Indeed, it is! I don't know who started that rumor, but obviously, it is someone who wants to ruin my reputation."

"The pirate is known for finding corrupt men and bringing them to justice."

"Exactly. However, I don't agree with the pirate's way of

justice."

"Forgive me for saying this, Uncle, but at times I would glad-ly join the pirate's crew just to rid Britain of these types of men."

Uncle Henry pulled his horse to a stop, and Broderick fol-lowed his example. Worried eyes stared at Broderick as he held his breath, still praying he hadn't said the wrong thing.

"My boy, this conversation must be kept between you, me, and none other."

Broderick nodded. "It shall."

"As I'm certain you are aware, there are still spies amongst us. I don't know who to trust."

"I feel the same, Uncle. But rest assured, you can trust me, and I hope I can rely on your secrecy as well." Deep in Broder-ick's heart, he knew confessing his secrets to his uncle would be a good thing to do right now. Taking a deep breath, he prepared his next words. "Uncle, I feel I must tell you something." Henry's unreadable gaze remained on Broderick. "For several years now, I haven't been the man my family believes me to be. In fact, before I came to stay with you for a spell, I was on the high seas, trying my best to find the lord chancellor's corrupt men."

"What are you saying, my boy?" Henry arched a thick eye-brow.

"I'm saying that the things I've been doing these past few years have been in secret."

Henry gasped so loud that it startled the horse. He stroked the animal's mane. "I beg you to explain more."

"I've been capturing enemy ships and obtaining secrets that will help us put a stop to lord chancellor's corruption."

Slowly, Henry's wide-eyed expression relaxed, and a hint of a smile touched his face. "How very interesting."

"I pray this doesn't ruin our relationship."

"On the contrary, my boy." He chuckled. "I think more high-ly of you now than I did before. I had imagined you to be a carefree man who skipped on responsibility. Now I can see I was mistaken."

"Indeed, you were, Uncle."

"No wonder you argued with me about accepting your position as a newly appointed marquess."

Broderick groaned. He had forgotten about that. "That is the very reason I hesitate on the matter."

"Oh, but you must see the positive side of that. Being an aristocrat will give you ample opportunity to gather information that would help in your cause."

"Yes, but it would also bring me closer to the enemy, and getting caught and hanged for treason is not what I want to happen at this point in my life."

Henry shook his head. "You are an intelligent man. I highly doubt anyone could catch you."

Broderick brushed a hand through his hair. "Regardless, I still have much to ponder on that subject, which I would rather not do at this time. However, I think we need to discuss Lady Sarah and why those men came looking for her."

Henry's forehead creased in puzzlement. "I still cannot fathom why they came. Do you suppose her father sent them?"

"No, Uncle. If her father had sent them, they would have mentioned it first, and they would have waited for Lady Sarah to return."

"Very true."

"So here is what I propose we do to keep her safe." He urged the animal closer to his uncle. Broderick explained how he'd asked Levi questions about the men who came, and what he realized. "We need to take Lady Sarah—and Miss Emmie this time—to another town, just for a visit. You cannot let the servants know where we are traveling. Lie if you must, but they cannot know. I don't want them to find us."

Henry's head bobbed. "I understand. Where shall we take them?"

"Brighton."

His eyes widened. "Why there?"

"It's just enough out of the way from your home, yet close

enough that I can have some of my crew meet us there in case these men know where we are."

"I do believe that is a wise decision."

"But remember, don't let any of your servants know of this plan."

"You can count on me."

"And Uncle, I shall inform Lady Sarah and Miss Emmie about our journey. I plan on taking them for a picnic this afternoon."

Henry studied Broderick closely as he rubbed his chin. "Tell me, Broderick, why are you so willing to protect the enemy's niece? If this cause is what you feel strongly about, you probably loathe the earl as well as the man's wicked brother."

"Indeed, I do, Uncle. But as much as I cannot stand—nor trust—these men, I want to protect Emmie—uh, I mean Lady Sarah and her companion. Unfortunately, I have another motive in mind while keeping them protected."

"Let me guess." Henry grinned. "You want to woo Lady Sarah?"

Broderick rolled his eyes. "Actually, I want to ask her questions about her uncle. The more I know about that man and what he has planned, the more I can assist my country."

"Now *that* sounds more like the nephew I know."

Chuckling, Broderick turned his horse and continued their ride. He didn't wish to further the conversation by going into more detail, especially when it came to Lady Sarah and Emiline. For certain, his uncle would be able to see how smitten Broderick had become with Emiline already. And until he could figure out this infatuation himself, he didn't want to discuss it with anyone.

EMMIE WAS NERVOUS, yet excited, to be traveling to Brighton. True to Broderick's promise, he arranged their journey, and they left the Cramptons' home without many servants knowing. The few servants who assisted in packing and loading the carriages also went with them.

To Emmie's surprise, they all left early in the morning. It was quite comical to see Mrs. Crampton and, especially, Rebecca sluggish and with puffy, sleepy eyes. Even Anna acted like she didn't want to get out of bed that early. Irritation for the maid's actions of late stung Emmie. How long had Anna been the maid? Yet now, after only a few short weeks, she was performing like a pampered, spoiled little rich girl. Emmie was put out, especially when *she* had never acted in such a way.

Although most everyone was tired, there was no way Emmie could sleep. Excitement pumped through her, and she couldn't wait to find her mother. She and Broderick had previously discussed how they would find her mother. Even though she had to argue with the man who made her heart flutter, she had finally convinced him that she would dress as his footman and go with him during his search.

She also couldn't wait to be with Broderick, alone. But this was the only way.

Curiosity niggled her mind, suddenly making her want to find out more about him. Whatever he did for a living must be successful, since his clothes were fancier than a mere farmer's would be. And his manners and intelligence proved he was far from being a mere farmer's son.

Emmie watched out the window as the morning sun brightened the trees and flowers, making them sparkle. Anna slumped against the corner with her head resting against the coach's wall, as heavy, sleepy breaths escaped her slightly parted lips. Across from them sat Mrs. Crampton. The woman's husband and daughter rode in the other coach, thank goodness. Emmie didn't think she could stomach being in close confinement with Rebecca for very long without voicing her thoughts, especially since she figured the other woman had put something in the tea to make her sick the other day.

The older lady had been dozing off and on since they left the estate an hour or so ago, but now she blinked to awareness and sat up straighter in the seat. She lifted a hand to tilt the bonnet that had fallen aside on her head. When she met Emmie's eyes, the woman smiled.

"Did you sleep well?" Emmie asked.

"As well as could be expected, I suppose. Are you not tired?"

"No. There is too much to see." Emmie glanced out the window again. "I love admiring the beautiful land."

"I've traveled to different countries, but I will always believe England has the best land." Mrs. Crampton smiled. "Miss Emmie, tell me… how long have you, eh… worked for Lady Sarah?"

Emmie didn't like the pause that followed. Obviously, she didn't think Emmie was a good companion. Then again, she really wasn't a good servant at all, so she shouldn't get upset that everyone else knew it, too. "Only for a few years. When my family fell on hard times, Lady Sarah's father invited me to be her companion."

"How very sweet of him." Mrs. Crampton offered an energetic smile that almost seemed too forced. "Lady Sarah's father is certainly a kind man."

"Have you met him? I know he is friends with Mr. Crampton, but did you know him as well?"

"Yes. Mr. Crampton and I were there when Bryon married Daphne." Her smile softened. "Daphne was so lovely and so in love with her husband. It was a marriage I thought would last forever."

Emmie blinked quickly to ward off the tears stinging her eyes. "That is what I heard," she said softly. "Unfortunately, fate had to change things."

"Yes. It was a terrible accident."

Silence lasted another few awkward moments as Emmie turned her attention toward the window to the passing scenery. The trees were so green and the flowers so colorful. This kind of beauty she could stare at forever.

"So, Miss Emmie, I have noticed you spending a lot of time

with my nephew, Mr. Worthington."

Emmie snapped her head toward the other woman. Panic rushed through her, yet she really didn't have anything to fear. Mrs. Crampton must know that nothing could come of Broderick and Emmie's friendship.

Slowly, she released her breath, hoping Mrs. Crampton didn't notice how uncomfortable she felt right now. "I suppose we have been spending time together. We became friends during our ride across the countryside."

"He has always been a kind boy, and as a man he has added adventure to his life."

Emmie chuckled. "You are correct. It was because of his love for adventure that we kept traveling farther away from your estate, and we were caught in the rain."

Nodding, Mrs. Crampton smiled. "He does love to ride."

"Mrs. Crampton, might I ask something personal about your nephew?"

"What would you like to know?"

"He doesn't talk very much about himself, and I wondered about his profession."

"Broderick works at the docks and helps to load and unload the ships. He must love it, because he spends most of his time there. In fact, a few times he has sailed with the cargo." Her forehead creased in confusion. "I don't exactly know what he does, but he does sail quite a bit."

"How very interesting."

For a few quiet moments, Emmie pondered what the older woman had said. If Broderick worked on the docks or ships, why did he dress so elegantly? She highly doubted men who worked on the docks made good money.

"Mrs. Crampton? Might I ask about his family? He has never told me about them."

"My husband and I are his only family now. Broderick's mother died when he was just a lad, and his father left this world a few years ago. Broderick is the only child. However, just recently, his grandfather passed away, and since Broderick is the only living male heir, the title of Marquess of Wilshire was given to him."

Shock vibrated her more than the movement the carriage made when the wheel ran over a rock. *Broderick, a noble?* "How wonderful for him."

Mrs. Crampton shrugged. "Unfortunately, someone will have to convince him of that. My husband tells me Broderick is struggling to accept the title."

"Why? He would live in his grandfather's estate and obtain all of his lands and money."

"You don't understand Broderick that well. He isn't the sort of man who believes his life revolves around money. He does what he wants—things that make him happy and uplift others. He is a very good person, but I fear that if he took the title, he would—"

Just then, a rifle shot rang through the air, and within seconds, the carriage came to a dead halt. Anna jumped in her seat, blinking awake with a frightened expression. Mrs. Crampton's eyes were wide as color slowly left her face.

Emmie's heart dropped. They were being attacked! She just knew it!

Chapter Fifteen

WITH A SPRING in his step and a happy tune on his mind, Broderick hurried out of his room at the inn and downstairs. The journey to Brighton had mostly gone smoothly—except for those blasted snakes slithering in the road that he had to shoot, which, of course, startled everyone. But once they reached the town, he had registered everyone in a room under his name so that nobody knew Lady Sarah was in Brighton.

Uncle Henry was in the main room visiting with the innkeepers. When he saw Broderick, he motioned to come over.

Broderick glanced around the spacious area as he walked toward Henry, hoping to see Emiline and Lady Sarah, but they were not there. He stopped beside his uncle and smiled. "Good morning, Uncle Henry. I trust you slept well."

"As well as could be expected." Henry chuckled and turned his attention to the innkeepers. "Mr. Brownstone, please excuse me. My nephew and I need to leave now."

The men bowed to each other before Uncle Henry led the way outside. Brighton's weather was lovely so far this morning, with the promise of getting better as the day progressed. This would be the perfect time to take a stroll along the boardwalk with a beautiful lady. Emiline would just love it. But the question was… would he be able to spend time alone with her?

"Did you have something to speak with me about, Uncle?"

Henry shook his head. "Not anything really important. I thought you and I could walk through town this morning. After spending all time confined inside a coach yesterday with a daughter who complained about everything, I would rather be with my nephew for a little while."

"I did hear how unhappy she was when I passed by your carriage a few times."

Henry rolled his eyes. "Unhappy? No, she was worse than that."

They both laughed.

As they walked, Henry talked about the weather and the town. Broderick agreed with everything and didn't have much to add. In a way, he wished his uncle would discuss something more important, mainly so that he wouldn't think about wanting to be back at the inn with Emiline.

Thankfully, the town was awake, and many people were doing their daily shopping. Soon, Henry's name was called, and both Broderick and his uncle stopped. A friend of Henry's came to greet them. From the introductions, Broderick realized the two friends hadn't seen each other for several years.

He tried to act interested in the topic the two friends were discussing, but as Broderick swept his gaze up and down the street at the different buildings, the only thing going through his mind was taking Emiline here. She would fall in love with this town, he just knew it.

When he recognized a familiar face, his thoughts stopped. It was one of Captain Hawk's crew members. Broderick acknowledged the man with a slight nod, not wanting to bring attention to either one of them. It was good to know the note Broderick had sent Phillip had been answered quickly. Now Broderick wondered where Phillip was holing up, or if his friend was even in Brighton yet.

Broderick turned back to his uncle and the other man and politely made his excuses. Uncle Henry gave him a curious stare, but Broderick just nodded and quickly left his relative's side. As he headed up the street, a few more familiar faces came into view, and he gave them each a nod as well.

He stopped in front of a glass shop to admire the pieces of art through the shop window. Within seconds, eeriness crept over him, and he got the distinct feeling he was being watched. Slowly, he turned and glanced up and down the street, hoping to see the culprit that made him feel this way, but he couldn't see anyone. Still, he couldn't shake the feeling.

He stepped away from the shop and slowly continued up the street, and when passing another window, he checked the reflection to see if anyone was following him. Finally, he noticed a man from across the street who had stopped when Broderick had. Out of curiosity, he continued. Once again, he slowed when passing another window, and the man was keeping Broderick's pace. This time, he noticed the man glance his way.

The man wasn't familiar, and he wasn't dressed as a naval officer. But that didn't mean anything. In these treacherous times, everyone was under suspicion.

As Broderick passed an alley, he quickly hurried toward the back of the building next to him. He turned the corner and took a quick glance to see if the man still followed. So far, the stranger hadn't ventured into the alley. Broderick flattened himself against the wall and waited.

After a few minutes, he heard a noise. The small rocks in the dirt were being crunched by someone's steps, and the uneven thuds let Broderick know the stranger was in a hurry.

When the other person came into view, Broderick grabbed the man. The reed-thin man gasped and jerked his head up to look at Broderick, his hat falling off in the process. Sweat beaded his forehead and the scalp shown by his thinning hair.

"What do you want with me?" Broderick asked with a growl.

"Nothin', sir. I don't even know ye." The man struggled to get away.

"If you do not know me, then why are you following me?"

The man gulped noisily. "I'm… uh, I'm not, sir."

The man continued pulling at Broderick's arms, trying to free himself. "Then what reason do you have coming up this alley?" Broderick tightened his fingers around the man.

"I, uh… Well, sir, you see…"

"Broderick? Where are you?"

His uncle's call startled Broderick enough to loosen his grip. The man took the opportunity to kick Broderick's shin. When he let go, the man sprinted down the alley toward the street, bumping into Henry. Broderick shot off after the stranger, but the pain in his shin kept him from running fast. When he reached his surprised uncle, he stopped.

"What in the blazes was that all about?"

"I wish I knew." Broderick bent and rubbed the bruise on his shin. "That man was following me, which is why I went up the alley. Before I could get anything out of him, you called."

Henry frowned. "Why was he following you?"

"Once again, Uncle, that's something I wish I knew." Grumbling under his breath, Broderick stood and met his uncle's worried gaze. "What is it that you want?"

"Well, you left in such a rush, I couldn't understand what was wrong."

"Forgive me, Uncle. I felt as if someone was watching us. I left to see if that person would follow," he said, not quite telling the whole truth. He limped back toward the inn, and his uncle walked beside him.

"Did he look familiar to you?" Henry asked.

"No. Did he look familiar to you?"

"Not at all." Henry shook his head.

"Well, hopefully, it was just some man waiting to rob me."

Henry gasped as he slowed his steps. "*Hopefully*? Do you mean you wanted it to be worse?"

"No, Uncle. I'm hoping it wasn't someone who had anything to do with Lady Sarah or Miss Emmie."

"Oh, I understand now." He lifted his chin and walked faster. "Well, I had not planned on taking Lady Sarah to any social gatherings."

"Good."

"However, Mr. Goodfellow has invited me and my family to his dinner party tonight."

It was Broderick's turn to stop. "What did you tell him?" He glared, hoping he didn't have to argue with his uncle out here in front of everyone.

"I told him we would be delighted."

Broderick quickly started planning. He would not go with his uncle to this dinner. However, this was the very excuse he needed to help Emiline find her mother. He would act as his uncle's driver, and hopefully, nobody would notice that Emiline came along as the footman. This opportunity would give her the chance to look for her mother. If this party didn't give them what they hoped for, Broderick would attend the next party his uncle was invited to, if only to ask questions about her mother's location.

"Well," Broderick answered, "*we* will not be delighted to attend Mr. Goodfellow's dinner. You, Aunt Martha, and Rebecca can go, but I cannot."

"Why not?"

"Because I have other plans."

"Like what?"

Broderick folded his arms. "Do you recall when I mentioned I was going to have my crew meet me here?"

"I do."

"That is what I'm doing this evening. However, to keep my disguise and not draw undue attention to myself, I need to act as your driver when you attend this gathering with Mr. Goodfellow."

"Are you jesting?" Henry's eyes widened.

"Not at all. People won't care about a servant meeting in secret with other men."

Henry shrugged. "Perhaps."

"Well, this is what I need to do. Will you help me without

saying anything to Aunt Martha or Rebecca?"

"Indeed, I shall keep your secret."

"I thank you, Uncle. Your silence will assist me immensely."

Excitement built in Broderick's chest, making him impatient to get back to the inn to tell Emiline. He clasped his hands behind him and rocked back and forth on his heels. This was the very thing he needed to be alone with her. The anticipation was almost too much to bear.

EMMIE PULLED HER hat lower on her forehead, for fear one of Broderick's family would recognize her sitting on top of the carriage. She waited while he helped his uncle, aunt, and cousin in the vehicle before he climbed on top and sat next to her.

He smiled at her and winked. "Are you ready?"

"Yes," she said softly, not knowing if his family would be able to hear their conversation inside the carriage. "But I'm more nervous than anything."

"Well, if it makes a difference, you look perfect for a footman." He tapped her leg.

She chuckled and shook her head. "I cannot believe you would admit that."

"Me either."

"Thank you for finding these clothes for me."

"You are most welcome."

He flicked the horse's reins, and their small journey began.

She folded her hands and rested them in her lap, but the jerky movements of the carriage had her bumping into Broderick much too often, and sometimes she didn't know if she would fall off or not. Finally, he glanced down at her. "Hold on to my arm."

Nodding, she did as he asked—then wished she hadn't. How could she have forgotten his muscular frame? He was built so perfectly, she feared she would not want to release him once they arrived at the party. Still, it was rather nice to sit so close and hold him in such a way. It reminded her of when they came back from her grandmother's house.

"Broderick?"

He glanced down at her. "Yes, my lady."

She giggled and shook her head. "You don't need to call me that anymore."

"Why? Our wager was for a whole week."

"I know, but because I cannot dress the way you asked for our wager, I don't think we should continue it."

"But it was so enjoyable. I don't want to stop playing."

"You are incorrigible." She smiled.

"Thank you for that compliment."

She nearly spat out a laugh. "But what I wanted to ask was… Well, do you think I will see my mother tonight?"

"My dear Emiline, I wish your dreams could come true to-night, but I don't want you to get your hopes up. I don't know Mr. Goodfellow, so I cannot tell you what kind of people he will have at his dinner party. However, since your mother is a companion of Mrs. Estelle Winterbourne, we first need to know if the old widow was invited. If not, we need to ask who knows this lady. Once we find Mrs. Winterbourne, we will find your mother."

She frowned and sighed. "I don't think it will be easy, but it's so hard not to hope."

"I understand." He placed his hand over her fingers still cling-ing to his arm and squeezed tenderly. "If I could make this night special for you, I would."

"You already have." She smiled again.

When they came upon the house, she pulled away from Broderick, preparing herself for the role of footman. Once Broderick stopped the carriage, she jumped down and opened the door. Mr. Crampton was the first to exit the carriage. His gaze met hers briefly as he stepped to the ground, but within seconds, he whipped his head around so fast she thought it might fall off.

When he met her stare, his eyes widened in shock. Inwardly, she groaned. *He recognizes me!*

Thankfully, he didn't say anything, but he helped his wife and then his daughter out of the carriage. Emmie closed the door and then proceeded to climb back up. Broderick's strong hand was there to assist. She grabbed it as he finished pulling her up. He then led the team of horses to the side of the house. After securing the brake, he jumped off then helped Emmie down.

"Are you ready?"

"Ready for what?"

"We are going to sneak around back and find a place to hide where we can watch the party and keep out of sight."

She grinned widely and nodded. She wanted so badly to take his hand, but other drivers were watching, so she didn't want to go with her first instinct.

Once they rounded the house and were away from curious eyes, Broderick made the first move to hold her hand. Her heart hammered with excitement, and she couldn't stop from cuddling close to him as they sneaked around to find a place to hide. The tall hedges would provide the perfect spot. From their spot, they could still see inside the large windows of the gathering guests.

She studied each woman carefully, hoping to see a resemblance to what she remembered her mother had looked like, but so far nobody had met those qualifications. As each minute passed, her hopes dropped lower.

A warm hand rested on her back and drew small circles. She looked up into Broderick's caring eyes.

"Don't rush things. It will happen, just maybe not today."

She nodded as tears stung her eyes. He turned her and pulled her into his embrace. She pressed her face against his chest, slowly breathing in his masculine scent of spice. Although she tried to fight the tears, they wanted to come anyway.

"Broderick, I know. I just never expected to see my mother again. And now that I'm so close—" She choked up.

"Shh… No need to explain. I understand."

She lifted her head and gazed into the shadow of his eyes. "I'm so happy you are here with me."

The corner of his mouth lifted. "Not as happy as I am to be with you right now."

When his gaze dropped to her lips, her heart raced with anticipation. But after a few seconds when he didn't kiss her, she rose on tiptoes and pressed her mouth to his. His arms tightened around her as he kissed her back with great urgency, slanting his mouth over hers to deepen the kiss.

Heavens, but she couldn't help but love him at this moment. He was such a kind, caring, and tender man. She never wanted this to end. She wanted to kiss him for the rest of her life.

Just as she prepared herself to tell him her feelings, the bushes rustled, and a loud gasp ripped through the air.

"Broderick Worthington! Pray, what are you doing with that… boy?"

Chapter Sixteen

STARTLED, EMMIE JUMPED away from Broderick. He swung around in the direction of the other man's voice, keeping his dignity—which was something she couldn't do. A man, dressed as if he had come from the party, stood not far behind them, his eyes wide and mouth agape. Even his face had lost color.

Embarrassment washed over her and scorched her cheeks. She wanted to dig a hole and crawl inside, or at least pull the hat over her face so that nobody could see her discomfort. Unfortunately, the hat wasn't large enough to cover her whole head.

Broderick chuckled, shaking his head. "No, Phillip. You have it all wrong." He glanced back at Emmie and took her hand to bring her forward. "My good friend, look closer." Broderick removed her hat and lifted her chin toward the sliver of moonlight pouring between the branches of the tree. "These delicate features don't belong to a boy, but a woman."

Phillip gasped again and stepped closer, his eyes now narrowed in scrutiny. "Indeed, she is a woman." He laughed. "Oh, thank the good Lord, Broderick. You had me worried there for a moment."

"Phillip, this is my friend, Miss Emiline Snow. Emmie, this is my friend, Phillip Daughtery—someone I, um, I have not seen for a while."

Emmie curtsied as well as she could wearing men's breeches,

and Phillip bowed like a true gentleman.

"It's a pleasure to meet one of Broderick's, uh… friends," he said.

Another blush spread over her face. Was this man hinting that Broderick had more than one *friend* like her? "It's nice to meet you, sir."

"So, Phillip, what are you doing here?" Broderick asked.

"I am friends with Mr. Goodfellow."

"What a coincidence. So is my uncle." Broderick chuckled. "But how did you know I would be out here?"

"I spoke to your uncle inside, and he hinted at your whereabouts."

Broderick's jaw tightened and he lost his smile. "Did anyone else hear him?"

"No, just me."

Broderick nodded and then looked down at Emmie. "I need to speak to Phillip for a few minutes in private. Will you be all right while I'm gone?"

She hiccupped a laugh. "Of course. I plan to continue watching the party through the hedges."

"Splendid. I shall return momentarily."

And I shall count the moments until your return so I can be back in your arms. She sighed. "All right."

Once Broderick and Phillip walked out of her sight, she turned back to the hedges. Making a space between the small branches, she peeked through. People still clustered together inside one of the rooms sipping their drinks. Apparently, dinner hadn't started yet. A few new people had joined the group, but the women had their backs to Emmie, and she couldn't tell if any were her mother or not.

Softly, she growled. If only she was closer, then maybe she could see more clearly.

Hastily, she surveyed the yard and spotted a large tree near the window. Her heart lifted. If she could climb the tree, she would be able to get a better look at the guests inside.

Without another thought, she sprinted across the yard, ducking behind bushes and keeping within the shadows for fear someone would see her. Within minutes, she scaled the tree as fast as her legs would push her. Although she hadn't done this for a few years, she had climbed so many trees in her life that this one was easy. She tried not to rustle any leaves or break any branches, but unfortunately, that was impossible. Soon she found a branch that could hold her weight and perched herself on it. Just as she'd expected, looking inside the window was now much easier.

Right away she noticed Mr. and Mrs. Crampton visiting with a couple of ladies, but the women had their back toward Emmie, so she couldn't see their faces. She studied each one, but none resembled the memories she had of her mother, or even the miniature Georgia had shown her.

From below came the thudding of footsteps mere seconds before someone called out, "Pardon me—you, up in the tree."

Fear sliced through her, and she froze. Closing her eyes, she wished the man would go away.

"I know you are up there, so you might as well answer me."

She sighed heavily in defeat. "I can hear you."

"Splendid. Now, will you come down and talk to me like a civilized person instead of thinking you are a monkey?"

She would have cried if she wasn't so upset. How dare this person refer to her as a monkey? And why had she been discovered so early in the evening before she could see her mother?

Slowly, she made her way down the tree until she could jump to the ground, landing right in front of the young man.

He was probably a few years younger than herself and swept his gaze over her length as his top lip curled in disdain. He rubbed his chin, which held a small patch of facial hair. Although she suspected he was slightly younger, he was a couple of inches taller and had wide shoulders. His hair was as brown as hers, and she couldn't tell his eye color because he was standing in the shadows.

"Who are you and why are you spying on this party?" he

inquired. "You obviously don't belong here."

"I'm actually the footman for somebody who is attending this function," she answered softly.

His eyes widened. "Oh, the Peeping Tom is actually a Peeping *Miss* instead."

"Yes, I'm a woman." She squared her shoulders and lifted her chin in defiance.

"Pray tell, why would anyone want their footman to be a girl?"

"If you must know, I'm actually in disguise. I'm here looking for the mother I thought died fifteen years ago. Just recently I discovered she is still alive. I also think she might be at this party."

He rolled his eyes. "That story is utterly ridiculous. Can you not come up with something better? Tell me, what is your name so that I can report you to Mr. Goodfellow?"

"Sir, my name is none of your business," she snapped, having had quite enough of his rudeness.

"If you will not give me your name, then give me the name of the person you are here with."

She couldn't possibly tell him. Mr. Crampton didn't need to know what she was doing, especially since he knew her mother. "Once again, that information is none of your business."

Glaring at her, he reached out and grasped her wrist. "Well, if you are not going to tell me what I want to know, then perhaps you will tell our host."

She panicked and tried to yank her arm away, but she could not prevail. "Unhand me this instant!"

"Not until you tell me your name or the name of your employer."

"She is with me."

Relief spread over her at Broderick's deep voice. She wanted to sigh aloud but didn't dare. Not until after this rude man had left.

Broderick stepped from the shadows and into the light. A small gasp escaped her throat—not from seeing him, but because of what he wore. Instead of wearing the hat and coat of the Cramptons' driver, Broderick wore a more elegant jacket and a different waistcoat, giving the appearance that he was attending the party. Where could he have possibly gotten those clothes so quickly? Unless… Wasn't his friend Mr. Daughtery wearing that color of coat?

The young man arched a haughty eyebrow at Broderick and released Emmie.

"And who are you?" he asked.

"My name is Broderick Worthington, Marquess of Wilshire."

Emmie nearly swallowed her tongue. Why was he using the title his aunt had mentioned he didn't want? Her heartbeat quickened. Perhaps this meant Broderick was now seriously considering the title.

The other man snickered. "A marquess? Do you think I will believe that rubbish?"

"I'm visiting my aunt and uncle—Mr. and Mrs. Crampton." Broderick stepped closer. "And this woman is with me and my relatives."

"But why—"

"It does not matter *why*." Broderick folded his arms and aimed his glare at the younger man. "Now why don't you go back into the party instead of sticking your nose into everyone's business?"

The other man's mouth opened and closed a few times before he nodded. "As you wish, my lord," he snapped before marching into the house.

"Oh, Broderick," she sighed as she walked into his arms. "You arrived just in time."

He slid his hands up and down her back. "Let us leave before others come outside and start asking questions." Nodding, she took hold of his hand as he led them back to the carriage. "Do you want to tell me how you got so close to the house when you told me you were going to stand behind the hedges?"

She looked up at him and grinned. "Do you want to tell me

why you are using a marquess's name and where you got that overcoat and waistcoat?"

He chuckled. "Fine, we shall play it your way for now and hide behind our secrets." Once they were on top of the carriage, Broderick grabbed the reins and got the vehicle into motion.

"Where are we going?"

"I'm taking you back home before anyone else sees you."

She frowned. "But what about your aunt and uncle?"

"I shall return for them later."

"What about finding my mother?"

"My friend, Phillip, told me he knows where Mrs. Estelle Winterbourne lives. We can call upon her tomorrow."

Excitement rushed through Emiline, as did a mixture of emotions—happiness for the time she would see her mother again, yet worry for when she would have to confess the truth to Broderick. "Oh, Broderick." She clutched his arm and pressed her cheek against it. "You are so wonderful."

"I promised I would help you, and I will not stop until I have you standing in front of her." He kissed the top of her head.

"Indeed, you are an extraordinary man."

BRODERICK CLUTCHED THE reins tightly, mainly so he wouldn't be tempted to take Emiline into his arms. Her mother was only a day away from seeing her daughter again, and Broderick was a step closer to never again seeing the woman who'd touched his heart so deeply. Once Emmie and her mother reunited, she would be out of his life. Forever.

He wasn't prepared for the emptiness that consumed him at the mere thought. He didn't want to let her go, but he knew he must. No other woman would be able to fill that void in his heart once she was gone.

Not another word was spoken until he drove back to the inn

and stopped the carriage. He helped her down, and they slowly walked upstairs toward their rooms. His room was closer than the one she shared with Lady Sarah, so before he could change his mind, he grabbed Emiline's hand and pulled her inside his room, shut the door, and turned on the lamp.

"Broderick? What—"

"Shh…" He gathered her in his arms. "I just wanted to hold you before returning you to Lady Sarah."

She wrapped her arms around his waist as she tilted her head to look at him. A soft smile graced her stunning face, her brown eyes sparkling with tenderness.

"Although I want nothing more than to stay in your arms, don't you have to go back to Mr. Goodfellow's party to get your family?"

"In a little while. My aunt and uncle will be there another hour at least." He removed her hat and stroked her silky hair that had been pulled tight in a bun. "For now, all I want to do is hold you."

"But why?"

"Because our time is limited." He carefully pulled out the pins holding her coil together, and her long hair cascaded over her shoulders and down her back.

"It is?"

He nodded. "Soon you will be reunited with your mother, and you will want to be with her. You and Lady Sarah will return to Devonshire, and… and I will never see you again."

"Never say never." She frowned.

"But it's true. You will soon forget about me, and eventually, I will forget about you." He cupped her face with both hands, caressing her cheeks with his thumbs. "But the way I'm feeling right now, I don't know if I'll ever be able to forget you." He bent his head and captured her lips.

Sighing, she leaned into him. The kiss was tender and thrilled him beyond anything he had ever experienced. His heart pounded so hard he thought it might break some bones in his chest. Yet the longer he kissed her, the more his heart ached with sadness.

Reluctantly, he broke the kiss and trailed his lips over her cheek. "Oh, Emiline, I don't think I'll be able to let you go. The mere thought of your leaving me is tearing my insides apart, and I cannot stand the pain." He moved his lips up to her eyes and brushed them across her closed lids. "Emiline, my love, I want you in a way I have wanted no other woman. You have somehow crept into my heart, and I cannot seem to get you out."

Her breathing had grown fast and heavy, as had his.

"Broderick? Why do you want to get me out of your heart?"

"Because this is wrong. We are wrong for each other."

"No, Broderick. We are alike in so many ways."

"No… no… You are all wrong for me. These feelings I have for you may just well destroy both of us."

She pulled away just enough for him to stare down into her smiling eyes. "What would you say if I told you I hold the same confused feelings?"

He drew his thumb across her bottom lip, wanting to kiss her again so badly. "I would say we were both in serious trouble, then."

"I don't mind it in the least. As long as we can be in serious trouble together."

Groaning, he pulled her in for another kiss, wrapping his arms around her to hold her as he devoured her mouth. Kissing her was heavenly, yet he knew he would be in hell if he enjoyed it any further. No matter how much he didn't want to be away from her, being with her was impossible. Indeed, his way of life and the way she was raised could never work.

Hesitantly, he broke the kiss and stepped away. Her lips were swollen due to his ardent kisses, yet her eyes were laced with desire. As much as he should remain strong, she would always be able to bring him to his knees.

"Come. Let's return you to Lady Sarah. I need to get back to the party." He pulled at the overcoat and waistcoat. "And I need to return these clothes to Phillip."

"No, Broderick." She grasped his hand, keeping him from going anywhere. "If you think this might be our last time together, then... let's make it memorable." Her beautiful eyes watered and her lips quivered. "I want you in my heart forever."

Helpless to stop the emotions inside of him, he gathered her in his arms again, bringing his mouth over hers. She clung to him, trying to pull him closer. The rogue inside of him desperately wanted Emiline. Now. Yet the gentlemen he knew he should be reminded him that she was too special to use. However, he didn't believe he was using her for his own satisfaction. After all, the feelings in his heart told him that this was, indeed, love.

Tonight, he would make this memorable for them both.

Chapter Seventeen

"WHAT IN THE blazes was Miss Emmie doing dressed as a footman?" Henry growled at Broderick after they had come back from the party. Thankfully, his uncle waited until Aunt Martha and Rebecca walked inside the inn before starting his tirade.

Broderick rubbed his forehead. An ache had already started to form in his skull. Not as great as the ache in his chest, but still painful, nonetheless. "It's a long story."

"Does it have anything to do with her mother?"

Broderick had just taken a step, but his uncle's comment made him stumble. He came to a halt and swung to face the older man. "What do you know about Emiline's mother?"

"I… uh, well, I…" Henry stammered as he swiped his hand through his thinning hair. Finally, after a few awkward seconds, he squared his shoulders and met Broderick's eyes. "Have you forgotten I'm friends with Lady Sarah's father?"

The confusion inside Broderick deepened, and he shook his head. "What does knowing the earl have to do with Emiline's mother?"

Henry growled and scrubbed his hand over his chin. "Oh, good grief. Will you stop asking so many questions?"

"I would if you were making any sense at all." Broderick folded his arms. "But I don't see how knowing the earl relates to

Emiline's long-lost mother."

"Augh!"

Henry threw up his hands and marched away from the inn. Broderick followed, wondering what made his uncle so irritable.

"I should not be the one saying this," the man grumbled as if talking to himself.

"Uncle, I think you should tell me. That will stop both of us from being confused."

Sighing in defeat, Henry slumped against the side of the building, holding his head as if it would explode at any moment. "But you don't understand. It's not my confession to give."

"Uncle," Broderick said sternly. "If you don't tell me now, I may just beat it out of you."

Dropping his hands, Henry looked point-blank at Broderick. "This evening I met a young man who claimed to be the son of my good friend Byron, Lady Sarah's father. After the confusion of his thinking my footman was a *girl*, the lad continued to perplex me even more. My first thought was that my good friend had sired a child out of wedlock, but the more the lad talked, I realized his mother was Byron's deceased wife, Daphne—and she was not dead at all."

As Henry's words registered in Broderick's brain, shock spread through him like icy fingers, numbing him quickly. The pain in his heart he'd had about Emiline leaving him changed and left a different hollow feeling—a pain that only deceit could create.

He swallowed the dryness consuming his throat. "If Daphne is Emiline's mother, then the earl is really her father?"

Reluctantly, Henry nodded. "I'm afraid so."

"Emiline is… Lady Sarah?"

"Yes." He shrugged. "Why she wanted to disguise her true identity, I don't know, unless it was a way to protect herself because of what her uncle had done." He placed a hand on Broderick's shoulder. "I have known about her switch for a little while now."

"Is her name really Emiline?"

"Yes. Her full name is Sarah Emiline Langston. Daphne called her daughter Emmie when she was young."

Broderick's mind swam in different directions, and he had a hard time putting two thoughts together, let alone trying to deal with all this information right now. The main panic rushing through him right now was that he had ruined her reputation. If he had known the truth, he would have been the perfect gentleman. This wasn't a mere servant any longer, but the daughter of an earl—the lord chancellor's niece! "Who is the woman playing Lady Sarah, then?"

"I'm assuming she is the maid."

"And the young man who found her in the tree is her brother?"

"Yes. He was attending the dinner party with a young lady and her parents."

Broderick rubbed his eyes, realizing the dull throb was moving from his forehead down his face. "I can't understand any of this."

He had never ruined a real *lady* before. Guilt ate at his heart, making his chest tighter. What was he going to do now? Yet there wasn't anything *to* do. She had outright lied to him. He wouldn't have even kissed her if he had known her identity.

Henry squeezed Broderick's shoulder. "My dear nephew, have you perhaps given your heart to Emiline?"

Broderick hardened his jaw and glared at his uncle. "I cannot abide women who lie, so giving my heart to her would be fruitless, wouldn't it?"

"But Broderick, I'm sure Emiline—"

Broderick flipped his hand in the air, breaking the contact between them. "It doesn't matter, Uncle." He breathed slowly, trying to maintain his anger. "I will do as I promised and help her locate her mother. After that, I will leave her in your capable hands to keep her safe, just as her father wished."

He spun around and marched away from his uncle. With any

luck, he would be able to leave Emiline within a day and never see her again.

EMMIE COULDN'T SLEEP. Knowing she would get to see her mother—and speak with her—kept her dreaming of their meeting all night long. Once in a while, she was able to think of Broderick and how wonderful he had been to her, especially his gentle and passionate nature, and their magical night together... and how she knew she was a ruined woman.

But today wasn't the day to stress about her feelings for Broderick, and especially how she would tell him the truth. She would worry about that later.

An hour ago, Rebecca had taken the fake Lady Sarah out to stroll through town with one of the servants. Emmie was invited—which surprised her greatly—but she declined. How could she enjoy Brighton when her mind would be preoccupied?

But now, as she paced her room, she rethought her answer. Perhaps she should have gone with Rebecca and Anna after all. At least she could have had something to do besides sit, pace, and create daydreams of how things would transpire with her mother.

When someone knocked on her door, she jumped and rushed to open it. Mr. and Mrs. Crampton stood in the hallway, both wearing sweet smiles. Remembering the role she was still playing, she curtsied and tried not to look them in the eyes. "Good day."

"Miss Emmie," Mr. Crampton began, "my wife and I would like a word with you, if you don't mind."

"I don't mind." She moved to step out of the room, but instead, the older pair walked inside and closed the door. Emmie brought over two chairs then sat on the bed as each took a seat.

"Miss Emmie... Emiline, my wife and I would like you to know that"—he paused, scratching his neck just under his collar—"um, well... we know you are really the earl's daughter,

Lady Sarah."

Emmie nearly choked on her gasp. She looked between the pair, trying to read their expressions. They should be very upset at her, yet they still wore the same tender smiles they had moments ago.

She wrung her hands together in her lap. "How… how did you find out?"

Mr. Crampton glanced briefly at his wife before chuckling and looking back at Emmie. "We actually realized it the day we went to London and took your maid. Because both Mrs. Crampton and I were friends with your parents, we recognized the resemblances right away, especially when your maid referred to you as Emiline."

Emmie licked her suddenly dry lips. "And you are not angry with me?"

"Of course not, dear." Mrs. Crampton reached over and patted Emmie's hands. "We understand why you did it. We know you were only trying to protect yourself."

Emmie shrugged. "Yes. The idea was my father's. He worried for my safety, even though I would be with you. That is why he wanted me and my maid to play different roles."

"I can sympathize, my dear. Being a father, we strive to do all we can to protect our daughters, but…" Mr. Crampton paused briefly, tapping his shoe against the floor. "But I hope you will want to return to being Lady Sarah today. I have arranged to pay a visit to Estelle Winterbourne's estate to see your mother, and I would like for you to join me so that I might present you to her."

Emmie's jaw dropped. "You also know about my mother? You knew she was alive?"

Mr. Crampton shook his head. "Not until last evening, while we were at Mr. Goodfellow's party."

Tears stung Emmie's eyes, and she quickly blinked away the moisture. "I would love to see my mother today. I just don't know how to act." Her voice cracked as a few tears slid down her face.

"Not to worry, dear." Mrs. Crampton's smile shook this time, as if she battled with her emotions, too. "Mr. Crampton and I will get things in order."

Emmie nodded as tears continued to fall. She wiped them away as she gave the Cramptons her most grateful smile. "You will never know how much I appreciate your help."

They rose to their feet, and she stood with them before they walked toward the door. Just as Mr. Crampton rested his hand on the doorknob, she quickly touched his arm.

"Will you do one more thing for me?" she asked.

"What is that, dear?"

"Please don't let Broderick know who I am."

A bright blush covered his face, and his wife's coloring looked almost identical. Emmie's heart sank. She knew their answer before they could say anything.

"Forgive me," Mr. Crampton muttered. "I confronted Broderick last evening, and, well… I did let it slip about your identity. I honestly felt I couldn't lie to him."

Emmie breathed deeply, her hopes dropping by the second. "Was he very upset that I had lied to him?"

"Yes, but I think if you explain things, he will understand."

"I will." She nodded. "Thank you again for everything."

Mrs. Crampton grasped Emmie's hands. "We will leave to go see your mother at two o'clock this afternoon. Do you need me to help you get ready?"

Emmie forced a laugh. "No. I shall have Anna assist me."

"Anna?" the Cramptons asked in unison.

"Yes, my maid—the one who has been playing the part of Lady Sarah since we came to stay with you."

"Then I shall make certain Rebecca has her back soon."

As Emmie watched the Cramptons walk down the stairs, her heart wrenched with the thought of confronting Broderick. Although she wanted to talk to him to explain why she'd lied, she couldn't worry about that now.

Tomorrow would be soon enough.

Chapter Eighteen

EMMIE PACED THE hallway just outside Mrs. Winterbourne's parlor door, half insane from the wait. Mr. and Mrs. Crampton were in that room talking about *her* with her mother. Emmie's legs shook, and she flexed her fingers, impatient for the moment that the door would open, and she would be invited inside.

It surprised her that Mrs. Winterbourne's servants hadn't bothered her, and nor had the widow herself. But that was all right, because Emmie didn't want to explain who she was. Introductions would come later.

Pausing by the door, she breathed deeply and smoothed her hands down her dress. For today's visit, she had chosen to wear the same blue-mint velvet dress, with the black lace over-bodice, that Georgia had given her. Would her mother recognize it from her sister's collection? Emmie shrugged. Probably not.

She took a deep breath and slowly released it as she pressed her ear to the door, hoping to hear something, anything, that would calm her jittery nerves right now.

Mr. Crampton's voice boomed through the room. From what she could gather, he was discussing last night's dinner party at Mr. Goodfellow's house.

Then she heard the loveliest voice, sweet and tender. *Mother.* Tears collected in Emmie's eyes, and her throat grew dry.

Feelings she hadn't experienced before blossomed in her chest, and she craved the moment she would be in her mother's embrace.

"Daphne," Mr. Crampton said, "there is something I must tell you, but I have avoided doing so thus far in our conversation."

"Why, Henry? What is it about?"

He cleared his throat. "As I mentioned earlier, it was quite a shock to discover you are alive when fifteen years ago we heard your ship had been attacked by a fearsome pirate. Anyway, I'm here to tell you that there have been others who thought you were dead, too."

"Henry, this is all such a shock to me. But my family knew the truth."

"Well... um, not *all* of them. There are a few family members who still thought you had died."

There was a pause, and Emmie held her breath.

"What do you mean by that, Henry?"

"Well, you see... um... As miraculous as it sounds, um..." He cleared his throat again.

"Henry," Mrs. Crampton interrupted. "Why don't we just bring her in?"

"Uh, yes. Splendid idea," Henry answered.

Emmie's heart nearly knocked right out of her bosom. Her hands were cold, yet sweaty at the same time. And she feared her legs would not be able to hold her up much longer. She took two steps away from the door, squared her shoulders, and lifted her chin, preparing herself for when the door would open.

Finally, it did, and Mrs. Crampton smiled as she motioned for Emmie to enter. On shaky legs, she walked the best she could into the room. When she rested her gaze on her mother, a knot of emotion caught in her throat, and immediately, her eyes watered. Never had she seen a lovelier woman. Dressed in a silver and white gown, the older woman had her hair tucked up neatly into a white cap, but her grayish-brown hair still showed around her forehead. Big, blue, wondrous eyes watched Emmie carefully.

Then her mother's eyes widened, and her face paled slightly. She ran her gaze over Emmie, from the top of her ringlet hair all the way down to her heeled shoes. When her mother's attention landed on Emmie's eyes again, they, too, were watery.

"You… you look like my sister, Victoria, but I know you aren't—" She stopped with a gasp, her hand flying to her mouth as a tear slipped down her cheek. "It cannot be…" She took a deep breath. "Emiline? My sweet little Emmie?"

Emmie's heart sang with gladness upon hearing the name she'd missed being called all these years. Tears swam in her eyes, impairing her vision. "Yes, Mother. I'm your little Emmie."

Her mother stood and slowly walked to her, tears streaming down her face. She gently touched Emmie's hair, and then her cheek. "Is it really you, or am I dreaming?"

"If you are, then I'm having the most perfect dream as well."

"Oh, my little Emmie." Her mother sobbed and threw her arms around Emmie, pulling her in for a tight hug. "I thought I had lost you."

"Mother," Emmie cried, wrapping her arms around her mother's waist. "We thought you had died. If we had known you were still alive—"

Daphne pulled back and looked into Emmie's eyes. "*We?* Who else are you referring to?"

Emmie offered a shaky smile. "Father and I."

"Your father is alive, too?"

"Yes."

"Oh dear. I had better sit before I swoon." Daphne pulled Emmie to the sofa, where they both sat, still in each other's embrace. "But this doesn't make any sense. I was told you and Byron were coming to join me here when your ship was attacked by the fearsome Captain Hawk, and everyone on board was killed."

"That is the same story we heard happened to you."

Daphne shook her head and pulled Emmie against her again.

"We'll find out the truth, but right now I want to hold my little Emmie."

Emmie breathed a sigh of relief and cuddled her mother, who smelled like fresh flowers. Lilies. Emmie smiled—just as she remembered from fifteen years ago.

As she glanced around the room, she realized Mr. and Mrs. Crampton had left them alone. *How very thoughtful.*

Her mother stroked Emmie's hair and kissed her forehead. "Sweetheart, I need to tell you something that will come as a shock to you. But if I don't tell you now, you will find out soon enough."

"What is it, Mother?"

"You have a brother."

Emmie sucked in a quick breath of air and sat up, breaking her mother's hold. Daphne clasped Emmie's hands in hers and nodded.

"Yes, my dear. You have a brother. From what he has told me—and from what Mr. Crampton said about last evening's party—I think you have already met Elias."

"I have?"

"Yes. He was the one that caught you climbing a tree."

Stunned, Emiline couldn't speak for a few moments. *I have a brother?* "But Mother, he was very rude. I cannot possibly have a brother who is that spiteful."

Daphne laughed. "When Elias told me about the girl he found in the tree last night, he said she was very ill-mannered, and he could not believe how disrespectful she was—for a footman."

Although Emmie should be insulted, she couldn't help but laugh. "Oh, Mother. I was only pretending to be a footman so I could spy on Mr. Goodfellow's party to find you."

Daphne cupped her daughter's face and smiled. "And now you have found me." She kissed her.

"But did you remarry?" Emmie held her breath. "Is that why I have a brother?"

"No, my dear. I was pregnant with Elias when I sailed to visit my family—although I didn't know I was with child. It wasn't until a month after I had heard you were dead that I realized I was going to have a baby."

Emmie grinned. "Father will be very pleased. He always wanted a son to teach to walk in his footsteps."

Her mother arched an eyebrow. "Pray tell, what has he done with himself all of these years?"

"He has been completely miserable. We both have."

Daphne placed a hand on her chest and breathed deeply. "As have I."

Emmie hugged her mother once more. "Oh, Mother, I'm so happy I found you. This time I will never let you go."

"And neither will I."

BRODERICK SAT AT the rickety table inside a tavern, sipping his ale. He wanted to drink himself into a stupor but had learned by now the consequences of drinking were not good. He needed a clear head to think—and because of his way of life, he had to be cautious from sunup to sundown.

A few times in his life he hadn't been cautious, which got him into trouble. He soon learned to be leery of everyone. So then why was he idiotic enough to let his heart get involved with a woman? Never had he felt this way, but he should have known better than to fall in love…

Groaning, he tipped back his mug and gulped down the remainder of the ale. "More ale over here," he called to the barmaid.

As he waited for the wench to bring him more, he gazed around the room at the other drunks. They were well into their cups, and it was still early afternoon. Apparently, their lives were more pathetic than Broderick's.

The tavern door opened, and he squinted against the blinding light. Once the door closed, he focused on the man coming his way. He smiled. "Phillip, would you like to join me?"

"I would, indeed." Phillip waved to the barmaid. "Bring me a mug, too." He sat next to Broderick and grinned. "It's been a while since we were able to drink like this."

"It has been quite a while, my good friend." Broderick patted his shoulder. "What's wrong with us? All work and no play?"

Phillip laughed. "Well, we are in hiding, so why shouldn't we play as well?"

"Exactly!"

The barmaid brought the drinks and left.

Broderick lifted his mug in a toast. "Here's to playing."

Phillip raised his mug and then clinked it against Broderick's before gulping the ale down. "Tell me, what has crawled into your head lately to get you like this? Not often do I see you this way. In fact…" He tilted his head, his narrow eyes studying Broderick. "If I'm not mistaken, I would think you are acting like a lovelorn fool."

Shaking his head, Broderick laughed. "Your eyes are not mistaken, Phillip." He frowned and stared at his mug. "Indeed, I have been a fool."

"Do you wish to talk about it?"

"No."

"Come now, my good man. How else are you going to work through your pain?" Phillip pointed to Broderick's mug. "You have learned by now that ale is not going to help you through this."

Broderick nodded. "You are wise beyond your years, Phillip." Sighing heavily, he raked his fingers through his hair as he stared at the grimy table. "Once again, in my wretched life, I have let a woman's lies woo me. I have only found a few women who could turn my thoughts to love, but they have lied to me. Now, I find a woman I can easily talk with who makes me feel desirable. She makes me feel like her hero. Then I discovered she lied to me. She isn't the woman I thought she was."

"What are you saying? You have charmed many women, Broderick. Have none of these others made you feel desirable?"

"Not one. Most of them were brainless twits, and conversing with them became futile. But then I met... *her*. She is well educated, and she knows how to make me laugh." A wistful smile tugged at the corners of his mouth, so he quickly took another drink.

"Are you talking about the woman I caught you kissing last night?"

"Aye. The very same."

"But I thought you were interested in wooing Lady Sarah."

Broderick snorted a laugh and looked at his friend. "I discovered an interesting tidbit last night after Mr. Goodfellow's party. Apparently, my Emiline has been masquerading as a lady's companion since the first time I met her." He shook his head. "She is the *real* Lady Sarah—not the woman we have come to know as Lady Sarah Langston."

Phillip's jaw dropped and he set his mug back on the table. "Are you jesting?"

"Not in the least."

"Why did she do that?"

Broderick shrugged. "I wish I knew. After my uncle told me of the switch, I didn't care to hear any more."

Phillip blew out a heavy breath. "Indeed, this is quite a shock."

"That it is." Broderick drank the rest of his ale. "But why am I so surprised that she lied to me? After all, I haven't met a woman who knows how to be truthful."

Phillip leaned in closer. "Did you tell her about Captain Hawk?"

Broderick scowled. "Don't be ridiculous."

"So, you lied to her as well. Two wrongs don't make a right, you know."

"But I *had* to lie to her. I cannot have people know I'm the fearsome pirate," he whispered.

"Then I assume she has her reasons for keeping the truth from you."

Broderick smacked the table. "Why are you defending her?"

"I'm not. I'm trying to make you see that sometimes people have reasons for lying to those they love."

Growling, Broderick pushed both hands through his hair, wishing the confusion in his skull would disappear.

Phillip slapped Broderick on the back. "Come. Let me get you out of here before you are too drunk to walk."

Nodding, Broderick dug into his pocket and threw some coins on the table to pay for both of their drinks. "I would appreciate that."

As Broderick stood, the room tipped for a moment. Groaning, he rubbed his forehead. He shouldn't have had that last mug of ale. Slowly, he walked to the door. When Phillip opened it, Broderick squinted against the bright light and moved outside. He inhaled several deep breaths of fresh air before proceeding to walk.

After a few minutes, his head began to clear, and when it did, thoughts of Emiline returned, as did the pain in his heart. His heartache and frown would be his constant companions until he figured out how to forget about her.

"Um, Broderick. You had better prepare yourself," Phillip muttered, glancing up the street.

Broderick focused in that direction until his fuzzy vision cleared. Up ahead, he saw Emiline walking with her mother and another man. She was wearing the same dress as that day they left her grandmother's house—the same one that had him tongue-tied and feeling like the most fortunate man alive.

He certainly didn't feel that way now, and he didn't want to see her, let alone talk to her. Unfortunately, her little troupe was heading right for him. Fortune wasn't on his side today, because her gaze met his and held.

How could he get himself out of this?

Chapter Nineteen

EMMIE SAW HIM and held her breath. Although he wasn't glaring at her as she'd suspected he would, the pain of betrayal was evident in his dark eyes and rigid jaw. Her heart clenched in sorrow. She really needed to talk to him in private. But they couldn't do that now.

When Elias noticed Broderick, he waved and quickened his step until he stood in front of him. "Good afternoon, Lord Wilshire."

Broderick's frown eased slightly into a smile. "Good day."

Emmie and her mother stopped beside Elias. Broderick looked dreadful, wearing wrinkled clothes—the same ones he'd worn last night—with unkempt hair, and—she took a deep sniff—smelling like he'd bathed in ale. Her heart broke even more, knowing he was this way because of her.

"I hope you remember me from the party last evening." Elias beamed.

"I do."

"Let me make proper introductions, then. I'm Elias Langston." He bowed.

Both Broderick and his friend's eyes widened in shock.

"And this," Elias continued as he pointed to Daphne, "is my mother, Lady Langston. And this lovely lady is—" He stopped then chuckled. "Oh, but I suppose I don't have to introduce my sister to you, since she was your footman last night."

Being the gentleman Emmie knew him to be, Broderick bowed. "My lady, it is a pleasure to make your acquaintance."

She smiled and curtsied. "If my little Emmie was your footman last night, then you must be Mr. and Mrs. Crampton's nephew."

"I am," Broderick replied. "And I would like you to meet Mr. Daughtery." He looked at his friend. "This is what Emiline looks like wearing a dress."

Although they all chuckled, Emmie knew Broderick's remark was meant to hurt. She curtsied and smiled at his friend. "It's nice to see you again, Mr. Daughtery."

"The pleasure is all mine." He bowed.

"We were all out for a stroll on this lovely afternoon," Daphne said. "Would you two like to join us?"

"I thank you for the offer, Lady Langston," Broderick quickly answered, "but I must decline. My friend and I have some business matters to take care of. I hope you understand."

"I do." Daphne smiled. "Once again, it was nice to meet you. I hope to see you again soon."

"I'm sure you will." Broderick and Phillip bowed again before walking away.

Emmie watched them leave, her heart dropping with each step. Then he glanced back, and her heart lifted. But seeing his frown and distrustful, judging eyes made her want to cry. She broke the contact by looking ahead of her as she continued her walk with her mother and brother.

"Strange, but I don't remember Henry or Martha telling me they had a nephew with a title." Daphne's forehead crinkled in confusion.

Emmie shook her head. "Broderick was offered a title, but he hasn't decided on whether he wants to use it or not."

"Indeed?" Elias asked. "So then why did he introduce himself as the Marquess of Wilshire last night?"

"I'm assuming it was because he wanted to look important

and powerful in front of you so that you would leave me alone." Emmie chuckled.

"He should not have done that." Elias pouted.

"Why? It worked, didn't it?"

Both Emmie and her mother laughed while Elias rolled his eyes, turned, and walked ahead of them.

Daphne linked her arm with Emmie's and patted her hand. "So, tell me, my darling daughter. What are your feelings for Mr. Worthington? Is there something I should be concerned about?"

Emmie's throat tightened. The only thing between them was that she loved him with all her heart. "What makes you think I have any sort of feelings for him?"

"My dear, I'm not blind. I can see you both have feelings for each other."

"No, Mother… We *had* feelings for each other. Broderick is upset with me right now, which I'm certain was obvious by the way he looked at me."

"Why is he upset?"

"Because I never got the chance to explain to him why I lied about who I was."

Daphne slowed her steps and looked into Emmie's eyes. "Then you need to find the chance to tell him, or both of you will be miserable. What if I invite him to Mrs. Winterbourne's home tonight, and—"

"No, Mother. I doubt he will come."

Daphne frowned. "Then we shall give him a few days to think about how miserable he is before he realizes he wants to see you again."

Emmie couldn't stop the smile sneaking on her face. "Yes, I think that is a splendid idea. And it will serve him right to be miserable right now."

As they continued their walk, she prayed that she would find a time—and a place—to speak with Broderick. And she hoped it would be soon. She couldn't go on being so happy with her mother, yet at the same time unhappy because of Broderick.

IT WAS LATE, but Broderick didn't care as he walked toward his room at the inn. The run-in with Emmie earlier this afternoon had left him in a fit of despair.

She was now *Lady Sarah*, and he felt like such a buffoon—as if everyone was laughing at him, knowing she had played him for a fool. Captain Hawk would have *never* allowed a woman to treat him as such, so why Broderick was allowing one to do so now, he didn't know.

Only a few candles were lit in the hallway, but he easily found his room. He opened his door and walked in—then stopped. A brighter candle lit his room. Strange, since the only time he had been in here today was to wash up and change his clothes after his night of drinking, and he certainly hadn't lit a candle.

Then movement from the end of his bed drew his attention, and a woman came toward him. As she walked into the light, he recognized her. Relief sprang from his throat in a sigh, yet the beating of his heart started another worry in his chest.

"Emiline. What are you doing here?"

"I must speak with you in private." She motioned around the room. "We cannot get any more private than this."

He opened the door again. "I wish you would leave. We have nothing to discuss."

"Close the door, Broderick. I'm not going anywhere, and if you try to make me leave by force, I shall scream and wake the whole inn."

Frowning, he closed the door and glared at her. "What makes you think I would use any force? Don't you know me by now?"

She shrugged and stepped closer. "I thought I did. But apparently, we both have secrets."

"Besides being the earl's daughter and lord chancellor's niece, what else are you hiding?"

"I want to tell you why I played the part of a lady's companion."

"Then I suggest you keep that hidden, because I don't want to hear what you have to say." He unbuttoned his overcoat and shrugged it off, laying it over the back of a wooden chair that stood near the window.

"You may not want to hear, but I'm going to tell you anyway."

Her tone of voice was stern. *Stubborn woman!* Then again, that came as no surprise. She had always been that way.

"Broderick, I did what I did not to play a trick on you and your family, but because I had to. My father was fearful of the danger I would be in if people knew who my uncle was. He trusted Mr. and Mrs. Crampton, but since he couldn't trust anyone else, Father had me play the part of Lady Sarah's companion. Then when you told me about the driver of our coach wanting to harm Lady Sarah—and then those men who came to your uncle's estate when we were riding the countryside—I knew I had to keep my identity hidden." She took a deep breath. "I know I should have trusted you, since we were growing close, but for years I have longed to feel normal—for someone to treat me normally, instead of as an earl's daughter. During my stay in Paris, men courted me, but I knew the only reason they were interested in me was because of my large dowry."

Broderick really didn't want to hear this, because the longer he listened to her sultry voice and looked upon her beauty, the more his heart softened. He didn't want that kind of reaction. She'd lied to him, no matter what her excuses were.

"Emiline, you must give yourself more credit than that. You are a very lovely woman."

She laughed lightly as a small blush touched her cheeks. "Apparently, only to you. Out of all the sonnets and flowery words told to me, my beaus never once called me a lovely woman."

"Then the men in Paris must be blind."

She shook her head. "Or perhaps you like me a bit more than

they did." Stepping closer, she kept her eyes locked with his. "Broderick, I know you like me, and I also know how upset you are right now. You have every right to be, but I pray you'll understand and forgive me."

"Emiline, a lie is a lie, no matter how much you sweeten it up, and I cannot condone it, or forgive you."

She arched an eyebrow. "Can you stand there and tell me you have never lied to me?"

He scowled. "What do you mean?"

"Or is it just the Marquess of Wilshire who lies?"

He rolled his eyes. "I'm not a marquess."

"Yes, you are, you just haven't accepted that fact yet."

"Who told you?"

"Your aunt."

More anger shot through him. "Did my aunt tell you why?"

"No."

Growling, he scrubbed his hand over his chin. "What else has she told you that I haven't given her permission to disclose?"

"She told me a little about your family. She also told me that you spend a lot of time on a ship—"

"Exactly! I spend time on a ship because that is what I enjoy doing. I love the taste of the salt air on my tongue, and the sea breeze blowing through my hair. I love commanding a crew, as well."

"Pardon me?"

"Oh," he shouted, flipping his hands in the air. "Let me guess… The high and mighty earl's daughter doesn't approve of a ship's captain? Is that too far beneath you?"

Fury shot through her eyes and her lips thinned. Before he could say another word, her hand sailed through the air, and her palm met his cheek dead center. The sound of the slap echoed through the room.

"That was uncalled for," she snapped.

He rubbed his stinging cheek. "Well, if that was uncalled for, I'm sure you will be very happy to hear that I cannot stand people like you. I especially loathe your uncle for all the people he has hurt." He stood straighter and lifted his chin. "Now, my dear *Lady Sarah*, what do you have to say about that?" He pointed to his other cheek. "This one hasn't been slapped. Feel free to release your anger on this side as well."

She gasped, her hand flying to her throat. Wide, surprised eyes stared at him for a few awkward moments as her bosom rose and fell quickly in uneven breaths. He had certainly caught her off guard with that confession. Thankfully, his anger didn't loosen his lips enough for him to tell her that he was also Captain Hawk. That bit of information would have her running back to tell her father and uncle.

Finally, she took a deep breath and released it slowly. Within seconds her expression changed, and anger was nowhere in sight. Instead, she looked almost pleased.

"You want to know what I *have to say about that*?" she inquired sweetly.

She stepped closer until she was right in front of him. Her gown even brushed against his legs. Now he could see her striking eyes better, and they were definitely not shooting fireballs at him.

Emiline toyed with the buttons on his waistcoat while staring up into his eyes. "Are you sure you want to hear my answer?"

What game was she playing with him now? He wanted to hear her answer, although he still waited for her to deliver another slap on the face—one he definitely deserved this time. "Yes."

"I think your confession was the most wonderful thing I have ever heard." Her gaze dropped to his lips for a brief moment before bouncing up to meet his eyes. "Although I'm related to the lord chancellor, I feel the same way you do about my uncle, and I sympathize with those he has destroyed. If only there was something I could do to help in your quest—"

He cut her off by grabbing her and pulling her against him, capturing her mouth in a fiery kiss. An overwhelming surge of happiness grew inside of him. Never had he expected such a confession, and hearing her sweet words melted his heart faster than a roaring fire could.

At this moment, he didn't care who her father was, and he couldn't care less about her uncle. Nothing mattered except showing this woman how much he loved her.

She wrapped her arms around his shoulders and hungrily returned his kiss. His heart burst in his chest as love poured out. He rubbed his hands over her back, pulling her closer, as if to make her part of him.

As she caressed his hair and neck, each touch, each stroke, let him know what was in her heart better than any words could at this moment. Then again, he didn't want to break the kiss to find out. He took pleasure in the way her mouth fit with his as their bodies practically melded together.

He lifted her and carried her the few steps to his bed, then laid her on the mattress. She broke the kiss and smiled. He caressed her hair as he stared dreamily into her eyes.

"Does this mean you have forgiven me for being a mule's hind end?" he asked.

"I don't know. I'm still considering it." She grinned teasingly.

"Will a few more kisses help you make up your mind?"

Her eyes twinkled. "It certainly couldn't hurt."

He placed his mouth over hers again, but this time kissed her with such gentleness that it nearly had him going insane for more. A soft groan escaped her throat as she cuddled closer.

Inwardly, he cursed. She would definitely be the death of him. But he also knew that if he didn't stop this insanity soon, he would give himself to her heart and soul—if he hadn't already. But he couldn't do that, especially knowing she was a true lady. Although he wanted her badly, she needed a normal wedding. Not one forced upon them by an irate father.

He broke the kiss again and smiled down at her. "How was that?"

She nodded. "Perfect. I do forgive you now."

"What would you say if I told you how much I love you?"

Her amazing, wondrous eyes swam with tears. "I would tell you I love you right back."

"You do?" His heart sang with happiness. "I never thought I would hear that from you, especially after the way I treated you." He kissed her forehead. "Please forgive me for not trusting you enough to hear you out before misjudging you."

"Why didn't you want to trust me?"

"Because I'm also in hiding."

She glanced at his hair. "Is that why you have colored your hair?"

He hitched a breath as his hand flew to his head. "How do you know it's colored?"

"Because the brown in your hair is fading into black."

"Then I suppose it's time to color it again. And yes, that's why I colored it—because I'm hiding from a man who nearly captured me."

"You know I won't say anything."

He caressed her cheek. "I know."

"I'm so glad I decided to talk to you. My mother thought I should wait a few days, but I knew I wouldn't be able to sleep without talking to you."

"Your mother knows about us?"

"She knows I care for you, but she doesn't know to what extent my feelings run."

He chuckled. "I'm so happy you found your mother."

"I wouldn't have found her without your help." She leaned up and kissed him. "I have you to thank for a lot of things." She wrapped her arms tighter around his neck and scooted closer to him.

Broderick groaned. He couldn't let things go too far. "And I have you to thank for loving me." He kissed her on the nose then moved off the bed, pulling her with him. "However, I think I need to get you back to your bedroom. If your mother—or father—knew you were in here, we would both be in trouble."

Giggling, she walked to the door. "Yes, you are correct. Being with you this late at night is definitely wrong—even though it's so very enjoyable."

"You are incorrigible." He touched her chin. "And that is one of the reasons I love you so much."

She took hold of his hands. "Be with me tomorrow. Spend the day getting to know my mother and brother."

He nodded. "I will, but only for a little while. I have a meeting to attend."

She gave him a skeptical look. "Here? In Brighton?"

"Yes. You met one of my crew, Phillip. He and I have a meeting tomorrow."

She grinned. "As you wish, just as long as I get to have you for a little while."

"My dear, sweet Emmie. You can have me forever if you wish."

"I definitely wish that."

He kissed her one last time then opened the door to his room. She sashayed out, dreamily gazing at him as she made her way up the hallway to her room and was safe.

At least for now.

But being the niece of a man hated so much definitely wasn't a good thing.

Chapter Twenty

BRODERICK WALKED INTO the inn, bypassing the section leading toward the bedrooms, and entered the dining area. Immediately Phillip raised his hand from his seat. Broderick nodded and proceeded to his friend's table.

"Good evening, Daughtery."

"And a pleasant evening to you." Phillip motioned to the empty chair. "I have already ordered us the inn's special for tonight, which they will bring shortly."

"Splendid." Broderick patted his belly. "I'm famished."

Phillip studied him with narrowed eyes for a few silent moments. "There is something different about you tonight."

"There is?" Broderick arched a brow. "Pray, tell me what is different." He glanced down at his shirt and waistcoat. "I'm dressed, so that cannot be what is different." He ran his fingers through his hair. "Perhaps it's because my natural hair color is returning."

"Yes, your brown color is fading, but it's not that." Phillip tilted his head. "What I see different from yesterday is that you are in much better spirits. No longer does your frown scare small children."

Broderick threw his head back and laughed heartily. "You are very observant. Yes, I'm feeling much better today."

"Do I dare ask why?"

"Because I'm in love, that's why."

"Love?" Phillip chuckled. "When only last night your heart was broken by a fair maiden? I don't think I've seen you move on so quickly, my good man."

"No, Phillip, I haven't moved on to another woman. The lady I'm madly in love with is my Emiline. She and I talked last night, and let's just say we worked out our problems. No longer am I upset with her for hiding her identity from me."

"That's wonderful." Phillip slapped Broderick on the shoulder. "And I must say, you do look much better when you're in love."

The barmaid brought their plates out, and another maid carried the drinks. Broderick thanked them and dove into his mutton and potatoes. It was hard to believe, but food tasted better now that he'd finally admitted his true feelings to Emiline.

Phillip took a small bite and, after a couple of chews, leaned closer. "Lieutenant Mercer was spotted in town," he whispered.

Broderick swallowed hard and nearly choked. His head was still reeling with Emiline's confession and the visit he'd had with her mother and brother earlier today, making it rather difficult to absorb what Phillip had just said. But now he had to clear his mind and focus on important matters. This was definitely not something he wanted to hear.

"Who told you that?"

Phillip lowered his voice. "One of the crew."

"Were they certain it was him?"

"Aye." Phillip lifted his eyebrows. "It's rather difficult to confuse Mercer with someone else because of his evil eyes."

"Very true." Broderick nodded. "But I wonder what he is doing in Brighton."

Phillip leaned his elbows on the table. "Do you suppose he is still looking for Lady Sarah? You mentioned the other day that you thought he was the one that came looking for her at your uncle's house."

Panic grew in Broderick's chest. Was his darling Emiline in

danger, especially now that the truth about her identity was out? "I still believe she might, indeed, be in danger. I just wish I knew why Mercer wants her so badly when the fool is working for her uncle." He scratched his neck, feeling like a noose was being pulled tighter around his throat.

"Hmm…" Phillip tapped his finger on his chin. "I wonder if Mercer has other ideas in mind."

"Like what?"

"Perhaps he knows about your relationship with the Cramptons, and since Lady Sarah is staying with them, maybe he wants to get her away from you for fear she might say something about her uncle that you could use."

Broderick shook his head. "That thought had crossed my mind, but if Mercer really knew I was staying with my uncle, the man would come to get *me*—not Lady Sarah. Remember, I have been on his kill list for a few years."

"All of this is so confusing," Phillip grumbled before taking a bite of his meat.

"Indeed it is."

A burst of laughter broke out in the far corner, making Broderick jump and reach for his knife. But the boisterous group of men were well into their cups and enjoying themselves too much to be of any bother. Slowly, he glanced around the room, suddenly feeling that danger lurked closely. He silently reminded himself nobody could be trusted.

As Broderick munched on his roll, his mind spun with ideas, none that made sense. He should be used to running from Napoleon's men, but now he realized he was completely sick of it. Was his crew tired of all this turmoil as well?

"There is only one thing to do to bring this to an end once and for all," he said before taking a swallow from his cup of wine.

"What is that?"

"Talk to Mercer myself."

Phillip choked on his food. "What? Are you insane?"

"I must be, but how else are we going to know what he is

planning?"

"Do you really believe he will tell you?"

Broderick shrugged. "Perhaps he won't, but Captain Hawk will find a way to loosen the man's tongue, even if it means torturing him. I'm sick of his games, and it's time Captain Hawk gained control once and for all."

Phillip grinned. "Shall I gather the crew together for a meeting?"

"Yes. As soon as you can."

"I'll let you know once I hear from them. There has only been a handful that came after I sent them missives. I suspect more will arrive."

"Splendid." Broderick lifted his cup. "I'm feeling better already."

"As am I." Phillip clinked his cup against Broderick's.

Unfortunately, Broderick wasn't feeling half as good as he should, especially when Emiline might still be in danger.

THE NEXT AFTERNOON, Emmie visited with her mother in Mrs. Winterbourne's flower garden. They sat at one of the decorative tables sipping tea, enjoying the fresh air. A warm wind blew against her cheek, stirring a lock of hair against her skin. It didn't bother her. She vowed not to let trivial things disturb her any longer. Life was too important to waste being upset or sad.

She glanced across the yard to the road on the other side of the fence. Not many people walked by today, but then, she had noticed this part of town wasn't as busy as the inn where the Cramptons were staying.

Being with her mother had been wonderful. Even Anna relished the fact that she was away from the high-and-mighty Miss Rebecca Crampton. Anna got along splendidly with Mrs. Winterbourne's servants, as well.

Emmie looked back at her mother, and a similar pair of eyes stared back. A small grimace tugged on her mother's mouth, and she wore a forlorn expression.

"Mother? What is amiss?" Emmie reached across the table and touched her mother's hand before withdrawing.

"Not to worry, my dear. I'm fine. I have just been thinking about what could have possibly kept us away from each other for fifteen very long years."

"I, too, have thought of that very thing lately." Emiline lifted the cup to her lips and sipped. "How could both of us have gotten the same kind of message?"

"Did your message state that the ship had been attacked by Captain Hawk?"

"Indeed it did, Mother. When Father wanted us to sail here, I worried that Captain Hawk might still be alive and attacking ships."

Daphne nodded. "That would frighten me, as well. Do you know if Captain Hawk is alive?"

"I couldn't tell you." Emmie reached out and grasped her mother's hand. "When you received the message about us dying, why didn't you come back to our chateau in France?"

"Because I was told the bodies were lost at sea, so there really was no burial service." Daphne frowned. "Why did you and your father not come here upon hearing of my demise?"

"The same reason—that your body was lost at sea." Emmie shrugged. "Not only that, but Father was quite upset with your family for wanting you to visit. At times I think he blamed them for making you sail across the sea to come see them."

Daphne shook her head. "There were times I blamed my family as well. My mother wanted me to stay with her after Elias was born, but I could not. A few years after that, I was introduced to Estelle Winterbourne. She needed a companion and didn't mind that I came with a small child. She has grandchildren, but they were never able to visit because they lived in Ireland."

Emmie released a wistful sigh. "If you would have stayed

with your mother, then I would have met you sooner. If not for Grandmother, I wouldn't have known where you were."

Daphne squeezed Emmie's hand. "The Lord was certainly helping us along, was He not?"

"Indeed. But that still doesn't explain why we received the same kind of notes fifteen years ago."

"No, it doesn't. Who would want us separated so desperately that they would go to such great lengths?"

"Well, Father thought Grandmother or one of your sisters was behind it at first."

Daphne shook her head. "My family didn't hate Byron. They just resented him for taking me so far away from them."

"Then who else would want to separate us?"

Daphne released Emmie's hand to sip her tea. Emmie sipped hers as well, hoping for some inspiration to strike. But the more they sat in silence, the more frustrated she became. Would they ever discover the culprit in this mess?

Suddenly, her mother's eyes widened. "Tell me, who signed the missive sent to your father that I was dead?"

Emmie tried to remember the events of that fateful day. "I was visiting a friend of mine, and when I returned home, Father had already received the letter. He was sitting in the parlor clutching your miniature and crying. The letter was on the table next to him." She paused, trying to remember more. "Come to think about it, my uncle, the lord chancellor, was there as well, consoling Father the best he could."

Daphne gasped and then muttered a curse that shocked Emmie, since she'd never heard a lady speak in such a way. Her mother stood and paced around the table.

"What is it, Mother?"

Stopping, Daphne closed her eyes and rubbed her forehead. "Oh, my dear. This makes no sense." She opened her eyes and looked at Emmie. "But your uncle was the one who sent me the letter about you and your father."

Emmie's body grew numb, and the teacup slipped out of her

hand, falling to the floor and shattering. Her chest tightened as if a house had fallen on it. Tears built in her eyes as she shook her head, not believing what she'd just heard. "But… why would he do that?"

Daphne rushed to Emmie and took her in her arms. "Oh, my little Emmie. Your uncle never approved of me. All the while your father was courting me, your uncle tried to convince Byron that I wasn't the right woman. Several times during our courtship, he tried to separate us."

"Why?" A tear slipped down Emmie's face.

"Because he said your father was meant for better things. The ruthless man wanted Byron to go into politics with him. He didn't want Byron marrying anyone unless they came from a well-to-do family."

"But why didn't he stop to think of the little girl who *needed* her mother?" Emmie sobbed against her mother's shoulder. "I thought he loved me, but he doesn't. All he cares about is himself."

"I know, dear. I know." Daphne stroked Emmie's hair, rocking her slowly back and forth. "I feel so bad that I didn't realize it was the lord chancellor until now. After he sent me the letter concerning your deaths, he came to visit to bring me a few things of yours and your father's so I could have something to remember you by. It touched my heart that he was so thoughtful when I knew he didn't like me." She blew out a frustrated breath. "I should have known better. He was being too nice."

Emmie jerked back and stared into her mother's teary eyes. "Oh dear. What will he do when he discovers we have found each other?"

Daphne shrugged. "I suppose he is not going to like it when Byron hears the truth."

"I pray someone arrests my uncle and hangs him for treason." Emmie sobbed. "If he tried this, what is going to stop him from trying to separate us again?"

"Hopefully, your father will take care of that." Daphne offered a shaky smile and caressed Emmie's wet cheek. "But nothing is going to tear us apart ever again."

Emiline glanced at the table. "I'm sorry I broke Mrs. Winterbourne's teacup."

"There is nothing to be sorry about. I shall have one of the servants clean it up. I think you should lie down on my bed. I'm certain a little rest will do wonders for you."

"I think I will." Emmie wiped her eyes and started walking toward the door. Her mother went to the servants' door to fetch someone to clean up the mess.

Before Emmie reached the door, she noticed a movement out by the street again. Elias was talking to some man with abnormally orange hair, and another man wearing a hat who had his back toward her. But the way he stood, a spark of familiarity hit her, but she couldn't put her finger on who the man could be. The orange-haired man and Elias were discussing something serious— as was evident by their drawn expressions.

She almost stopped and called out to Elias but decided against it. She was certain her face looked a fright after she'd been crying. She didn't feel like talking to anyone right now, especially anyone new.

Slowly, she walked to her mother's room, her heart wrenching with sadness over her uncle's betrayal. How could he do that to his family?

Her head pounded with anger as well. She wanted to inform her father of what his self-centered relative had done, yet she needed to tell him face to face and let him see his wife as well. Soon all would be out in the open, and she prayed someone could stop her uncle once and for all.

She lay down on the bed, but the stuffy air and warm room made resting impossible. She rose and opened a window to let in the breeze before returning to bed. Just as she rested her head on the pillow, the sounds from outside drifted through the air, making her hear almost everything going on outdoors. More specifically, she heard her brother and the two men. Why did the street have to be so close to her mother's room?

Groaning, she rose once again to shut the window, but then one of the men spoke a name that made her pause. They couldn't have said what she thought.

Moving closer to the window, she peeked outside. All three men were hidden by the leaves from the bushes, but their voices were much clearer.

"You cannot let her near him," one of the men said. "He is a dangerous man. There is a reason Captain Hawk's name strikes fear into women and children."

She sucked in a breath and quickly slapped her hand over her mouth. *Captain Hawk is still around after all these years?*

"But how can I stop her from seeing him if you don't want me to let her know what is going on?" Elias asked.

"That, Mr. Langston, you will have to figure out on your own. We just came to inform you of what might happen to your sister."

"Does she know about Captain Hawk?"

"No, and I don't think you should tell her. Just protect her the best you can, and whatever you do, keep your sister away from him."

"As you wish. I shall try my best."

The two men left, but she couldn't see them very clearly as they walked up the street. Elias stood watching them for a few brief moments before he turned and headed back toward the house.

Her heart pounded fiercely. Why would they discuss her and Captain Hawk in the same conversation? Nothing made sense, and fright consumed her, almost as much as it had when she was younger and thought about sailing across the sea. At this moment, she felt vulnerable, which was something she could *not* feel.

Broderick will protect me.

Yes, she must go tell Broderick.

As she hurried out of the bedroom to find her mother, Emmie's mind was scrambled with thoughts about why her name would be connected to Captain Hawk's. Helplessness washed over her. If asking her brother would help, she would do it in a heartbeat, but she received the impression from listening in that her poor brother was nearly as confused as she was.

She found her mother quickly as she was coming from the kitchen. Emmie ran to her and clutched her hands.

"I must leave immediately. I need to talk to Broderick."

"Why so suddenly?"

"I don't know exactly what is going on," Emmie continued in a rush. "I shall explain later. I must leave." She tore away from her mother and strode toward the front door.

"My dear, let me come with you."

"Not this time, Mother. I shall be fine." She hurried out the door before her mother could say any more.

Halfway down the street, Emmie realized she hadn't grabbed her shawl or her bonnet. Nevertheless, she couldn't turn back now. She must find Broderick and tell him of what she'd heard, and she prayed he would be able to figure out this most confusing puzzle.

She turned a corner and quickened her steps, anxious to walk the five blocks to the inn. She passed couples strolling down the street as if they were standing still. At the moment, she didn't care what people thought of her. They didn't know her and wouldn't remember her once she left this town to return home to Devonshire.

As she passed an alleyway, she recalled there was a shorter way to get to the inn. Without giving it another thought, she turned up the alley and hurried faster. But from the echoes of quick footfalls stomping behind her, she wasn't the only person going this way.

She glanced over her shoulder briefly to see who it was. There was something recognizable about the man coming at her—besides the fact he had stood beside the man with orange hair that her brother had talked with.

Emmie stopped suddenly and faced him, ready to speak her mind and ask him why he would think Captain Hawk would be after her. "Why are you following—"

The man snickered and threw a blanket around her head, then wrapped his beefy arms around her so tightly she didn't think she could breathe. As she struggled and tried to scream, the man cackled.

"Now Captain Hawk will be mine very soon."

Chapter Twenty-One

BRODERICK SAT AT the small desk inside his room at the inn jotting down notes for how he would bring Lieutenant Mercer to him, and, in return, find the location of the lord chancellor to capture him. There were few ideas floating around in his head, but he was determined. Wanting to be a normal man again and marrying Emiline was his motivation.

He was certain that all the men who played the role of Captain Hawk had felt the same as Broderick. There was still need for the fearsome pirate, yet soon he would fade away.

The knock on the door brought Broderick out of his thoughts of the future. "Enter."

The door opened and Uncle Henry peeked inside. "Are you busy?"

"I'm just finishing some correspondences. Why? What is wrong?"

"Nothing. I'm just bored."

Broderick chuckled as he set his quill back in the ink bottle. "I would invite you in, but this room is small." He pushed away from the desk and stood. "Would you like to venture downstairs to visit? Or take a walk instead?"

"I think we should take a walk."

Nodding, Broderick grabbed his overcoat and shrugged into it. "A walk sounds refreshing."

They moved down the stairs in silence. "Where are Aunt Martha and Rebecca this afternoon?"

"Aunt Martha has a headache, so has taken to her bed, and Rebecca has been in a fit ever since she found out Lady Sarah's role was played by Emiline's maid all this time." Henry rolled his eyes. "Rebecca left a little while ago with her personal maid to do some shopping. That is what your cousin does when upset, you know."

Broderick laughed. "And chumming up with a maid and treating her like an actual person is so far beneath her that she has to throw a temper tantrum? Really, Uncle. That is just absurd."

Henry threw back his head and laughed. "Well said, dear boy. But yes, she has been in a foul mood for a few days."

Broderick scratched his head. "I pity the man who marries her."

Henry chuckled. "Watch your tongue—she is my daughter, you know. But…" He glanced around the spacious room. "I, too, pity the man," he ended softly.

They walked out of the darkened inn and into the sunlight. Broderick squinted against the brightness until his eyes could adjust. "Speaking of marriage…"

Henry looked at him with raised eyebrows.

"I'm going to ask Emiline to be my wife," Broderick said happily.

Henry beamed and slapped him on the shoulder. "What an excellent choice. She is a wonderful young lady, and I think you and she will be very happy, indeed."

"I believe we will, Uncle. I do love her, and have for a while now, even though I didn't want to admit it."

"Admitting our love is very hard. It means we must commit to a relationship, and for some men, that's nearly impossible to do."

"So true, Uncle. I'm glad to know it's not just me who thinks that way."

"But marriage to Emiline is a good thing, I assure you."

"No need to assure me, Uncle. I know how special Emiline is."

Henry slowed his footsteps and leaned closer. "You are not marrying her because of who her uncle is, are you?"

Broderick stopped, his head spinning. Strange, but he really hadn't thought of that since he'd confessed his love to her. Even though Emiline agreed with him about her uncle's actions, the man was still Broderick's enemy. He prayed she wouldn't think he wanted to marry her to get closer to capturing her uncle.

"Actually, I want to marry *her*—not her family. Although I must remember to be very careful about what I say around her father."

"Yes, you don't want to slip and say something that might give away your secrets."

Broderick shook his head. "Not to worry, Uncle. I have been hiding secrets for a few years now."

Henry's jaw hardened. "I honestly don't know how you or others can live your life in such a way—always cautious, for fear of being captured." He placed his hand on Broderick's arm and squeezed. "But I do admire you for being so dedicated to helping your country any way you can."

"I only want to make our country stronger, Uncle. I want a better life for my posterity."

"As it should be."

Up ahead, he noticed a woman hurrying up the street toward him as if dogs were nipping at her heels. Beside her was Emiline's brother. When they spotted Broderick, Daphne's footsteps quickened, and Elias aimed a glare in Broderick's direction. It surprised him to see Emmie was not with them.

"Good day," Broderick said when they met.

"Lady Langston, what a pleasant surprise," Henry added.

"Mr. Worthington, Mr. Crampton." Daphne's tone was clipped. Elias continued to glare. "Mr. Worthington, do you know where my daughter is?"

Broderick frowned. Worry started to grow in his chest. "No,

my lady. I thought she was with you."

"She was with us earlier today, but then suddenly she stated she had to see you and rushed out of the house before I could stop her."

"When was that?" Broderick asked.

"Not more than an hour ago."

"I assure you, I have been in my room at the inn until my uncle and I left for a walk." He studied their worried faces before glancing at Henry, who wore the same type of expression. Panic filled Broderick completely.

Elias stepped up to him, and the lad poked his finger into Broderick's chest. "I demand you tell me what you have done with my sister."

Broderick held up his hands. "Whoa there, Elias. There is no need to get testy. I assure you, I have done nothing with your sister. I have not even seen her today."

"You are lying!" Elias accused.

"Pardon me," Broderick snapped as the worry to find Emiline expanded, "but why would I lie? I love your sister and want to protect her." He switched his attention to Daphne. "Tell me what happened. I need to know so I can find her."

Lady Langston studied Broderick for a few silent moments before her face relaxed and moisture coated her eyes—eyes that looked so much like Emiline's that it tugged at Broderick's heart. Helplessness settled in his gut, and he didn't know what to do about it.

"I wish I knew, Mr. Worthington. My daughter and I were having a most serious discussion, and I could see how upset it made her. I bade her to rest in my room for a little while. After several minutes, she came back down in a fit and said she needed to find you posthaste. Before I could discover what was wrong, she ran out of the house." Her lips trembled as she placed a shaky hand on Broderick's arm. "Please help us find my daughter. I cannot lose her again."

He grasped her hand and squeezed. "I assure you, I will locate

Emiline. I love her, and I don't wish to lose her either."

"You do not love her," Elias snapped. "You only want to use her."

Broderick released Daphne's hand and glared at the boy. "Why are you saying such lies? What have I done to make you hate and distrust me?"

"Because… Well, I know about you." Elias narrowed his eyes. "I know who you *really* are."

Broderick's heart sank like a boulder in the sea. He glanced at Henry, and the color on his face had disappeared as well. His eyes were wide with fright.

Broderick swallowed hard and looked back at Elias. "And who do you think I am, *really?*"

"Two men told me you were Captain Hawk."

He licked his suddenly dry lips, his mind scrambling for something intelligent to say. He snuck a peek at Daphne, who, thankfully, didn't look as condemning as her son.

"From the stories I have heard about Captain Hawk for many years," Broderick began, "the man would well be into his eightieth year, wouldn't he?" He swept a hand around his face. "Do I honestly look like I'm that old?"

Slowly, the angry expression on Elias's face changed. No longer was he cocky and assured—now doubt snuck across his creased forehead and tight lips.

"Well, I suppose you aren't that age, but the men assured me—"

"Who were these men?" Henry said. "Why do you trust them over the man your sister loves?"

Elias shrugged. "The naval officer was so convincing."

Fear clutched Broderick's heart once again. "A naval officer, you say? What did he look like?"

Elias shrugged again. "A middle-aged man, I assume. Freckled face, with an abundance of burnt-orange hair."

Sickness rolled in Broderick's stomach, making him want to throw up. Somehow Mercer had connected the pirate to

Broderick. But how? And that still didn't explain why the lieutenant would take Emiline. Was it to bring Captain Hawk out of hiding?

Taking a deep breath to control his fear, Broderick nodded. "Tell me everything these men said. I need to find Emmie. She is in grave danger."

"Oh," Daphne groaned as she swooned. Henry rushed to hold her up. Thankfully, she hadn't lost consciousness.

"Not to worry, Lady Langston," Henry said, patting her arm. "My nephew will find Emiline and bring her home safe."

"I will. I promise." Broderick helped to hold up Emmie's mother then looked back at Elias. "Hail a hackney to take you two home. Your mother is in no condition to walk."

Nodding, Elias scampered down the street.

Broderick and Henry exchanged worried glances. Perhaps the only way to get Emiline back was for Broderick to turn himself in—which he could not do. But she depended on him to rescue her, and right now, she was more important.

There was only one decision to make. He loved Emmie with all his heart, which meant he would find her. He prayed his crew would be able to come up with a rescue plan, because he feared he wouldn't be able to save both himself and the woman he loved.

NOISES GREW ALL around Emmie as she slowly became alert. Her head pounded, and she recalled the moment one of the men who had taken her had hit her, rendering her unconscious.

Groaning, she shifted, but couldn't move. As sounds and feelings slowly came to her, she realized her arms were tied at her back, and her feet were secured tightly to the chair in which she sat. A blindfold had been placed over her eyes. Her body ached from being in this position, and panic welled within her chest.

Voices from not far away echoed in the room. She kept still and listened intently as she tried to clear her head of the fog she'd just left.

"How soon do you think he will come?" asked a woman.

Although the woman's voice was low, Emmie suspected she'd heard it before. But where?

"If I know Captain Hawk, he will come today."

Forgetting that she was going to keep quiet, Emmie sucked in a quick breath. *Captain Hawk?* Impossible! Why would he come? Her head pounded for different reasons now. Was he somehow connected with her uncle?

All these unanswered questions were so frustrating. She wanted to know what was going on now, but she continued to act as if she was still unconscious. She prayed her captors believed that.

"And when will I get my money?" The woman's voice came out stronger now, and more determined.

"Not to worry, my sweet lady," the man said charmingly. "When Hawk arrives, you will be paid accordingly."

Emmie didn't like the sound of that. She wondered if the woman was way in over her head as well. Apparently, this man wasn't someone to be trifled with.

"I better be paid *very* well. I didn't stick my neck out for you for nothing, you know. If Broderick Worthington knew what I have done—"

"He won't, I assure you."

Once again, Emmie gasped. Broderick? How was the man she loved involved in all of this? Somehow there was a missing piece of the puzzle, and she didn't know what it was.

"My dear Miss Crampton. Your cousin will never know." Once again, the man spoke with confidence.

Inwardly, Emmie groaned. *Rebecca?* What had that wretch of a woman done? Emmie had never liked Broderick's cousin, and now she knew her first instincts were correct. Rebecca was definitely the hind end of a mule. Worse, actually. She was the devil's own child. Obviously, Broderick had done something very damaging to her cousin that hopefully Emmie would discover soon.

Another set of footsteps pounded on the floor. "I believe everything is in place, Lieutenant Mercer. The trap has been set. When Worthington arrives, there is no way for escape," the man said with quick breaths.

Emmie boiled inside, knowing that Broderick would be as helpless as she was now. And that second man's voice… Why did it sound familiar?

"Splendid," the man referred to as Lieutenant Mercer answered gleefully. "Finally, after all these years, Captain Hawk will be mine."

Emmie's mind skidded to a halt. They were just discussing Broderick, and now the pirate's name had been mentioned again. It sounded like Broderick and Hawk were the same person. But that definitely couldn't be correct. Broderick was too young to be that pirate.

Wasn't he?

Dread washed over her like filthy water. Broderick was probably in his mid- to late twenties. Fifteen years ago, the pirate would have been about the same age or older. Yet the lieutenant seemed to think Broderick was Hawk. Could it be possible that Broderick had taken over as Captain Hawk after a friend or family member? She knew his father was dead, so what were the chances that the original pirate was Broderick's father?

Not only that, but Broderick had promised her that Captain Hawk didn't attack passenger ships. And she believed him. So, why was Captain Hawk being blamed for things he didn't do?

Her headache grew worse the longer she pondered all these confusing questions. But one question remained. If Broderick was indeed Captain Hawk, then the pirate couldn't be as ruthless as rumors indicated. Broderick Worthington was now—and had always been since she first met him—the kindest and gentlest man she'd ever known. There would be no way he could be anything else. She had gotten to know the *real* man, the man who fought with his fellow countrymen trying to keep their country safe from the controlling lord chancellor's grasp. Broderick was the man who would do anything to help the woman he loved locate her mother. And he would do anything to help Emmie now.

Once again, panic wrenched her heart. He didn't know he was walking into a trap. She must not allow that to happen. She needed to figure out where she was, and how to get out of these ropes that bound her to this very uncomfortable chair.

She tried to smell the things around her. As she took a deep sniff, she nearly gagged. Wherever she was being kept prisoner, it was moldy and dusty. She prayed she didn't sneeze.

The more she concentrated on her whereabouts, the more she realized the floor rocked slightly, and she felt off-center. *A ship?* She'd gone sailing enough times with her father when she was younger to know the feeling well. Without a doubt, she was on some kind of ship, and by the fetid scent, she was below deck in a room that wasn't used very often.

Her mind returned to the group still talking. Oh, why hadn't she been paying better attention? She trained her ears on what the other two were saying.

"Whatever happens, I cannot be here," Rebecca said. "I don't want my cousin to see me."

"What will it matter?" the lieutenant asked. "He will die soon enough."

Rebecca huffed. "It's the principle of the matter."

The second man laughed, and once again, Emmie felt she knew him from somewhere.

"Oh, Miss Crampton. You are so two-faced, it's almost laughable. You are the very reason we can capture Broderick Worthington, yet you think all you have to do is use a little soap and your sins will be washed away?"

"How dare you insinuate—"

"Miss Crampton, I don't need to *insinuate*. Your actions speak loud enough."

"Lieutenant Mercer?" Rebecca stomped. "Are you going to allow *this man* to speak to me in such a condescending tone?"

Mercer chuckled. "Miss Crampton, you act as if you are royalty. You're not, so if I were you, I would shut my mouth and keep it closed."

"I don't need to stand here and take this kind of treatment."

"No, you don't," the lieutenant answered, "but if you want your money, you will."

If Emmie wasn't so upset over Rebecca's betrayal, she would have laughed. Indeed, Rebecca was two-faced, and Emmie was glad the other men knew it. Still, deep down inside, she felt Rebecca's life might be in danger now because of what she'd done.

"As for you, my friend," the lieutenant continued, "I think you should depart posthaste. You don't need Mr. Worthington seeing that you are working for me. And our prisoner doesn't need to see you, either."

"You are correct, Lieutenant Mercer, as always. From what I have heard of Lady Sarah, she is a little spitfire." The other man chuckled. "I will definitely be in touch, soon, to find out how everything transpires."

"I'm in hopes that our plans will flow smoothly."

Irritation grew inside her. Whoever this man was, surely he hadn't heard the correct information about her. She was *not* a spitfire. Still, it bothered her that she hadn't pinpointed his identity.

After the unknown man left, silence stretched in the room for a few moments. Emmie tried to keep her breathing slow instead of what her quick heartbeat was dictating. She was certain the other two were watching her now. She must not appear as if she'd been awake this whole time.

"So, Miss Crampton, I suppose we should see to our prisoner now."

"As long as you don't remove her blindfold. I don't want her seeing me."

Mercer chuckled. "You are so typical. Always thinking of yourself."

Rebecca huffed again. "Well, considering I'll continue to live a normal life, as well as Lady Sarah, I don't need her knowing the identity of the one who planned her kidnapping."

"Actually, my dear, confused woman"—the lieutenant's voice turned charming again—"I was the one who planned her kidnapping."

Their footsteps neared Emmie. She feared they would notice the bodice of her gown moving so fast due to her erratic heartbeat. Silently, she prayed they would not. She remained in the same position she'd been when she had awoken, with her chin resting on her chest. She smelled them near her, and although the man didn't stink, he definitely didn't smell as pleasant as Broderick.

Calloused, dry fingers pressed against her neck, and it was all she could do not to jump out of her own skin.

"She is alive. I worried that when I hit her to knock her out, it might have been too hard."

"It's what she deserves, if you ask me," Rebecca answered matter-of-factly.

When Emmie was finally free of these binds, she'd be sorely tempted to claw the other woman's eyes out for that comment.

Two hands grasped Emmie's shoulders and shook. Her head rocked with the movement and made her headache that much worse. She groaned loud enough for them to hear her this time.

"She is waking up now," the lieutenant said. "Lady Sarah? Can you hear me?"

She moaned again. "Yes." Struggling against her ties, she tried to put on a good performance. "What... what is going on? Why can't I move? Where am I?" she ended, her voice pitched higher than before.

"Lady Sarah, you are my prisoner. Where you are is of no consequence, since you cannot do anything about it."

"Why am I here? What have I done to become your prisoner?"

"You have done nothing—except capture the heart of the notorious pirate, Captain Hawk. Because I would like to kill him, I'm using you as bait."

She struggled against her ties again for show. "I'm afraid you are wrong. I don't know Captain Hawk. I have never met the pirate."

Mercer laughed loudly. "Oh, you have met him, I assure you. His real name is Broderick Worthington."

She paused for effect, and then slowly chuckled. "As much as I know you might not like me proving you wrong, I fear I must. I heard stories of Captain Hawk fifteen years ago. The man would have to be at least eighty years old. Mr. Worthington is certainly *not* that age."

"Lady Sarah, you must believe me to be addled. I assure you, I'm not. Would I have made it to the rank of lieutenant if I were that futile? Mr. Worthington wasn't the first Captain Hawk, and I'm certain that after he dies, another man will take his place."

"Then why are you so willing to kill Mr. Worthington if you know another man will take his place?"

"Because I want the recognition of capturing the elusive man. Since he has stepped into the role of pirate, he has captured many of my men. My brother was one of those who lost their life at Mr. Worthington's hand. Several years ago, I vowed to do all I could to stop him and slowly torture him until he dies."

A cold shiver ran over her. Lieutenant Mercer's voice was evil and unfeeling. She didn't need to be told how ruthless he was. Indeed, he would do as he'd planned. But who would stop him? Did Broderick know what kind of danger he was in?

And most importantly, would she be able to save him?

Chapter Twenty-Two

B RODERICK COMBED MOST of Brighton, even going into every shop just to inquire about Lady Sarah's whereabouts. For those few who knew her or had seen her with Lady Langston, they couldn't tell him where Emiline was, and they certainly couldn't remember when they had seen her last. As the day passed, his hopes of finding her sank lower, and he feared he would never find her. Thankfully, Uncle Henry helped him search. If Broderick had had to do this all by himself, it would have taken much longer.

As the sun began its descent, Broderick knew he wouldn't give up until she was found. He had asked Elias over and over again what exactly Mercer and the other man had told him, hoping there would be a clue as to where they had taken Emiline, but they had left no clue.

Feeling frustrated, Broderick wanted to scream and find a random person in town just to shake them until he got some answers. But he feared that wouldn't work. Mercer must know of Broderick's love for Emiline, which was why the lieutenant played this game of cat and mouse. Broderick didn't like this game. He wanted to be one step ahead of Mercer, as he'd always been. Unfortunately, the naval officer had now bested him.

Humiliation was a hard emotion to swallow.

From down the street, a familiar face caught his attention.

Without making a scene, Broderick hurried toward his friend. When Phillip noticed him, his eyes widened first, then seconds later, his forehead creased in worry.

"I'm so relieved I found you," Broderick said breathlessly.

"Good heavens, captain. What is wrong? You don't look like yourself. Your face is white."

Broderick nodded. "I'm not myself at all. Emiline has been taken by Mercer."

A loud gasp exploded out of Phillip's mouth. "No. Tell me you are jesting."

"I'm not. I have been searching for her for hours, and I cannot find her."

"What can I do to help?"

"I don't know. My uncle and I have been all over town." Broderick shook his head. "But I know that when I finally locate her, Mercer will be waiting to capture me." He took a deep breath. "Can you locate as many crew members as possible? We must formulate a plan for my escape."

"I can. But as I told you last night, only a handful are here."

"Gather them and meet me at the tavern at midnight."

"Aye, captain. I will try to find them." Phillip turned and hurried back up the street.

An ounce of relief was taken off Broderick's shoulders, but no more. There were still so many things that had to be done. Growling, he raked his fingers through his hair. This madness had to stop immediately, or he would not be able to think straight.

The air had turned slightly cooler, so Broderick bundled his overcoat tighter around his neck. Standing in front of a shop, he closed his eyes and mentally tried to focus on what his next course of action would be.

From across the street, a lad scurried across the road before a carriage whisked by. Just as the boy reached Broderick, he lifted his eyes. His shocked gaze clashed with Broderick's immediately, and the lad gasped. Quick as lightning, the boy broke into a run.

It took only a second for Broderick to register the identity of the boy. What was the kid doing in Brighton, instead of back at Henry's house taking care of the stable?

Broderick chased after Levi, determined not to let Henry's servant get away. But the boy was fast, and it took all of Broderick's willpower to keep on him. It wasn't until Levi tripped and fell that Broderick was able to catch up.

Levi sprang to his feet and was off again, but this time Broderick was close enough to grab the boy's jacket. The sleeve tore, but at least it helped Broderick in capturing the lad.

He tightened his fingers around Levi's arms, imprisoning him as he glared into the kid's frightened eyes. "I demand to know what you are doing in Brighton—and why you chose to run from me when you realized my identity."

"Let me go!"

"I shall when I receive some answers."

"I'll scream!"

"Then scream. I'm certain the constable will side with me." He gave Levi a hard shake. "Now start talking."

"No. You can't make me." Levi struggled, but to no avail.

Broderick arched an eyebrow. "I may not be able to make you, but I'm quite certain my uncle can. Do you want to keep your employment with Mr. Crampton? If so, you had better start talking."

Levi scowled, and his mouth tightened.

"Why are you in Brighton?" Broderick raised his voice, turning it more threatening. After a few moments of silence, he gave the boy another bone-rattling shake. "Tell me now, or so help me, you'll wish you were never born."

"I'm here to keep an eye on you. I'm being paid well."

That was definitely not the answer Broderick thought he'd get. He met the boy's glare with one of his own. "Who is paying you to watch me?"

"The man who came looking for Lady Sarah that one day you were gone."

"Lieutenant Mercer?"

Levi shook his head. "I don't know his name."

"You told me the man had orange hair. Is this the same man paying you?"

"No. The man paying me has black hair."

Shock vibrated through Broderick, but he kept his tight hold on the boy. Then again, Lieutenant Mercer was too cowardly to play this game of cat-and-mouse with the fearsome Captain Hawk alone.

"How did you know we were in Brighton? None of the servants—save for the ones who traveled with us—knew where we were going."

"I overheard Miss Crampton telling one of the maids."

Broderick gnashed his teeth. Leave it to his blabbermouth cousin to put a kink in things. "So, tell me why the man with black hair wants you to follow me?"

Levi's eyes turned a darker color, coated with malice. "You are Captain Hawk. I don't want a murderer in Mr. Crampton's house—family or not. You should be hanged for your crimes."

Broderick nodded. "I commend you for being so devoted to your employer, but the man paying you is wrong. If I kill people it's because I'm trying to protect myself from their attack. Perhaps you should have talked to Mr. Crampton about my loyalty before condemning an innocent man and feeding him to the wolves."

Within seconds, the anger fled from the boy's face, replaced with a white color. "But he assured me—"

"And he was wrong." Broderick released Levi. "I promise not to say anything to Mr. Crampton about this if you hurry back home as soon as possible—tonight, even."

"I-I-I promise, sir. Please forgive me. I was only trying to do my civic duty—"

"I understand, Levi. I'm quite certain you will hear things about people's characters quite a bit in this day and age, but unless you seek out the truth before you lay judgment, you are no better than the traitors themselves. Please remember this in case it happens again."

"That I will, sir. Thank you for understanding."

"Now be off with you before Mr. Crampton sees you."

Nodding, the boy turned and fled as fast as he could. Broderick prayed Levi would take his advice and leave posthaste. There were already enough problems happening at this moment. He didn't need a snot-nosed heathen around to cause more.

EMMIE'S BODY ACHED terribly. They hadn't moved her from this tied-up position on the rickety chair. And to make matters worse, she had to use the privy. Although she seriously doubted they had one on this ship. Still, if she waited any longer, well… She didn't want to think of the consequences.

Lieutenant Mercer and Rebecca had moved away from her. Emmie assumed they were sitting at a table, because earlier she'd heard other chairs scraping the floor as if someone was moving them out to sit. And she'd heard their whispers. Unfortunately, this time she didn't know what they were saying. Emmie suspected if they knew she was still awake, they would be more secretive.

As she opened her mouth to get their attention, the bang of a chair being knocked over echoed in the room.

"Miss Crampton, I grow tired of your constant complaining. You shall receive the money once Mr. Worthington arrives, and not a moment sooner."

"But you promised me—" Rebecca whined.

"I said, *enough!*"

A hard slap resounded through the air mere seconds before Rebecca wailed. Emmie shook her head, having known something like that would happen to Broderick's cousin at least once. Mercer was correct—Rebecca complained a lot. Emmie was the prisoner here, yet she hadn't complained once.

Although now was a good time, because she *really* needed to use the chamber pot.

"Pardon me, but I need some help over here." Emiline still couldn't believe that her captors would forget about her. Apparently, they didn't know how to handle women prisoners. "I know you are there, even though I'm blindfolded. I can hear you, and I can smell your foul scent."

Footsteps pounded on the floor, coming her way. She cringed, wondering if Mercer would hit her, too.

"What do you want?" he demanded.

"I need… Um, well, I have womanly necessities I have to take care of."

"What in the blazes are you talking about, woman?"

Inwardly, Emmie groaned. He was really simple-minded. "I need to use the chamber pot, you jackanapes."

She held herself still, readying for his hard hand across her face. Instead, he started chuckling.

"You definitely are the spitfire we heard you to be. I suppose I will allow you this necessity, but you will remain tied and blindfolded."

She nodded, not really wanting to upset him, but if he was too stupid to figure it out, she must spell it out for him. "But how can I attend to my *problem* if I cannot move my hands or legs—or see?"

"You make a good point, so I will untie your feet only. Someone else can assist you."

A gasp sprang from across the room. "You want me to act as her *maid*? I refuse! I will not help Lady Sarah do *that*!"

Emmie groaned silently. Had Rebecca not learned her lesson yet?

Mercer marched across the floor away from Emmie, and then came Rebecca's shriek. "Stand up and go help our prisoner, or you will not see a shilling of the money I promised you."

Rebecca's soft sobs grew closer to Emmie, followed by Lieutenant Mercer's heavy footsteps. Her legs jumped as he untied the ropes securing them to the chair. Feeling rushed to her feet, making them tingle, then burn. She wouldn't complain. At least she could feel them now.

"The chamber pot is in that corner," the lieutenant growled. "Go get it."

Rebecca's sobs turned louder as she did as the man instructed. For a moment, Emmie almost felt sorry for her.

"Where shall I take her?" Rebecca asked in a compliant tone.

"Behind that stack of crates will work just fine."

A strong hand grasped Emmie's arm and yanked her up. She almost couldn't stand, and so stumbled when they started walking. She feared she would fall into some object and not be able to brace herself with her hands tied behind her. But thankfully, she made it to their destination without any problems.

"I shall allow you only five minutes to take care of things, then I'll be back."

"Thank you, sir," Emmie answered. "You are most gracious to allow me such luxury." She ground her teeth through the outright lie.

Chuckling, Lieutenant Mercer moved away from her and Rebecca, and then the door closed. Emmie breathed a relieved sigh.

"I know this menial task is not something you usually do," she told Rebecca, "so if you will untie my hands, I'll see to my womanly needs by myself."

"As much as I would like to comply, I fear it would take me five minutes just to untie you. So, I must help you as much, as I hate doing so."

"I thank you," Emmie whispered.

Within minutes, Emmie felt much better. After she was finished, and she stood, Rebecca helped put her clothes back together.

"I know who you are, Miss Crampton."

The other woman gasped as her hands stilled. "How do you know?"

"Although we have not talked much, I still know your voice. And I feel I must let you know, you are in danger if you stay here."

"You know nothing," Rebecca snapped.

"Yes, I do. I know the lieutenant isn't going to release you, even if he gives you the money. Greedy, controlling men like that are not nice, and they never follow through with bargains they make. You need to escape, Rebecca. Get away from him and tell your father what you have done so he can protect you."

"Quit trying to frighten me." Rebecca shoved her.

Emmie stumbled, praying she wouldn't step into the chamber pot. Thankfully, she didn't. "Miss Crampton, I'm not trying to frighten you. I'm telling you the truth."

"What do you know, anyway? Nothing! You are a pampered daughter of an earl and have no idea about things like this."

Emmie now wanted to slap the woman herself. No, she'd let Lieutenant Mercer do it—little good it would do, anyway. Rebecca was hardheaded and wouldn't believe anyone. "Fine. But if we both live through this, I expect to hear an apology from you when you realize I'm right." If Lieutenant Mercer didn't kill them both first.

"Just hush up and let me take you back to your chair."

Rebecca tugged on Emmie's arm. She followed, trying to keep up with Rebecca's quick steps as they moved back to the chair. When Broderick's cousin pushed Emmie, she feared she would fall once again, but thankfully, the chair stopped her, and she was able to sit. Seconds later, Rebecca's fingers gripped Emmie's shoulders painfully.

"This is a warning, *Lady Sarah*—if you do happen to live through this, you had better not tell my father that I was the one who turned Broderick in. Know this now: I will deny it until I'm old and gray. And my father will believe me over you, anyway."

She was unbelievable. Rebecca was acting more like a pampered, spoiled child than a grown woman.

"If your father will believe you over me, then why threaten

me at all?"

Rebecca growled and slapped Emmie across the face. Her cheek stung for a moment. She wouldn't give Rebecca a reply. It wasn't worth the breath, anyway.

Lieutenant Mercer returned and tied her feet back to the chair. Tears stung her eyes, and she prayed that God would send someone to rescue her. Anyone but Broderick. If he came, he'd be killed, and she couldn't live knowing he'd risked his life for her.

BRODERICK BLEW OUT a breath. Time was wasting away, and he was frustrated beyond belief. Perhaps he needed to be the one to find his crew. He alone couldn't capture Mercer, especially since the man obviously had others helping him.

Not far from him was another inn. Broderick hurried toward that establishment. As he walked inside the building, his foot caught on the rug, and he stumbled into a man. Righting himself, he opened his mouth to apologize as he looked into the other man's eyes.

"Pardon my clumsiness, sir—" Recognition hit as excitement shot through Broderick. "Benjamin Spencer, you are just the man I came looking to find." He grasped the man's shoulders. "You don't know how happy I am to see you." It was then he noticed a traveling satchel in Ben's hand, as if he were leaving.

"Mr. Worthington. What a pleasure it is, indeed. I was just on my way out, but we could sit at the table and order drinks if you would like."

"There is no time." Broderick lowered his voice. "I need you and the others. Mercer is in town and has kidnapped someone I hold dear."

Ben frowned. "Are you certain?"

"Yes."

"But then why did you order us to leave Brighton?"

Broderick blinked. "I did?"

"Aye, captain. Yesterday, George and I were told that you no longer needed our presence here, and to meet you back at the ship in a fortnight because we'd be sailing again."

"You received this information yesterday? What time were you told this?"

"In the evening."

Something wasn't right. A painful throb began in the base of Broderick's skull as he collected his thoughts. There was only one man who would give such instructions. And because they were deliberately false and meant to lead Broderick astray, this only meant one thing.

With a sinking, saddened heart, he realized he had finally found the traitor amongst his crew.

Chapter Twenty-Three

EMMIE DIDN'T KNOW how she could doze off while sitting in an uncomfortable chair with her arms and legs tied with ropes, but she had. She shook her head, forcing herself to wake up. Her stomach growled, and she really didn't want to have to ask Lieutenant Mercer for something to eat, yet she needed food in her stomach. When someone finally came to rescue her, how could she help if she didn't have the strength?

She listened for any sounds around her, but couldn't detect any. It had been a while now since she'd heard Rebecca's whiny voice, and her fear returned. Had Mercer killed the poor, misguided, stubborn woman? Emmie prayed for Mr. and Mrs. Crampton's sake that their daughter was still alive.

Silence grew in the room. Everything seemed so very still. Once in a while, she heard the waves slapping against the ship, but by the slow rocking of the vessel, she could tell they weren't sailing. Perhaps there was a wind tonight.

What worried her was that she couldn't hear Lieutenant Mercer, either. Earlier, he had been talking to another man, but as before, they whispered their conversation so she couldn't hear any words. Not knowing how much time had passed, she could only hope that Mercer had retired to bed. But if he expected Broderick, she was certain the lieutenant would not sleep until the man she loved was captured.

"Is anyone there?" she asked softly, and waited.

No noise. Nothing different was detected from a few moments earlier. So perhaps she was by herself after all.

Her arms and legs were pretty much numb by now, but she tried to struggle out of the ropes binding her wrists. She tugged and tugged with all her might, and after a few minutes, she had to stop and catch her breath. Being so weak, there was no way she could get out of these ropes.

Tears pooled in her eyes, and she didn't have the willpower to hold them back from falling down her face. It didn't matter, since her blindfold soaked up the moisture anyway.

Helplessness swept over her, and for the first time since she was kidnapped, she felt as if her doom was very near. Lieutenant Mercer would kill her just as soon as Broderick arrived. And she had no doubt he would come for her, not thinking about his own safety at all. She at least hoped the lieutenant would let her tell Broderick she loved him before he killed her. If only she could have told her mother, brother, and father the same thing. If only…

Her thoughts skidded to a halt. Had she just heard a noise? Holding her breath, she listened again. After a few moments came the same scrape she'd heard.

She held still, listening intently. Although she wasn't really frightened of mice, she was tied up and so wouldn't be able to shoo the rodent away if it neared her. The noise definitely couldn't be Mercer, because he made enough commotion to let the whole ship—and the fishes under the sea—know he was walking. So, where could that noise be coming from?

Another scrape sounded, from the door this time. Maybe Rebecca was returning. Emmie almost hoped so, because then she'd be reassured Broderick's cousin hadn't been killed after all.

Holding her breath, Emmie listened for more. Silence lasted another few minutes before she heard a different sound. It was the squeak of the door opening. She even felt the brush of cooler air across her feet. From underneath the blindfold, a tiny amount of light came into the room. It wasn't until now that she realized how dark the room had been.

Very soft footsteps—more than set—came inside before the door squeaked again, followed by the click of the door closing. If Rebecca had returned, who was with her?

Within seconds, the footsteps quickened—but were kept light—and coming her way. Someone neared, and she felt the warmth of another body kneeling beside her chair as tender hands touched her tied ones. A familiar masculine scent filled her senses and made her heart sing with joy.

"Broderick?" she whispered.

His hands squeezed hers. "Yes, my love," he replied softly. "Keep quiet. My uncle and I are here to get you out of this wretched place."

Tears streamed from her eyes like a waterfall. "No, Broderick. You must leave now. You have put yourself in danger by coming to rescue me," she whispered brokenly.

His lips brushed hers briefly. "Do you honestly think I would let that stop me?"

Another pair of fingers worked the binds at her feet while Broderick untied her hands. "But it must. As long as you are alive, they will not hurt me."

"And as soon as I get us out of here, they will not hurt either of us."

"But Broderick—"

His mouth pressed against hers again, silencing her protests. The kiss was slightly longer, but not long enough for her to thoroughly enjoy. He pulled away, and seconds later, her blindfold came off. Because her eyes had been hidden for most of the day, she squinted at the small amount of light coming from the lantern.

Broderick's face was before her, love glowing in his eyes. Her heart flipped with excitement, and she prayed he could get them out of there safely.

"Shh..." he whispered. "We don't want to alert Lieutenant

Mercer, or whoever else might be helping, that we are here."

She nodded, then quickly glanced at Mr. Crampton. She couldn't see his face, since he was still bent over untying her feet. She needed to tell him about Rebecca, but then the poor man might get angry, or worse… make noise. Still, they couldn't leave here without Broderick's idiotic cousin.

"Broderick, there is something you must know about who is helping Mercer."

"I already know, my love. Phillip is the traitor amongst us."

She gasped as her heart broke for the man she loved. Not only had his friend betrayed him—but his cousin as well. Now she realized that was why the other man's voice seemed so familiar. She *had* heard it before, if only once. "I'm sorry to hear that. But there is more."

"I'm quite certain there are more people assisting the lieutenant, but let's get you out of here first. I will return with other members of my crew, and we will fight them all." He grinned.

"No, it's not that—"

"There," Mr. Crampton said as he rubbed her ankles, looking up at her. "The binds are off. Can you stand?"

She shrugged. "Considering my legs have been numb for hours, I don't know how well I can stand, let alone walk."

"I shall carry you," Broderick told her softly.

"No. That will only slow us down. Give me a moment to regain feeling in my feet."

She stood and tested her footing. Broderick's muscular arm wrapped around her waist to help her to stand. Mr. Crampton tiptoed to the door and placed his ear on the weathered wood. She needed to tell Broderick now, without his uncle close by.

"Broderick," she whispered, and leaned up to his ear. "Rebecca is here."

Broderick quickly pulled back, his eyes widening as he stared at her. Emmie took a quick peek at Mr. Crampton to make sure he was still by the door before leaning back to Broderick's ear.

"Rebecca turned you in. She was the one responsible for my

kidnapping, too." He pulled away again, shaking his head. She nodded and leaned toward his ear again. "Your cousin isn't very wise, but she is still your cousin and Mr. Crampton's daughter. We cannot leave without her."

Where is she? he mouthed.

"I don't know where Lieutenant Mercer took her." She shrugged. "I don't even know if she is still alive."

Frowning, Broderick swiped a hand over his face. Her heart went out to him. He'd had too many people betray him lately. She prayed there were no others. She feared his heart wouldn't be able to bear it.

"I cannot think of that now," he answered. "We must get you out of here and safely home. Then, and only then, will I be able to figure out how to return to save her." He sighed heavily.

The burning tingles in her legs had returned, but she couldn't concentrate or worry about that. As long as she could walk, she was fine. She tested her legs by taking a few steps. When she was confident she would be able to walk off this ship by herself, she said, "Let's go."

Mr. Crampton pulled away from the door and motioned with his hand. "I don't hear anything on the other side. I think all is well."

"I pray you're correct, Mr. Crampton." She touched his arm and smiled. "Thank you so much for helping Broderick."

"Think nothing of it." He stroked her cheek. "And you are the daughter of my good friend, as well. I'm doubly blessed to be helping."

Broderick picked up the lantern before moving to the door. He turned off the light before carefully opening the door and peeking out into the hallway. Emmie held her breath, hoping they would be able to leave without any problems.

Finally, Broderick looked back and nodded. He took her hand, and she tightened her fingers around his, never wanting to let go—ever again. They all took careful and very slow steps down the hallway. Darkness was thick through these halls, and she trusted Broderick would lead them out without any difficulty.

A sliver of light shone up ahead, almost a bluish color. She wanted to sigh with relief, knowing it was probably the moon reflecting off the ocean, but she didn't dare. They weren't out of danger yet. The closer they came to the light, the quicker their footsteps became. It was hard to walk carefully when hope—and freedom—were so close.

The few stairs leading to the top deck were just ahead. Broderick strode up the stairs first, pulling Emmie's hand as she followed. As his head cleared topside, several clicks of pistols resounded in the night. Broderick froze, and her heart sank.

They'd been caught!

"Welcome to my ship, Captain Hawk." Lieutenant Mercer's voice boomed in the quiet night. "Please come up, and bring your friends with you."

Broderick's hand tightened around her fingers, and she clutched his overcoat with her other hand. Once they were on deck, he pulled her close against his body, protecting her.

Mr. Crampton followed with his head lowered in defeat. Her heart went out to him as well. He had yet to learn about what his own daughter had done to bring all of this about.

She glanced around the deck. Only three other men stood beside Mercer, and Phillip wasn't one of them. As she scooted closer to Broderick, she felt the weapons Broderick had on him. If only they could beat these other men back, they might get out of here alive.

Lieutenant Mercer released a grating laugh. "Now see, Lady Sarah. Did I not tell you that Mr. Worthington would come for you?"

"Yes, you did," she answered softly.

"And I'm so very happy you're both together, once again. I want Captain Hawk to watch the woman he loves die a slow and painful death."

She sobbed and buried her head in Broderick's chest. His arms tightened around her.

"I'm afraid, Lieutenant Mercer, that your plans won't happen that way," Broderick said. "You see, Captain Hawk *never* loses a fight, and he for certain doesn't allow those he loves to die in front of him."

Emmie turned her head slightly to look at the lieutenant to see his reaction.

He laughed again. "Oh, but you haven't been Captain Hawk as long as the others before you. I'm quite sure I can best you yet again."

"And I'm quite sure you cannot," Broderick replied boldly.

Lieutenant Mercer's attention moved from Emmie and Broderick onto Mr. Crampton. "And what a pleasure it is to see you again, Henry. I thank you for assisting me with the capture of Captain Hawk. I'm so glad you brought him here. Well done, my good friend."

Emmie's heart sank once again. Beside her, Broderick stiffened in shock.

No! Not Mr. Crampton!

Chapter Twenty-Four

BRODERICK'S MIND TURNED numb. This couldn't be right. His uncle wouldn't betray Broderick's trust. Would he?

He swung in his uncle's direction, still holding Emmie against him. Henry, who had been standing with his head lowered, suddenly looked up and glared at Lieutenant Mercer.

"How dare you tell that outright lie." Henry squared his shoulders. "I'm *not* your good friend, Lieutenant Mercer. And the only reason I agreed to bring Broderick to you was because you threatened to kill my daughter if I didn't heed your command."

Henry turned and looked at Broderick. "You must believe me, Broderick. I would never hurt or betray you, but..." A tear slid down the older man's cheek as he swallowed hard. "Lieutenant Mercer told me he would kill Rebecca if I didn't bring you here. Please, forgive me."

Broderick's heart tugged from his uncle's pleading. He'd already been hurt by his friend. Yet things added up where Phillip was concerned. When Broderick pieced together all the times he had thought there was a traitor on his ship, at least he knew he was right to suspect *someone*. But things didn't add up with his uncle. That could only mean one thing.

Broderick nodded. "I believe you, Uncle. And I forgive you." He turned and glared at Mercer. "Only men like this can sink low enough to threaten family members to go against each other.

Lieutenant Mercer, you are not human. You have no heart."

The man marched up to Broderick with hatred in his evil eyes. "It's because of you that I have no heart. You killed my brother."

Broderick shrugged. "I can only assume that your brother deserved to die, because I don't kill unless to protect myself or my friends. Who was your brother, may I ask?"

"He was one of Napoleon's soldiers. His name was Harold Mercer, but you probably don't even remember him."

"You're correct, I don't recall that name, but if he was one of Napoleon's soldiers, and he tried to harm me or one of my friends, then indeed, he deserved to die."

Growling, the lieutenant lifted his pistol and pointed it to Broderick's forehead. Broderick held his breath, tightening his embrace of Emiline.

"*You* deserve to die," Mercer ground out through his teeth. "Right here and now."

"Oh, but you forget," Broderick quickly said. "You were not going to kill me right away. Remember?"

The other man scowled and jerked his weapon away from Broderick's head. He dared breathe in relief. Now, if he could only figure out a way to get out of this situation without being killed, he'd be doing better than he first thought.

He surveyed the other three men standing around them, their pistols aimed at Broderick and his uncle. It surprised him to see Phillip wasn't with them, but he figured his first mate wasn't present because he was trying to remain the traitor amongst the crew. Well, Broderick would deal with him soon enough. First things first. He needed to somehow figure out how he could draw his own pistol and kill at least one of these idiots here without getting Emiline or Uncle Henry shot in the process.

Slowly, Broderick moved his hand toward his pistol, but Lieutenant Mercer saw and shook his head.

"Tsk, tsk, Captain Hawk. I would not do that if I were you. Keep your hand away or the woman dies now, in your arms."

The lieutenant tilted his head. "Wouldn't that be *romantic?*"

If Broderick could strangle the man at this moment, he would, but a quick death would be more to his liking. He must remember the lessons in patience his friends William and Marcus had taught him.

"Then again," Mercer continued, "perhaps dying in each other's arms would be more romantic? Eh, Captain Hawk?"

Subtly, Emiline's hand slid into the pocket of his overcoat… the same pocket where he had tucked one of his pistols. His heartbeat quickened. This would get her killed, and he couldn't let that happen.

"I'm not going to die, and neither is Lady Sarah." Broderick hoped to keep Mercer and the other three focused on him and not Emiline. "Is that not correct, Uncle? None of us will die tonight—only the ones with the lieutenant."

"Uh, yes."

Broderick's ploy worked, because all four men switched their attention to Henry. Emiline slowly slid the pistol out. Broderick sneaked his free hand around his back as she handed him the weapon.

"It's not my intention to die tonight." Henry lifted his chin. "And from all the things I have heard about Captain Hawk, I happen to think that my nephew will prevail this evening as well. Haven't you ever heard that the bad guys *always* receive their comeuppance?" His gaze moved from one man to the other.

Lieutenant Mercer moved closer to Henry and gave him an evil stare. "You're too cocky, like your nephew. And your daughter is a lot like you as well—stubborn to a fault."

Henry took a shaky breath. "Where is she?"

The lieutenant nodded down toward the floor. "She is below deck sleeping. I was tired of her complaining, so I knocked her out."

Henry's jaw tightened, and Broderick prayed his uncle wouldn't do anything foolish yet.

"You *hit* her?"

Mercer shrugged. "How else could I knock her unconscious?" He shook his head. "I'm surprised you haven't done that to your daughter a time or two. She is certainly annoying enough."

Emiline slipped her hand inside Broderick's overcoat this time, sneaking her way to his other pistol. He hoped his uncle kept talking to keep the men focused on him instead of what she was doing.

"I swear, Lieutenant Mercer, if you lay one more hand on her, I'll…" Henry stepped closer to the other man, going nearly nose to nose.

"You'll *what*, pray tell?" Mercer snickered.

"I'll kill you."

Lieutenant Mercer threw back his head and laughed. "What humor you possess, Mr. Crampton. From what I have learned about you, you cannot harm a flea."

"That is because a flea has never given me the motivation to do so."

Growling, Henry lunged forward and wrapped his hands around Mercer's throat. The lieutenant gasped and dropped his pistol as he tried to pull Henry's fingers away from his neck. Two of Mercer's men stepped closer, pointing their weapons at Henry.

"Let him go," one shouted.

Just as Emiline closed her fingers around one of the pistols, Broderick moved away from her, aimed, and shot the man who was about to kill Henry. Within seconds, the second man swung and aimed his pistol at Broderick, but before he could pull the trigger, Emiline shot him in the chest.

Not wasting any time, Broderick reached for his sword, but the third man had turned his weapon onto Emmie.

"Drop your sword or I'll shoot her," he warned.

Emiline's gaze met Broderick's, and she shook her head. "Kill him. Don't worry about me."

Before Broderick knew what was happening, Henry was knocked to the ground, holding his knee as Mercer loomed over him, still gasping for air. He quickly bent and retrieved his pistol before glancing at the two men who lay dead on the deck in a pool of their own blood.

"Hawk!" he shouted. "You have not won. You will *never* win again."

"Actually, I think you are wrong, Mercer. Captain Hawk *will* win."

The familiar voice that boomed through the air was followed by several clicks from pistols. Broderick swung his head to look in the direction of the voice to see Phillip standing with two other crew members, Spencer and Stephens, all holding pistols and pointing them at Lieutenant Mercer and the other man.

"Daughtery, what in the blazes are you doing?" shouted Mercer. "Kill Broderick Worthington. And for heaven's sake, shoot Mr. Crampton and Lady Sarah as well. I'm fed up with this game, and I want them all dead now."

Mercer's last man turned his weapon toward Phillip, but Spencer shot the bloke before he had a chance. He, too, fell by his deceased comrades.

Smiling, Phillip walked toward Mercer, shaking his head. "Looks like you are all alone now."

"What is wrong with you?" the lieutenant yelled.

"I'm not going to kill my best friend, Broderick Worthington, and I'm never again going to do what you tell me to do."

"What?" Mercer asked, and both Broderick and Emiline echoed him.

Phillip glanced briefly at Broderick before focusing on the lieutenant once more. "You see, Mercer, I have *never* been a traitor. But the only way to bring you to your knees and capture you was to make you believe I was one and, in doing so, helping you to get Captain Hawk."

Spencer took the pistol from Mercer's hand. Phillip turned to Broderick and frowned.

"Please forgive me for putting you through this turmoil. I had to make Lieutenant Mercer believe I was working with him. That was the only way we—you and I and our crew—could finally win and be free of this imbecile."

Broderick's mind whirled with the unbelievable confession. He didn't know whether or not to trust Phillip, yet his heart told him to believe. If Phillip had really been the traitor, he would have been standing with Mercer, not Spencer and Stephens, and the pistol would be pointed at Broderick instead.

Speechless, all Broderick could do was nod at Phillip. Emiline returned to his side and wrapped her arms around his waist, laying her head on his chest. Still, he was too stunned to do anything. He couldn't even remember sliding his arms around her shoulders, but how else would she be in his embrace right now?

"You *lied* to me?" Mercer yelled, and lunged for Phillip.

Phillip tried to ward off the attack, but the lieutenant was able to grip his weapon. They struggled, but Broderick knew Phillip was stronger. Within seconds, the pistol fired. Mercer staggered back clutching his bleeding chest. He stared at his bloody fingers and then switched his shocked gaze back to Phillip before staggering to the ground in a dead heap beside the others.

Finally, Broderick was able to breathe a relieved sigh. Emiline did so as well before hugging him tightly.

"We are alive," she whispered brokenly.

"Yes, we are." Broderick nodded, looking at Phillip as his friend walked closer. "Phillip… I don't know how to thank you."

His friend clapped his hand on Broderick's shoulder. "As many times as you have saved my life, this is the least I can do."

Emiline lifted her head, tears filling her eyes as she stared at Phillip. "You really are not the traitor?"

"No. I'm sorry that I didn't tell you about my plans, Broderick, but I had to make Mercer believe I was with him and against you. If Mercer thought I was lying, we would both be dead, my friend."

Broderick nodded. "Very true. You are forgiven this time, but for the love of God, don't put me through that agony ever again."

Phillip chuckled. "I assure you, I went through agony too,

and I will never do it again."

"Pardon me," Henry said, walking up to Phillip. "But do you know where my daughter is being held?"

"Yes. I shall take you below deck and show you. Once she awakens, she shall be fine—just with a splitting headache, I'm sure. Hopefully, she has learned her lesson about making deals with the devil."

"I pray you are right," Henry muttered.

Phillip looked at Broderick. "Will you wait for us?"

"I will."

After Phillip led Henry back down the stairs, Broderick moved Emiline away from the dead bodies, over to the corner of the deck behind some crates, where it was more peaceful. He gathered her tighter in his arms and gazed into her beautiful eyes, still watery even through her smile. "I love you."

"Oh, Broderick. I love you so much. The whole time I was kept prisoner, I prayed you would come rescue me, yet I knew if you did, you would be walking into a trap, and I didn't want you to die."

"No, my love." He caressed her cheek. "I would never let you die for me."

She arched an eyebrow. "And it's all right for you to die for me? That makes no sense at all, Mr. Worthington."

He laughed and kissed her forehead. "I have a plan. Let us just forget about dying altogether. We will marry, raise a family, and live together—happily forever and ever."

Sighing, she leaned against him and shook her head. "That does sound wonderful, but I fear I cannot marry you."

Not sure he'd heard her correctly, he withdrew enough to look down into her eyes. "What? You cannot marry me? Pray tell, why not?" His heart clenched. He was not sure he was going to like her answer.

"Because, my dear man, you haven't asked me to marry you yet. And for certain, you haven't asked permission from my parents."

Relief swept over him, and he smiled. He stepped away from her and went on one knee, taking her hands in his. "Lady Sarah Emiline Langston, would you do me the great pleasure of becoming my wife? I promise to spend every waking moment making you as happy as you have made me since we first met. And I promise to move heaven and earth to please you. I will accept the title of marquess if you wish me to, or I can remain Captain Hawk. Your wish is my command."

He glanced up at the sky. The yellow moon floated high in the sky, stars hung suspended around it. The night was beautiful and so perfect. If he listened closely, he knew he would hear heaven's angels singing as well.

"Emiline, my dearest," he continued as he gazed back into her eyes, "say yes and make this night our paradise. Even though we have been through much turmoil tonight, all I want to do when I think back on this night is remember us, and your accepting my marriage proposal."

She sighed and nodded. "Yes, Broderick Worthington, my captain enchanter. I accept your proposal, and I will always remember tonight as our wonderland. I will only want you to be a marquess if that is what *you* wish. And I will accept your being a pirate if you can promise me you will not get yourself killed." She grinned. "There is no way I want to lose you ever again."

"Whatever our future is, we will decide together." He winked. "Is that all right with you?"

"It's perfect."

Placing his mouth over hers, he sealed the promise with a kiss. A kiss that started out simple, but soon turned into more. Much more.

Epilogue

"THIS IS PERFECT, don't you agree?" Emmie asked excitedly as she glanced at her mother sitting across from her in their carriage. "Father's brother has been arrested and awaits sentencing, and Father decided to come get us and meet us at Mr. Compton's estate. The timing couldn't have been better, I think."

Her mother nodded. "I agree. That man is a threat to everyone, so locking him away is the best thing, in my opinion. I will never understand men who want to run England their own way."

"Did you tell your father about the surprise?" Broderick asked.

Emmie looked at him and smiled. She reached over and patted his hand. The coach they were riding in seemed cramped, since her mother and brother were sharing the same vehicle. But her mother wouldn't allow Emmie to ride with Broderick alone, since it would ruin her reputation.

"When I replied to Father's letter, I told him we were in Brighton, but that we would return to Greenwich. I let him know that I had couple of surprises for him." Emmie grinned. "So, Mother, you and Elias stay in the carriage until Broderick comes to get you."

Her mother nodded as she twisted her hands in her lap. This was all so exciting for Emmie—and nerve-racking—and she could only assume her mother felt more jitters than her at this moment.

Emmie looked out the coach's window as they came upon Mr. Crampton's estate. She couldn't wait to let her father know that his brother had been lying to them all for fifteen years. Emmie was relieved that her father had already disowned his brother after his arrest.

Nervously, she wrung her hands in her lap and noticed her mother doing the same. Broderick had his arm around Emmie's shoulders, and he squeezed lovingly. When she met his eyes, he winked.

"You will be all right. I just know it."

She smiled. "Thank you for everything. We wouldn't have been able to do any of this without you."

He kissed her forehead and pulled her against him tighter. Across the seat, Daphne tried to hide a grin as she looked away. Elias, however, chuckled as if it were funny to see his sister kissing a man.

When the coach stopped, Broderick opened the door and hopped out before assisting Emmie down. She glanced at the second coach that had a few of her mother's servants along with Anna as they rode with the trunks. Emmie didn't want to wait for Anna to climb out to instruct her on what to do, so she hurried toward the house, Broderick following closely behind. Thankfully, Mr. and Mrs. Crampton had decided to stay in Brighton for another day to allow Emmie's family to use the house for their special homecoming.

When they reached the door, she inhaled deeply before entering. She looked at Broderick and smiled. "Let me do all the talking."

He chuckled. "Yes, dear."

She rolled her eyes. "You know what I mean."

"I do."

She hurried inside, peering in every room until she noticed her father reading a book on the sofa in the sitting room. Moistening her suddenly dry throat with a swallow, she stepped inside.

Her father's head jerked toward her. Immediately, he set the book down and stood, holding out his arms. He beamed with happiness. "Welcome back, my little Emmie."

She rushed into his embrace and hugged him tight. "Oh, I have missed you so."

"Not as much as I have missed you." He kissed her cheek and pulled away.

It was then when his attention moved behind her. "Father," she said quickly before he could ask, "I told you I was bringing you a couple of surprises, and this is one of them." She motioned to Broderick. "Father, meet the Marquess of Wilshire, Broderick Worthington. He is Mr. and Mrs. Crampton's nephew."

Broderick stepped forward and offered his hand. "It's a pleasure to meet you, sir. I feel as if I know you, since your daughter has talked nonstop about you."

Her father shook Broderick's hand. "It is always a pleasure to meet Henry's family. I fear it's been years since I have seen my good friend. How is he faring?"

"Quite well. He and my aunt will be home tomorrow. I'm sure my uncle will enjoy catching up on old times with you."

Her father nodded. "I would certainly enjoy that."

She dared to move closer to Broderick, even right up next to him. Slowly, Broderick slid his arm around her waist. Her father watched every movement until his eyes widened in understanding.

Once again, she quickly offered up explanation before her father said anything. "And Father, Broderick and I have become… um… very close lately. And he would like to ask you a question."

Broderick cleared his throat and squared his shoulders. "Lord Langston, I have fallen deeply in love with your daughter, and I would like your permission to marry her."

Emmie held her breath as her father's focus darted between her and Broderick. Smiling, she cuddled closer to him and laid her hand on his chest. "Father, I love him with all my heart, and I cannot imagine life without him."

Blowing out a gust of air from between his lips, her father scratched his brown hair, sprinkled lightly with strands of white.

He scrubbed his chin, studying Broderick closely.

She removed her attention from her father and gazed lovingly at Broderick. He had colored his hair brown again to hide the natural black. He did this so as not to get noticed. One of these days she would like to see him with his natural color. Their children would have raven hair, too, she just knew it.

"Well," her father finally said. "I must admit this is quite a surprise—a shock, in fact. Emiline, my dear, I had no idea your *surprise* would be bringing home a man."

She chuckled. "Actually, I brought home more than that, but right now, I wanted to have you meet this wonderful man who risked his life to save mine."

Her father's eyes widened. "What is this you say?"

Shaking her head, she waved her hand through the air. "That is another story, which I will gladly tell you, but for now, we are anxiously awaiting an answer."

He paced in front of the hearth with his hands behind his back. "I suppose I need to know where the marquess plans to live if I give you both my blessings."

"Actually," Broderick said, "we plan on living in Devonshire. I have recently been given this title and some lands in that location."

Finally, her father stopped and faced them, a smile stretching across his face. "Now that is the answer I was seeking." He stepped forward and clapped his hand on Broderick's shoulder. "Welcome to the family, son."

Emmie sighed in relief and hugged her father. Broderick moved to shake his hand again, but her father gave him a hug instead. They all laughed together. It was then she realized Broderick was even taller than her father, and she'd always thought he was a large man. And even though her father's shoulders were wide, Broderick's were even wider.

Taking a deep breath, she prepared herself to give him the next big surprise. "Well, now that is all settled, do you want your next surprise?"

Her father tilted his head, narrowing his eyes in suspicion. "It depends. Is it anything like this surprise was?"

"Oh, no, Father. This surprise is much better." She glanced at Broderick, giving him the nod to go fetch her mother and brother. Once Broderick left the room, she took her father's hands and held them. "This trip to Greenwich has opened my eyes to a lot of things, which Broderick was all part of. But one of the things I discovered was how your devious brother has tricked you and me for years now."

Her father's forehead creased. "How so?"

"Well, fifteen years ago he told us some disturbing news that was nothing but a lie."

Slowly, color faded from his cheeks. She knew he was thinking of her mother.

"Your brother made us believe that my mother—your wife— had been killed. But that is not the truth." She took another deep breath. "Father, Mother is alive. I found her living in Brighton."

He swayed slightly and then stumbled to the chair where he'd been sitting. Tears collected in his eyes as he stared at her. "Daphne… is alive?"

"Yes." Emmie sat on the footstool and took his hands again. "Your brother orchestrated this whole thing, Father. He gave us the note that said Mother had died, and he gave Mother a similar note that told her *we* had died."

"Are… are you certain he did that?"

"Yes, I'm quite sure." Emotion stuck in her throat, making her voice crack. "I pray your brother pays dearly for what he has done to our family."

Anger blazed across her father's expression. "I pray that, too. I'll never let him—or anyone—break up my family again."

"I'm so glad you think that way," she said.

Silence stretched in the room for several moments. The only sounds were the wood crackling in the fireplace and her father's ragged breaths as he tried to hold back tears. Then she heard the floor in the hallway creak, and she knew Broderick had returned.

Emmie stood and walked to the door then opened it. She smiled at her mother and brother, motioning them to enter.

When Daphne glided into the room, looking lovelier than Emmie could remember, her father jumped to his feet. His gaze nearly devoured his wife. Tears streamed down Daphne's cheeks as she held her hands out to her husband.

"Oh, Byron." Her voice broke. "You are really alive!"

Emmie's father released a sob and ran to his wife, sweeping her in his arms. Emmie placed her fisted hand to her mouth to keep the cries from spilling forth from her own throat as she watched her father and mother hug and kiss—something she'd missed seeing for all these years.

The presence beside her alerted her that her brother was also seeing his father for the first time. She took hold of Elias's hand and squeezed. "What do you think of him?" she asked softly.

"He is amazing." Even Elias's voice was choked with emotion.

Daphne turned, still in her husband's arms, and reached her hand out for Elias. "Byron, I want you to meet your son, Elias Byron Langston."

A hoarse laugh escaped Byron's throat as he pulled Elias in for a hug. "I have a son," he shouted in joy.

Everyone laughed, still with tears in their eyes.

Standing beside Emmie, Broderick wrapped his arms around her and held her close. "I love you," he whispered in her ear.

She smiled up into his eyes. "I love you more."

He bent and kissed her lips briefly. "I love you higher than the sky."

"I cannot beat that, now can I?"

"Not unless you are an angel in heaven."

She turned and wrapped her arms around his waist. "You *are* my heaven."

Meet the first Captain Hawk

Readers, if you enjoyed this story, let me direct you to my first pirate story about Captain Hawk, Marcus Thorne.

A Notorious Pirate...
Marcus Thorne wants only to find the secrets the Royal Navy is hiding from him—the perfect revenge against his absentee father. His life goes smoothly until he captures a ship and meets the daughter of the man who stole from him. Now Marcus wants a different revenge, and this one will be more enjoyable.

An Inquisitive Lady...
Isabelle Stanhope should be quaking with fear when she is taken prisoner by the masked man. Instead, his kisses set her on fire, and she sees a different man from the fearsome pirate he tries to be. Now she wants more, but can she convince him she is a better prize than what he seeks from the Royal Navy? If not, she will have to journey to New York and find the man she has never seen—the one her father wanted her to marry.

With revenge, arranged marriages, and furious fathers, can these two really find love?

Other published stories by Marie Higgins
www.authormariehiggins.com/books

Join my Newsletter
www.authormariehiggins.com/newsletter

About the Author

Marie Higgins is an award-winning, best-selling author of clean romance novels that melt your heart and have you falling in love over and over again. Since 2010, she's published over 100 heartwarming, on-the-edge-of-your-seat romances. She's broadened her readership by writing mystery/suspense, humor, time-travel, and paranormal, along with her love for historical romances. Her readers have dubbed her "Queen of Tease" because of her twists and unexpected endings.

Website – www.authormariehiggins.com
Facebook – facebook.com/marie.higgins.7543
TikTok – tiktok.com/@author.mariehiggins
Instagram – instagram.com/author.mariehiggins
Bookbub – bookbub.com/authors/marie-higgins
Twitter – @mariehigginsxox